HOW HOT?

Alex refused to feel guilty for the primitive satisfaction that coursed through him at the knowledge that Isabel didn't have a lot of experience. She was unique in every other way, why not this one, too?

Her passion belonged to him.

He could tell that her own responses were surprising her and that added an excitement all its own to their lovemaking. What man did not want to be *the one* to bring out his woman's sensuous nature? But for all her passion, she was also nervous, and he didn't want her nervous. He wanted her hot.

Leaning down, he kissed the corner of her mouth, teasing the edge of her lips with his tongue. She sighed and her body melted into him. He kept up the tender kisses until he felt the fires that had been banked by their little discussion rekindle in her. Her breathing grew ragged once again.

BOOK YOUR PLACE ON OUR WEBSITE AND MAKE THE READING CONNECTION!

We've created a customized website just for our very special readers, where you can get the inside scoop on everything that's going on with Zebra, Pinnacle and Kensington books.

When you come online, you'll have the exciting opportunity to:

- View covers of upcoming books
- Read sample chapters
- Learn about our future publishing schedule (listed by publication month *and author*)
- Find out when your favorite authors will be visiting a city near you
- Search for and order backlist books from our online catalog
- Check out author bios and background information
- Send e-mail to your favorite authors
- Meet the Kensington staff online
- Join us in weekly chats with authors, readers and other guests
- Get writing guidelines
- AND MUCH MORE!

**Visit our website at
http://www.kensingtonbooks.com**

LUCY MONROE

Come Up and See Me Sometime

ZEBRA BOOKS
KENSINGTON PUBLISHING CORP.
http://www.kensingtonbooks.com

ZEBRA BOOKS are published by

Kensington Publishing Corp.
850 Third Avenue
New York, NY 10022

All Kensington titles, imprints and distributed lines are available at special quantity discounts for bulk purchases for sales promotion, premiums, fund-raising, educational or institutional use.

Special book excerpts or customized printings can also be created to fit specific needs. For details, write or phone the office of the Kensington Special Sales Manager: Kensington Publishing Corp., 850 Third Avenue, New York, NY 10022. Attn. Special Sales Department. Phone: 1-800-221-2647.

Zebra and the Z logo Reg. U.S. Pat. & TM Off.

First Printing: May 2005
10 9 8 7 6 5 4 3 2 1

Printed in the United States of America

For Kate Duffy, an extraordinary editor and person. Your zeal and passion are unparalleled in this industry. Every time we talk, you continue to amaze me with your ideas and genuine concern for both the books you edit and the authors who write them. You are a visionary among visionaries and I am so honored to be working with you. You've made an immeasurable difference in my life, and I constantly thank God for the tremendous blessing the rest of the world calls Kate Duffy.

Chapter One

"I think we've got a spy."

Marcus Danvers's announcement erupted in Alex's mind like Mt. St. Helens on a bad day.

Pushing his chair back slightly from the massive walnut desk that sat in the center of his office, Alex met Marcus's expectant stare. "Why?"

Leaning in the open doorway, Marcus's six-foot-two-inch frame exuded casual relaxation, while his blue eyes glittered with anticipation and amusement. "Harrison's daughter called this morning."

The closer they got to seeing John Harrison's company dismantled, the less humor Alex found in anything.

"Explain."

Marcus crossed the oversized office and sat down in one of the chairs facing Alex's desk. "She wanted to know if I liked the idea of changing employers. Ms. Harrison said that she had a client interested in someone with my skills and experience."

Alex shrugged, making a concentrated effort not to overreact and feed Marcus's offbeat sense of humor. "She works for one of the most exclusive headhunting agencies in the Portland area. She makes a lot of calls like the one you received this morning."

Although he'd never met Isabel, Alex had no doubt she was a lot like her father. He stole men's ideas. She stole employees, specializing in the hi-tech industry. According to his sources, she was very good at her job.

Marcus stretched out his long legs and crossed them at the ankles. "If you ask me, it's too much of a coincidence right now. Our client is only months away from closing the deal on her dad's company and she calls your most valuable employee trying to lure him away."

"My most valuable employee being you?"

"Well, yes." Marcus attempted a modest look of acceptance. "Not to mention an employee with inside information about St. Clair's plans to take Hypertron apart."

Alex nodded. "I'll look into it."

Marcus stood up to leave.

"What did you say to her?"

Marcus turned around, his brows raised in mockery. "If I'd said yes, I wouldn't have told you about the phone call, now would I?"

"With your twisted sense of humor, that's not a given."

"I told her no, boss. I'm not interested in leaving CIS. Working for you gives me a chance to use my hunter's instincts without dressing up in fatigues and chasing some poor animal through the forest."

With a sardonic smile, Marcus left.

He was right. Operating CIS satisfied something both male and primitive inside Alex as well. Some called him a corporate raider, but that wasn't accurate. He was a purveyor of highly specialized information. He evaluated companies, identifying their strengths and weaknesses for investment groups. A few of those groups were led by true corporate raiders, men who made their money in the warlike world of hostile takeovers.

Alex had created CIS—Corporate Information Systems—on the advice of his dad, a few years before his death. Just out of college, Alex had considered pursuing a career in the field of arbitrage. His dad had suggested that Alex would be happier participating in the hunt than in the kill. He'd been right.

Providing information that could help companies to grow and change the landscape of the hi-tech industry was a deeply satisfying job. He'd discovered that building up was more satisfying than tearing down, hence the reason he seldom took on corporate raiders as clients.

Guy St. Clair was one of those exceptions. Alex looked forward to being in on the kill for the hostile takeover of Hypertron, with the primal anticipation of a predator ready to bring down its prey.

John Harrison owned Hypertron. Both the man and the company had played their roles in the untimely death of Alex's father. Alex had been biding his time for two years, waiting for an opportunity to redress that injury. It had finally come three months ago when two unrelated but fortuitous events had taken place.

The first had been John Harrison's overextension of his company in an untimely bid for expansion. The second had been when Guy St. Clair, a true corporate raider, had approached Alex for information on several companies including Hypertron. St. Clair bought companies and made his money in taking them apart and selling off the pieces—in this case, product patents.

Alex considered the takeover the perfect ending for the company that had destroyed his father by refusing him the right to patent the results of his personal research and development.

One hour and several information-gathering phone calls later, Alex surveyed the notes he'd taken. No overt behavior on Harrison's part or that of his company indicated that he knew of the impending hostile takeover or of CIS's role in it.

There was a chance Harrison was playing a deep game, though. If he suspected anything, his first order of business would be to secure accurate inside information. Hiring Marcus away from CIS would be a brilliant move in that direction.

Alex tapped his pen against the yellow pad on his desk and then opened a file next to it.

A picture of a young woman stared up at him. The black-and-white image couldn't tell him her hair or eye color, though that information was listed on her fact sheet—Hair: light brown; Eyes: green. The photo taunted him as it had for the two years since he'd opened the file on Hypertron, John Harrison, and his family. Because in that candid shot, Isabel Harrison looked innocent and too damn appealing for Alex's peace of mind.

The heart-shaped face and sparkling eyes called to him on a level he didn't understand.

He had had women in his life, on a very temporary basis, but he'd never found himself fantasizing about one of them when he was on a case. Yet this photo regularly found its way into his conscious mind. Had she been any other woman, he would have made her acquaintance by now, dated her, bedded her, and gotten rid of this longing.

But she wasn't any other woman. She was John Harrison's daughter, not exactly Alex's enemy, but a woman destined to hate him when his plans for her father's company came to fruition. Using the evidence of what she did for a living, he'd managed to convince himself the picture lied.

He had managed to stay away from her.

Until now. His options were limited in gathering the information that he needed on this new development and what he had avoided for two years seemed inevitable.

He would have to meet her because every possible line of inquiry led back to the same source: Isabel Harrison.

Isabel propped her feet on her desk and admired her new Italian leather pumps. Dark mauve, they were the perfect shade to complement the tailored jacket of her pantsuit. Sometimes size six feet had their advantages. She'd gotten her new pumps for a song off the clearance rack at her favorite trendy shoe store in Washington Square.

Smiling in remembered satisfaction, she shifted her gaze to the clipboard lying across her legs and wondered if she should put "an appreciation for footwear" on her list but decided against it. That might be pushing the male chromosome just a bit too far. And it was definitely the Y chromosome she needed, or at least the result of it . . . a man.

A small sound made Isabel swing her attention from the clipboard in front of her to the doorway of her office.

Her breath lodged in her throat.

A man stood there. Undoubtedly not *her* man but an impressive man just the same.

A nighthawk, she thought fancifully. There was just something so dark about this guy, and not only his appearance. Dark and intense. She could *feel* him standing less than a dozen feet away. His probing, deep brown gaze momentarily froze her in place, and she stared back at him with helpless fascination.

Black hair, cut just a little long, framed a face that was not pretty-boy handsome but drew a shocking response from her just the same. Attraction, strong and undeniable, slammed into her like an express train. Sensual lips above an aggressively square jawline snagged her attention before she got hold of her focus and sent it elsewhere.

He hadn't even worn the customary white shirt to relieve the dark charcoal gray of his suit. Instead, he wore a crisp black shirt with a Neru collar. At least eight inches taller than her own five feet four inches, he dominated her office and her breathing space.

The thought that this man probably had no appreciation for footwear flitted through her brain before she banished it. He was a potential client, not a potential date, and definitely not a potential mate. He was too overwhelming.

Summoning a smile, she scrambled to present a more professional appearance and whipped her feet off her desk. In her haste, she forgot about the clipboard resting against her legs, and it went tumbling to the beige carpet.

"Excuse me. I'll be right with you." She bent down to retrieve it.

Heat crept up her neck and into her face as she opened one of the drawers in her oak desk and shoved the clipboard inside. He'd come farther into the room while she'd been busy dealing with the clipboard and now stood on the other side of her desk.

Remembering her manners, she stood up and extended her hand. "Isabel Harrison. What can I do for you?"

Nanny Number Four had drilled courtesy into her: "Courtesy is not merely a sign of good breeding, my dear, but it is more importantly a mark of respect from one person to another," she had repeatedly said. Isabel tried always to be courteous and had put the trait down on her list, wondering all the while if it would weed out too many potential candidates.

Not many men bothered with polite gestures anymore.

The man towering over her desk took her hand in his.

Heat transferred from his strong, masculine fingers to her own and she hastily pulled her hand back before she made a complete fool of herself over nothing more than a common gesture of courtesy. A lot of people had warm hands. Hers were probably uncommonly chilled for some reason and that is why his skin had felt so hot against her own.

It was not some kind of primitive female reaction thing.

Surreptitiously glancing at the calendar on her desk, Isabel confirmed that she had no appointment scheduled. She rarely did during the lunch hour, but it wasn't unusual to have a client drop in unannounced. It was very unusual, however, for a client to have the effect on her senses that this man had. She didn't even know his name.

She indicated a floral-covered chair in front of her desk. "Won't you have a seat, Mr. . . ."

Folding his body into the chair she had offered, he said, "Alex Trahern, and I think you know why I'm here."

So this was Alex Trahern, owner of CIS and boss to the man she had called this morning to discuss career options. She barely stifled a sigh. She didn't want one of *those* confrontations this morning. She really didn't. If employers would just realize that she wasn't the enemy. It wasn't her fault that they often underpaid and undervalued their employees, making her job of placing them with other companies that much easier. She wouldn't *have* a job if all employees were satisfied with their positions.

However, her phone call to Marcus Danvers earlier that morning had been a complete failure. He was one of the rare employees who had absolutely no interest in moving on. Perhaps if she told Mr. Trahern that, he would forego the whole warning-her-off-of-his-employee routine.

She summoned her most convincing smile, the one she used to encourage her clients to offer a higher salary or better benefits for the employees they wanted her to find. "Mr. Trahern—"

"I prefer Alex," he interrupted.

Nanny Number Four would be appalled, but Isabel nodded. "Alex, then. Although I am not at liberty to discuss my clients or potential clients, I can say that if I had contacted one of your employees, you can rest assured that he or she showed no interest in changing companies."

Instead of looking placated, he frowned. "I don't like games, Isabel. I know that you called my assistant, Marcus Danvers, this morning with an offer to lure him away from my company. I want to know why."

So Mr. Danvers had told Alex about her phone call. She wasn't surprised. Some employees found that mentioning she had contacted them increased their leverage when negotiating for employment benefits. Others merely felt that they owed knowledge of the phone call to their employers as proof of their loyalty. She didn't disagree with either stand, but it sometimes made her day less pleasant.

"Strictly speaking, I did not call Mr. Danvers with an offer this morning." The conversation hadn't gotten that far.

"The fact that an offer was not extended is unimportant. You called Marcus and I want to know who put you up to it."

Oh dear. This was going to be worse than usual. Being

warned away from an employee who had exhibited no interest in changing companies could be handled relatively smoothly. However, when an employer started asking questions about her clients, she knew she had to tread very carefully.

"I'm sure you will understand," she said, with more hope than certainty, "particularly considering the type of business that you run, that I cannot breach the confidentiality of my clients."

Alex leaned forward, his brown eyes intent. "What exactly do you know about my business, Isabel?"

Squelching the ridiculous urge to back away from her desk, she straightened her shoulders. "I make it a policy to investigate the companies of the employees that I contact. It's good business practice. Naturally, when an employer expressed an interest in hiring Mr. Danvers, I gathered what information I could on CIS. I must admit that it wasn't a great deal." She looked at Alex, trying to gauge what he was thinking.

The tensing of his jaw indicated that he wasn't satisfied with her answer. "What did you learn?"

There was no harm in telling him what she had discovered. After all, it wasn't anything he didn't already know. "I discovered that your company sells a service rather than a product. You are apparently a purveyor of information."

He nodded, his expression still very intent and somewhat forbidding, and yet she had this strange compulsion to reach out and touch him. She swallowed a groan at her own stupidity. Touch him. Right.

"I also learned that you have very low turnover in your company. I could not find anyone locally that had worked for you in the past."

Satisfaction momentarily gleamed in his eyes.

"This morning I discovered that your company engenders fierce loyalty in its employees as well." She couldn't help smiling with her own satisfaction over that fact. "It's always a pleasure to come across someone truly content in his job."

Alex leaned back in his chair and considered her with an air of wry disbelief. "I can't see a headhunter finding pleasure in an employee's job satisfaction. Wouldn't that make it a little challenging to lure the employee away?"

Darn. Just when she thought things were getting pleasant. "I don't care for the term headhunter. I consider myself more along the lines of a career guidance specialist, and I assure you, my primary goal is to see people content in their jobs. Certainly, sometimes that requires helping them find positions with new companies, but it is always in the best interest of the person making the move."

"Is that how you justify stealing a company's most valuable asset?" He didn't even blink when launching that insult.

Irritation started to replace her desire for diplomacy. "I do not *steal* anything. Employees are people, not things. They have the right to fair compensation for their work, competitive benefits, and a comfortable work environment. If that means moving to a different company, then the ones to blame are the managers and owners of the companies responsible for a lack in any of those three areas."

"Convenient philosophy for someone in your line of work."

She'd had enough. "Okay. Let's get this over with. Tell me not to contact your assistant again. I'll tell you that he's made it clear he isn't interested in moving, so it's not an issue." She stood up and indicated the door with a wave of her hand. "You can leave and I'll get back to work."

Alex didn't even shift in his chair. "Do you get a lot?"

"A lot of what?" she asked with exasperation.

"Employers warning you off of their employees."

She went to run her fingers through her hair and remembered belatedly that she'd twisted it into a French knot that morning. She felt strands of hair slip loose of the knot and fall against her face. Things were just not going her way. She immediately removed her hands, but the damage had been done. Another lock of hair slid from the neat coil, and she knew that within seconds it was going to look like a rat's nest. Darn it.

She yanked the clip from her hair, intending to pull it back into the twist. "Yes, as a matter of fact I do. It's one of the hazards of the job. You wouldn't believe what I've had to put up with."

He paralyzed her with a lazy smile. "Try me."

She stood there like a simpleton with her hands stilled in their attempt to repair the damage she'd done to her hairstyle. He had a dimple and goodness only knew why, but it had an astounding effect on her insides.

Giving up on trying to fix her hair without a mirror and with hands that shook for no apparent reason, she finger-combed the strands and let it fall in its customary blunt cut to her shoulders. Obviously, he wasn't going to leave immediately, so she sat back down.

"I've had employers threaten me, call me names, and throw temper tantrums right here in my office. The worst as far as I'm concerned, though, are the ones that come by and offer me money to not have contact with their employees."

Alex brought his hands together in a loose grip in front of him. "Why does that bother you? It seems like good business sense. You still get what amounts to a commission and the employer keeps his employee. It's a win–win situation."

He clearly didn't get it. "Win–win for whom? The employee is stuck with a boss who would rather pay what amounts to protection money than improve the quality of life at work. Believe it or not, I'm not interested in earning my commissions that way. I'm a career guidance specialist, not the mafia, for heaven's sake."

Surprise and something else flickered in his dark brown eyes. If she didn't know better, she would have thought it was desire. She must be mistaken. For goodness' sake, she had just met the man. Besides, he couldn't be attracted to her. He didn't like her.

"So you only called Marcus this morning because you wanted to provide him with a better job opportunity than working for me? Your client's needs had nothing to do with it." The sarcastic disbelief in his voice grated against her nerves.

She didn't know why she'd given in to the urge to try to convince this man to see her differently. It was obviously a wasted effort.

"I called Mr. Danvers because my client specifically asked me to. I had other potential candidates for the job on my books with qualifications I thought were a better match, but I always try to please my clients, whether employer or employee. I had no personal desire to lure your assistant away from a job he enjoys. Once I discovered that he wasn't interested, I congratulated him on finding a good position, told him to call if he ever felt the need for a change, and hung up."

"That still doesn't tell me who hired you to go gunning for my assistant."

Really. The way this guy thought. "I didn't *go gunning* for anyone and as I mentioned, confidentiality prevents me from telling you who my client is."

Alex nodded and stood. He extended his hand in an unexpected show of courtesy. "Thank you for your time, Isabel. I apologize if my comments or attitude have offended you. I can see that you take your responsibility to your clients, both the employer and the employee, very seriously."

She shook his hand, nonplussed at the abrupt change in his demeanor. She was pretty sure he had meant to offend her. So, why the apology?

"I can understand your concerns." So many employers truly had something to worry about in this situation. However, Alex didn't. "In your case, I believe they are unfounded. Mr. Danvers is obviously content to stay where he is."

Alex let his hand linger on hers for just a second longer than a formal business handshake required and then let her go.

As he left her office she couldn't help wondering how he would do against the requirements on her list.

Alex walked through the anteroom to his office and tossed instructions at his secretary as he passed her. "I don't want to be disturbed for thirty minutes, Miss Richards."

Veronica Richards looked up from her meticulously organized desk and smiled a cool, professional smile. "Very well, Mr. Trahern. I've updated your task manager with this morning's messages. When you get a moment you might wish to review them."

He nodded and headed into his office. How did she manage to make a politely worded request sound like an order? No doubt about it, he might be the boss, but Veronica ran the office. Not that he would call her Veronica to her face. His young but very proper secretary would never countenance such familiarity, though she'd worked for him practically since he'd opened CIS.

Sitting down at his desk a few seconds later, Alex

emptied his mind of all thoughts related to his zealously efficient secretary and concentrated instead on the information matrix he was building around Isabel Harrison.

The image of her running her fingers through her honey-brown hair kept superimposing itself over the data he was trying to compile. He finally gave up and allowed himself to focus on the woman, not the facts surrounding her. Isabel in person had not met any of his preconceived notions of what John Harrison's daughter would be like. In fact, she had been the living, breathing embodiment of everything a two-year-old, black-and-white photo had implied: innocent, trusting, and somewhat naive.

He had expected a calculating businesswoman, not a self-proclaimed career guidance specialist.

And he had not expected to be physically attracted to her, but why the hell he hadn't realized that his reaction to her in person would outshine his reaction to a photo, he didn't know. He was usually a lot less self-delusional than that.

From the moment he'd walked into her office, he'd found it difficult to keep his concentration on the task at hand. Isabel kept getting in the way. Her hand had felt delicate in his own, and her guileless green eyes had spoken of warmth and gentleness rather than calculation and greed.

Then, it had been the little wisps of hair falling from her sleek twist behind her head and flirting around her face. He'd wanted to touch them, a completely uncharacteristic response for him when he was in an information-gathering mode. Hormones had no place in business.

When she had pulled her hair down completely, he'd felt his heartbeat accelerate while his hands actually itched to reach out and touch her. From the matter-of-fact way she had finger-combed the silky strands, it was obvious she had no clue how sexy the gesture was.

It had only compounded the reaction he'd had when she stood up from her desk. Her tailored jacket and trousers had emphasized all-too-tempting feminine curves.

He wanted her and the knowledge rattled him.

He could not afford to let things get complicated at this juncture. He needed a clear head. He needed to know who had hired Isabel to approach Marcus.

She had said it was someone who would have done better with one of her other employee clients. That implied either Isabel was ignorant of her father's plans or that it hadn't been John Harrison who got her to contact Marcus.

Or Isabel had been lying.

She could be a consummate actress. The little routine with her hair could have been planned. The air of innocence and naïveté put on for his benefit.

Adept at reading people, Alex didn't like the fact that after this brief meeting he had more questions than answers.

The only solution was to see her again.

Chapter Two

Alex Trahern had a dimple.

That fact kept flitting in and out of Isabel's thoughts the morning after the devastating male had visited her office.

She was supposed to be calling recently placed clients and checking on their job satisfaction. However, each break between calls grew longer and longer as her mind insisted on going back to the meeting she'd had with Marcus Danvers's employer the day before.

If she didn't get herself together soon, she'd mess up her morning schedule and have to shift the calls to another spot on her busy calendar.

A short knock, followed quickly by her office door opening, came as a relief. Bettina, Isabel's dearest friend, walked in carrying two steaming, brightly colored mugs.

Isabel smiled in welcome as the rich aroma of coffee teased her. The other woman set one of the cups in front of Isabel before gracefully sliding into the same chair Alex had sat in the day before.

One long leg crossed over the other and Bettina cocked

her head to the side. "Ready for some coffee and girl-chat?"

"Yes." More than ready. "I'm having a lousy time concentrating this morning. Maybe a short break will help me get my focus back."

Bettina's rich laugh filled Isabel's office. "Girlfriend, don't lie to yourself. After a visit from Mr. Tall, Dark, and Dangerous yesterday, a coffee break isn't going to get you back on track. You might as well give up the game and go shoe shopping." She pretended to wipe perspiration off her forehead with one chocolate-brown hand. "Man, that dude was hot!"

Isabel gave her friend a mock frown. "Bettina, you are a married woman with three children. You aren't supposed to notice *hot men*."

Bettina's black eyes widened in amazement. "I may be married, but I'd have to be dead not to notice that dude."

Isabel laughed.

Far from dead, Bettina was one of the most vibrantly alive people Isabel had ever met. The same age as Isabel, Bettina had been married for six years and had three adorable children, not to mention one adoring husband.

It was easy to understand Tyrone's affection for his wife. Bettina was gorgeous. She could easily be mistaken for a teenager, had a figure that even looked good in biking shorts, and hair that Isabel would kill for.

They'd spent their first meeting laughing over PMS and had been fast friends ever since.

"He's not *that* good looking."

Bettina, serious for once, nodded. "He's not handsome like my Tyrone, but he's got presence in spades. I saw the way you watched him leave, girlfriend."

So what if she'd watched the guy walk out? A woman

had to have a sense of self-preservation in situations like this. It meant nothing. "He was just another disgruntled employer, offended that I would have the temerity to contact one of his 'assets' with a competitive job offer."

Bettina groaned. "Aw, nuts, I was sure he stayed in your office so long because you were finally going to get lucky."

"I don't need to *get lucky*, Bet. I'm not looking for someone hot and dangerous to share a wild night of sex with." Though just thinking of what such a night might be like with Alex had her temperature spiking. "I'm looking for father-and-husband material."

"The two do not have to be mutually exclusive, you know."

"Right. If a man is good looking, nine times out of ten, he's gay or a player. The other one is usually married."

"Well, my Tyrone is married . . ."

Isabel took a sip of her coffee. Bettina had added hazelnut syrup and cream. It was divine and slid over her tongue like a warm wake-up call to her senses.

"There is only one Tyrone Fry, my dear friend, and you've got him. The rest of us poor souls will have to make do with what's left."

Bettina complacently nodded her head—long, curling braids that looked like ringlets swaying against her shoulders as she did so. "That's right, but that doesn't mean you've got to give up all hope."

"I haven't. That's why I've got my list. I'm hopeful, not hopeless."

Her friend looked unconvinced, which was no surprise. Bettina thought Isabel's approach to her problems was worse than unorthodox, it was a recipe for disaster.

"Bet, let's not get into that again right now."

Bettina sighed and nodded. "Was it awful, your meeting with Mr. T, D & D? I feel terrible. I thought you were in here having fun, or I would have interrupted with some dire emergency you had to see to that very minute."

"His name is Alex Trahern. He's the president of CIS. And no, it wasn't awful. He was really pretty decent there at the end."

"Meaning he put you through the wringer first," Bettina surmised after taking a sip of her coffee.

"I guess. A little." She'd certainly experienced *something*. "But it wasn't awful, so don't worry about it."

Her friend's intense scrutiny made Isabel squirm.

A slow smile spread across Bettina's face and her eyes lit with knowing amusement. "So, you do have the hots for him. I knew it."

Rather than deny the ridiculous accusation, Isabel said, "You know I don't mix business with my personal life. It's too messy. Besides, now that I have my list of requirements, I'm not going to date just any man that comes along. He's going to have to pass muster."

Bettina's face softened in understanding. "Honey, don't let that unfaithful lecher turn you off good men."

"He hasn't." Isabel wrapped her hands around her mug, enjoying the warmth. "Didn't you hear me? I've got my list. I'll be able to tell a good man when I meet him."

"And Alex Trahern? How does he stack up against your *job description*?" Bettina asked slyly, for once not arguing the merits of Isabel's list.

There were definite drawbacks to working with your best friend. "It doesn't matter. He's a business associate."

"Not technically." Bettina drew the words out.

"What do you mean?"

The ringing of Isabel's phone prevented her friend from answering. Giving Bettina an apologetic smile, Isabel picked the headset off the cradle and fit it to her head, then pressed the talk button. "This is Isabel Harrison."

"Isabel. Alex here."

Giving Bettina a warning glance, she said, "Hi, Alex. Was there something I could do for you?"

Bettina mouthed, "I told you so," her brows raising in a parody of lecherous intentions.

"Yes. You could have dinner with me tonight."

It took a moment for Isabel to comprehend what Alex had just said and when she did, it felt as if all the air had been sucked from the room. "I, uh, I have a policy."

"I hope it's to say yes to dinner invitations."

"Uh, no. Not exactly. My policy has to do with not dating business associates. I'm sorry, Alex."

Bettina glared at her and made a show of pretending to hang herself. Isabel spun her chair so her back was to her friend.

"Isabel?" Alex asked.

"Yes?"

"I'm not your business associate. I've never hired you to work for me, and I assume I'd know if someone had hired you to offer me a job."

"Well, yes."

"So, what time can I pick you up?"

He certainly had no problems with self-esteem.

"I didn't say that I'd go."

"Will you?" His voice came right across the fiber-optic phone line and took hold of her feminine instincts with a seductive grip that did not let go.

She tried to weigh the pros and cons of saying yes, but all she could think of was that darn dimple.

"Yes."

A whoop of delight sounded from behind her and Isabel gripped the phone receiver closer to her ear.

"I'll pick you up at seven. We can have dinner downtown."

The phone clicked in her ear. He hadn't said good-bye.

She had not told him her address or how to find her condo. For a man with his business background, that would be an easy detail to attend to, she supposed.

Still, he could have said good-bye.

Isabel applied her makeup, all the while running through the requirements on her list. If she was going out with Alex, she wasn't going to make her usual interpersonal relationship mistakes. Not this time.

Too much was at stake.

Her entire future and the future of her yet-to-be-conceived children.

Children she wanted desperately.

Her friends told her that at twenty-eight, she was still too young to be hearing her biological clock. Unfortunately, she couldn't seem to get the darn thing to stop chiming so loudly. She found her gaze following women with strollers in the mall, and these days she actually spent as much time in baby apparel and accessory stores as she did in shoe stores.

She watched the birthing channel on television and had even cried over one successful delivery. Her obsession with babies might not be normal for a twenty-eight-year-old woman with a well-established career, but it wasn't going away.

She wanted her own baby to love.

The fact that in some ways she was quite old-fashioned necessitated that the man who fathered that baby be her husband as well, a man who would be involved in the life of his children. *Not like her father.*

Staring blindly at the vanity mirror, she thought about how she couldn't remember much about her own mother. But she did remember how it felt to have a much-absent father and the string of nannies, the host of strangers who tucked Isabel in at night instead of her one surviving parent.

She wanted something different for her baby.

Only she hadn't had any more success in her dating than she'd had in creating a bond with her father. After her last relationship had ended in disaster, she decided to take a more pragmatic approach to finding what she sought.

Clearly, going on instincts wasn't working.

Brad had looked so perfect on the surface. Handsome. Charming. Urbane. A successful businessman. But those characteristics had been mere camouflage. Underneath had lurked a deceitful wretch. Not good father material at all.

Once she'd gotten over the trauma of their breakup and of making a hash of yet another personal relationship, she acknowledged that she'd ever done only one thing really well. She was unparalleled in her ability to match employees with the appropriate employment opportunity.

It was only natural that she would decide to apply her skills in that area to her current dilemma and treat it much as she would filling a job vacancy for a client.

She had set about creating a list of requirements for a potential mate with the same focus and attention she gave to writing up a comprehensive job description.

She mentally ticked off the items on her list so far. The first level was superficial, like her ex-boyfriend Brad. She didn't leave it off, however, because she'd discovered that the superficial elements in a job environment could make or break a working relationship. So, she had carefully detailed her desires regarding outward appearances and the sorts of things he and she needed to have in common.

The second level was more complicated and a lot harder to judge. She wanted to find a man who had his priorities straight. She looked down at her list. Number six was "good work habits."

Brad had had terrible work habits. She should have paid attention to that telling fact, but she'd overlooked the many times he dealt with pages and cell phone calls during their dates.

She'd told herself that unlike her father, her ex had at least taken time away from the company to go out to dinner and the theater. He rarely cut a date short to handle a business emergency. Not like her father, who had frequently ended up leaving the table halfway through dinner on the rare nights he had made it home to eat the meal at all.

Brad had worked some weekends, but Isabel had convinced herself that an occasional weekend at work wasn't the end of a relationship. Learning that those weekends were spent working at something other than his job had proved Isabel wrong.

His efforts at keeping his female boss satisfied sexually had definitely put a damper on his and Isabel's relationship.

She pushed the memories away with a mental shove strong enough to send them out of her head and into the next universe.

Tonight was about Alex and what she would be watching for in his behavior and speech. Just like an employee interview.

She grimaced as she considered the next level of requirements. Assuming a man passed Level One and Level Two, he still had to show an aptitude for the extremely important Level Three: 'interpersonal relationships'—her own particular Waterloo.

The first item on her list was physical compatibility. This wasn't about the way a man looked, but rather how she responded to him on a wholly physical level. Something she'd dismissed before as unimportant. Not so. If she had listened to her body when her ex kissed her, she would have stopped dating him long before the embarrassing experience of walking in on him with another woman.

His touch had been pleasant but nothing more. She wasn't looking for fireworks and overwhelming passion, but she wanted something more than pleasant. She wanted at least a spark of desire, something that would tempt her to give herself completely to a man.

She'd only risked that kind of vulnerability once and that was another memory she did not want to dwell on.

No doubt a psychoanalyst would have a heyday with her current situation. She wanted a family badly enough to search for a husband, but did not want to risk letting down her emotional barriers in order to make love to a man. She hadn't with Brad, but then she hadn't wanted him, either.

The deeply religious Nanny Number Seven had told her that intimacy with a man was meant for marriage and a woman gave bits of herself away when she made love, so Isabel should be very careful who she gave those bits to. The advice had had a huge impact on a young woman who had already experienced a lot of pain from opening herself to others.

When her peers had started experimenting sexually in high school and later in college, she had simply not been interested. No one had ever affected her enough to make her want to go against Nanny Number Seven's advice. Well, almost no one, and she wasn't sure that counted.

Sometimes she wondered whether she was capable of the kind of sexual response necessary to fuel the passionate side of a relationship. If that was true, she didn't know how she would ever have the family she craved.

Relegating the disturbing doubts to the furthest recesses of her mind, she finished applying her makeup.

Alex's black Aston Martin rolled forward as the traffic control light for the entrance onto Hwy 26 briefly turned green and then red again. He resigned himself to taking as long to merge onto the freeway as it had taken him to travel from his house to the on-ramp.

When he had bought the place, which he also planned to use as the base for CIS, he'd decided he wanted to be where the majority of the electronic firms in Oregon were located. That meant moving west of Portland to what many termed Little Silicon Valley.

Not so little—hundreds of electronic firms, including several sites for the biggest chip manufacturer in the world, made their homes within a fifteen-mile radius of Alex's strategic location.

His small farm had a Portland address, but was closer to Beaverton than to Portland's city center. And every time he walked into the barn, which had been remodeled into modern office space, he felt a measure of satisfaction. It belonged to him, as did the farmhouse he was renovating in his spare time.

Considering the romantic décor of Isabel's small office, he guessed she would appreciate his desire to strip the wood moldings of their paint and varnish them with a natural, clean finish. Not that she would ever see his farmhouse or his offices.

Once he knew who wanted to hire Marcus, Alex would not see her again, period.

She deserved that much consideration. It wouldn't be fair to build a friendship with her that would undoubtedly end in recriminations and anger once his role in St.

Clair's hostile takeover of Hypertron became known. The thought irritated him and he pushed it away.

St. Clair's plans for Hypertron had nothing to do with Isabel, and although they were the culmination of Alex's desires, he could not be blamed for the mess Harrison was shortly going to find himself in. Alex hadn't made the decisions that put Hypertron in such a vulnerable place to take over.

No, that had been John Harrison himself, the same man responsible for Alex's father's death.

Shifting the Aston Martin into gear, he accelerated onto the highway, immediately transferring into the left lane as he continued to accelerate. A quick glance at the digital numbers of the clock on his dash confirmed that he was right on time. No need to rush, but he didn't ease his foot off the accelerator. Soon he would be at Isabel's condo.

Would she wear another business suit to dinner, or would she dress in something more feminine? He knew she was leery of him. He'd seen it in her eyes in her office that morning.

What the hell was he thinking? He and Isabel Harrison had no future. They had no relationship. He would be a fool to try to take them beyond anything more than a surface involvement. His words reminding Isabel that they technically did not have a business association came back to haunt him.

Was she going to expect romance? Perhaps asking her out had not been the most effective way to get the information he needed. It had seemed like an expedient plan at the time, but now he could imagine countless complications.

Unwanted complications.

He said a word that he reserved for severe frustration. He was not used to being unsure of his judgment, and his doubts were unnerving. As unnerving as the anticipation he felt at seeing Isabel again. She was the daughter of his sworn enemy, and yet he couldn't get the image of her sweet smile and clear green eyes out of his head.

Alex rang the doorbell at Isabel's condo, unaccountably irritated that she chose to live in an unsecured building. Didn't she realize how many dangers a single woman faced when living alone?

The door swung open and Alex's curiosity about Isabel's attire was answered. Her shimmery black dress with spaghetti straps clung in all the right places, covering about as much of her legs as would an oversized T-shirt. Her feet looked sexy as hell in a pair of black satin shoes with three-inch spiked heels.

Alex's body reacted like a teenager on an overload of hormones. "Don't you think you will be a little cold in that?"

This wasn't exactly southern California. And although it was still early fall and an Indian summer made for warm days, the nights were plenty chilly.

Her smile faltered and her face took on a decidedly cool cast. "I have a jacket. I'll be fine."

Was her jacket going to cover the long expanse of exposed legs? He doubted it. "Where is it?"

"In the living room." She pivoted on her heel. "I'll get it."

He followed her inside, closing the door behind him.

She stopped in the living room when she realized he'd followed her. "Would you like a drink before we go?"

A drink sounded good—anything to get his raging libido under control. Too bad they didn't have time. "We have reservations in half an hour. We should leave in case we hit traffic going into downtown."

She nodded and grabbed a little jacket off the arm of her white leather sofa. The entire room was done in white and shades of light brown. Beige, his mother would have called it.

He stepped forward to help her. She gave him a startled look, but allowed him to adjust the stiffened black silk across her shoulders. She'd pulled her honey-brown hair into a twist again, leaving the tantalizing, womanly column of her neck exposed. It took tremendous willpower not to brush it with his fingers.

If he didn't do something fast, he was going to lose objectivity in this information-gathering expedition.

He refused to think of it as a date. The word was rife with too many unwanted possibilities. He took a hasty step away from Isabel and out of temptation's way. It didn't help. Her fragrance, some kind of flowers, reached out and wrapped itself around his senses so that he might as well have been holding her in his arms.

She turned and faced him, giving him a tentative smile. "Ready."

She didn't look ready. The tiny jacket looked no warmer than her sexy little dress and both did more to accentuate the high curve of her full breasts than to disguise them.

He was glad the heater was already warmed up in the Aston Martin. He hoped he could find a parking spot close to the restaurant. He didn't want her walking outside in such flimsy clothes, and he wasn't about to tempt fate by putting his arm around her to keep her warm.

"We'd better get going, then," he said.

Isabel allowed Alex to push her chair in for her and wondered how to deal with schizophrenic courtesy when it came to her requirements for a potential mate.

Alex had insulted her dress upon arriving at her door, then helped her into her jacket as if the small act of courtesy came as natural to him as breathing. Upon leaving, he had lectured her on security and been appalled to learn that she rarely remembered to check the peephole before opening her door. He had then held the car door open for her to get in and had come around to open it for her once they reached the restaurant.

He certainly had good taste in restaurants.

He'd made reservations at one of her favorites, the dining room in the Heathman Hotel. She loved the ambiance of the restored hotel and could *feel* the history in the room, even sitting in a canvas director-style chair that was more appropriate for Hollywood. She wasn't going to get sidetracked by her surroundings, though. She had a real dilemma. Did she mark Alex down as an inconsiderate jerk or a polite charmer?

She covertly studied him over the top of her menu as the waiter recited that night's specials to them. Alex had changed from his business suit of the morning into a pair of charcoal gray slacks and a raw-silk shirt in the same shade. The top two buttons were undone, revealing curling black chest hair. Sexy. Definitely sexy . . . and dangerous.

He ordered a bottle of white wine without consulting her. *Typical male arrogance or old-fashioned courtesy?*

The waiter left and she put down her menu. "I can't decide."

"Try the salmon almondine. It's very good."

She played with the stem of her water glass. "That's not what I meant. I'm going to have the Chef's Special. I like eating things that aren't on the menu."

"Entrees that make it to the menu are ones that other customers have liked well enough to order over and over," he replied, as if explaining an important concept to her.

"I'm not interested in following the pack. I like to try new things."

"That's a good way to end up burned. I prefer calculated risks." He set down his menu and took a sip of water.

"I imagine you do. After all, you are in the business of gathering information so that others can minimize their risks and calculate their odds of winning."

He considered her a moment before answering, his intent scrutiny sending warm shivers through her. "Marcus says that we're hunters."

"But hunters are predators. You just supply the information." She didn't understand how the term applied to what CIS provided.

Alex shrugged. "It's both the method and the product that defines what we do."

His words sent a sharp sense of unease through her. He was right. She didn't know anything about his methods. Were they honest? Somehow, she couldn't imagine them not being, and yet there was a ruthlessness about him, a throwback gene that she could not deny.

"I have to admit that before you came into my office, I had pictured you as the scholarly type." How wrong could you get?

Alex was a lot more like a panther than a professor.

"*The scholarly type.*" He said the words as if tasting them for flavor. "What does that mean?"

She waved her hand airily, wishing she'd kept her mouth shut for once. "You know, someone who spends a lot of time in libraries or in front of a computer screen. Sort of nerdy, maybe."

"How do you see me now?"

As a predator. She almost blurted the words out, but managed to hold them in check. "You aren't nerdy at all. My office mate called you Mr. Tall, Dark, and Dangerous."

He didn't smile at her small joke, but eyed her with a sort of bleakness she didn't understand. "Do you think I'm dangerous to you, Isabel?"

The waiter appeared with their wine before she could answer.

"Well?" Alex said as soon as they were once again alone, "Do you think I'm a dangerous man?"

He wasn't going to let it drop.

"I'm not sure what to think about you," she blurted out in all honesty.

He considered her words and his wine before raising his Hershey-chocolate eyes to fix her with a questioning gaze. "Is that what you meant earlier when you said you couldn't decide?"

She played their conversation back through her mind and remembered her comment. "Yes. In a way. To be honest, you aren't a man easily cataloged."

"I would think that wouldn't bother a risk taker like you."

"Risk taker?"

"Yes."

"Why do you say that?" She wasn't like that at all.

He didn't quite smile, but she sensed that he was amused. "You work in a job that puts you on the receiving end of some pretty irate customers—"

"My clients are all very happy with my performance," she interrupted.

He waved that aside. "I was using the word customer loosely. I meant others like me, who don't like knowing that you've gone after one of their employees."

Was he still angry about that? "Oh."

"You live alone in an unsecured community."

She gave a soft laugh. "This may surprise you, but I'm one of several single women that own condos in my complex. Trust me, we aren't a bunch of bungee jumpers."

He let that slide. "Then, there's the way you like to order your food."

He considered ordering the Chef's Special a risk?

He sat back in his chair and pinned her with his powerful, dark, eyes. "However, the biggest piece of evidence that you aren't a cautious person is that you agreed to have dinner with me tonight."

She agreed but probably for reasons entirely different from the ones he was implying.

"*Should* I be worried? Are you planning something nefarious for later in the evening, or is this part of some devious plot that's going to leave me devastated?" She asked the questions facetiously and couldn't have been more surprised when the square line of his jaw tensed.

"Maybe you should be a little more worried about things like that, Isabel. You know nothing about me."

She had him there. "I know a great deal about you. I investigated your company, remember?"

His frown did not lighten. "You thought I was the scholarly type."

She chewed on her lip. He had a point.

"Look. Is there a purpose to this?" He was making her nervous.

His expression lightened. "You asked me why I thought you were a risk taker."

Her fingers relaxed their grip on her wineglass stem. What would he think if she admitted to him that she was practically a virgin at the ripe old age of twenty-eight? He'd have a hard time justifying his view of her then. Or perhaps not. Maybe she made up for her emotional wariness by taking chances in other areas of her life.

And where was all this navel-gazing taking her? Exactly nowhere.

She took a small sip of wine. "You could be right, but to be honest, I've never thought of myself that way."

She didn't like to go along with the flow, but she'd never equated that with a willingness to step out on the edge. She still wasn't completely sure she agreed with him.

His hooded dark eyes were unreadable. "We rarely see ourselves as others see us."

She frowned in thought over that. "Do you think that's because we don't allow the world to see all that we are, or that sometimes we are too close to ourselves to see clearly?"

"A little of both, maybe."

Was she really sitting here having a philosophical discussion on self-perception with *Mr. Tall, Dark, and Dangerous?* Bettina would be appalled. Isabel could hear her friend's words as if she were there. *Get with the program, girlfriend. This is a date! Flirt, already.*

Yeah, right. Flirt. She didn't even know *how* to get with the program. Something about Alex's mood discouraged chitchat and yet that was a woman's best weapon on a first date. Silence reigned until the waiter brought their food.

Alex looked up from his salmon. "How is it?" he asked pointing to her plate.

She smiled. "Fabulous." The shrimp and pasta in garlic sauce was delicious.

"Some risks pay off."

"That's nice to know. After all, I wouldn't want to think the risk I took in going out with you, a virtual stranger, wouldn't be rewarded." She smiled and winked at him with flirtatious recklessness.

Bettina would be proud of her.

He contemplated her statement far longer than should have been necessary while his long fingers drummed a melody on the tabletop. "Only time will tell."

She shivered but wasn't sure why. What was that cryptic statement supposed to mean?

He frowned. "I told you that dress would be too cold."

Not again. "Has anyone ever told you that you practice schizophrenic courtesy?"

His body gave a small jerk and his dark brown eyes widened, for once clearly expressing his thoughts—surprise and a little confusion.

She experienced a measure of satisfaction that she'd managed to knock him off-kilter, even a little.

It seemed only fair, as she had felt off balance since the moment he'd arrived in her office the day before. "It's true, you know. You can be very polite and then say or do something incredibly rude. The most amazing part is that you appear completely oblivious to it."

"My comment about your dress offended you?"

She wanted to laugh at his honest disbelief.

"Both times you said it, yes. And the fact that you lectured me on where I live, implying I'm a naive ninny for not checking in the peephole every time the doorbell rings."

"Why should my concern for your physical comfort and well-being offend you?"

She stared at him. "You really don't get it."

"Why would you be offended that I might offer a suggestion for your well-being?" He shrugged. "No, I don't get it."

"I didn't miss anything here, did I? This really is our first date. We met this morning. I haven't got amnesia about a several-month-long relationship, or something. Right?"

His eyes narrowed. "We don't have a relationship."

And from the tone of his voice he wasn't interested in one, either. Why had he asked her out then? All evening, she'd felt like something was missing from the equation. He didn't treat her as if they were on a first date. He'd just made it clear that he didn't want a relationship, but then he didn't seem to be angling for a bout of casual sex, either.

"That's just my point. No, we don't have a relationship. *This is our first date.* On a first date, you are supposed to compliment my dress, not criticize it for impracticality. You aren't supposed to remind me later that you were right, either. It just isn't done. That sort of stuff is supposed to be saved for petty disagreements down the road."

He stared at her like she'd lost her mind. Maybe she had.

She frowned at him. "Well?"

His eyes narrowed in wariness. "What?"

"Compliment my dress."

Now, his chocolate gaze filled with incredulity. "You're serious?"

It shouldn't be so hard for him, but then maybe the disconcerting attraction she felt wasn't mutual.

She frowned at the thought. "As a heartbeat."

"It's sexy as hell and so are your shoes. Is that good enough?" He looked and sounded harassed.

He'd noticed her shoes? A funny feeling unfurled in her stomach at the compliment. She might have ordered him to say it, but she still liked hearing it. How shallow could you get?

"Thank you."

"You're welcome. Now, would you like to put your jacket back on? It's damn cold in here."

It didn't feel that way to her. Not now.

"I'm fine. Maybe later," she conceded when he frowned, and then wished she'd agreed as her nipples tightened under his intense regard.

Trying to ignore the unusual situation, she returned to her dinner. They had finished their meal, and the waiter had gone to get the dessert tray when Alex spoke again.

"Tell me about the A.A. Placement Agency."

Wary, as she always was when people wanted to discuss her work, she asked, "What do you want to know?"

"What does the 'A.A.' stand for?"

She had a hard time believing a man with his penchant for digging out information didn't already know, but she answered anyway. "Above Average. We pride ourselves on matching the best employee with the job."

"Except with Marcus you were willing to go with someone not as well qualified because the client requested it, right?"

She smoothed the napkin in her lap. "Right."

"How long have you worked there?"

Relieved that he wasn't going to pursue the topic of his assistant, she answered immediately. "Ever since I graduated from college."

The waiter returned with the dessert tray. Alex chose tiramisu, and she selected a wickedly decadent looking slice of cocoa fudge cake.

"I'm surprised you didn't go to work for Hypertron."

Isabel's head snapped up. Of course he would know about her father. Alex knew more than the average person about the local hi-tech industry. "Because my dad's the head of the company?"

"Yes."

"That's probably the single most important reason why I didn't take a job there," she said.

"You wanted to prove that you could make it on your own, without his help?"

"That was part of it but not all. My dad has lousy work habits." At Alex's look of disbelief, she smiled. "I didn't say work ethics, I said work habits. Nothing comes before his company. I didn't want to work for a boss that would expect that kind of commitment. I want a life outside of my job."

"I guess you don't place a lot of your clients with

him, then. He wouldn't be your idea of the ideal employer."

She grimaced. "Exactly. I have, um, helped several of his employees find more fulfilling positions elsewhere, however."

Alex laughed and the sound captivated her.

Entranced at the recurrence of his dimple, she smiled. "To be honest, once in a while I look for someone for him. Call me a masochist, but I keep trying to convince him to change his attitude toward his employees."

Thinking of how impossible the task was, she lost her smile. "I wait until he's desperate, then I lecture him about how he wouldn't be in his predicament if he didn't demand so much from his employees that they end up getting divorced, burning out, leaving, or all three. Then I find him a new employee."

Alex's laughter dried up, too.

"Someone like my assistant?"

Chapter Three

"That's what this is all about, isn't it?"

Alex didn't like the look of dawning understanding in Isabel's eyes, because it was accompanied by a wounded expression that dug at his heart.

"What do you mean?" he hedged.

"I've been wracking my brain trying to figure out why you asked me out."

Her typical female need to analyze everything concerning the male–female relationship had come at a damned inconvenient time. He didn't want to have a major confrontation here at the restaurant. He didn't want one, period. He just wanted a name.

"It's not something you need to dissect, Isabel."

"Right." She rolled her eyes, her disdain clear. "I may be naive sometimes, but I think I've got this one figured out. No wonder you found it so easy to break the first date rules and criticize my appearance. You don't care about my appearance. You aren't attracted to me *at all.* You're still trying to find out who hired me to approach Mr. Danvers, aren't you?"

He would feel a hell of a lot better if all of what she said was true. "You're wrong."

"I don't think so." She pushed her unfinished dessert away and picked up her purse from the empty chair next to her. She started rifling through it.

"I *am* attracted to you."

She looked up from her purse, her hands stilled in their search, a flicker of hope flaring in her eyes. "Are you saying you didn't ask me out in order to obtain information about one of my clients?"

He could lie to her. He *should* lie to her, but he wasn't going to. She wasn't her father.

There was something too trusting in her expressive green eyes for Alex to ignore their appeal for honesty. "No, I'm not saying that."

Her lip trembled, but she clamped it between her teeth.

She nodded. "I see. Well, I guess this is where I tell you that it didn't work and I'm going home." She stood up, dropping two twenties on the table as she did so. "That's for my dinner. I wouldn't want you to feel like you paid for information that you didn't get."

He should let her go.

She was right. He wasn't going to get any more information from her. She might as well hate him now as later. But at the sight of the two crisp bills against the white tablecloth, the tenuous hold Alex had on his control—since picking up the all-too-tempting Isabel— snapped. He shot to his feet and wrapped his fingers around her wrist in a loose grip that still prevented her from leaving.

She gasped and stared at him with wide, startled eyes. He grabbed the money and handed it to her. "I'll pay for dinner."

She made no move to take the money.

"Fine. You can leave it as a tip for the waiter." He tossed the money back on the table and headed toward the front of the restaurant dragging Isabel with him.

"You can't leave a forty dollar tip. Let go of me. You're acting like a caveman. This is ridiculous." Isabel kept up her litany of complaints all the way to the maitre d's station.

"If you didn't want to leave a forty dollar tip, you should have taken back your money," he informed her as he stopped in front of the maitre d'.

"Is there a problem, sir?" the maitre d' asked.

"No problem. We're ready to go."

"You're supposed to wait for the waiter to bring the bill to the table," Isabel hissed from behind him.

He almost smiled at the outrage in her voice. It was better than her sounding betrayed and hurt.

The maitre d's expression remained impassive. "Of course."

He clicked his fingers and the waiter who had been serving them materialized at Alex's side.

Without letting go of Isabel's wrist, he managed to extract his American Express card from his wallet and hand it to the waiter. The man disappeared and returned a few minutes later. Alex took perverse pleasure in adding a twenty percent tip to his charge receipt. A sharp intake of breath from behind him indicated that Isabel had been watching over his shoulder.

"Will there be anything else, sir?" asked the maitre d'.

"I'd like you to call me a cab," Isabel said.

Alex turned his head and smiled grimly at Isabel. "That won't be necessary."

She fixed him with a steady gaze and pulled at her wrist until he let go. "I'm afraid it is."

The maitre d' said, "There's usually a taxi out front."

"Thank you," Isabel said as she turned to leave.

Alex muttered a curse under his breath and followed her.

When they got to the hotel lobby, she stopped and turned to face him. "I would thank you for a lovely evening, but that would be hypocritical. I'll just say good-bye."

He bit back an irritated retort. "I'll take you home. You've already wasted forty dollars on a tip for the waiter. Do you really want to waste more money on a cab ride?"

Her expression turned mulish. "I've already wasted an evening on you, what are a few dollars on top of that?"

"Damn it, Isabel. I take my dates home and I pay for their dinner. Got that?"

He felt ready to explode. How had she gotten him to this point? He was furious. He rarely got angry, never furious, and never this fast. On top of that, the sight of her in the sexy black dress kept feeding all sorts of impossible ideas into his head. What the hell had he gotten himself into?

"More schizophrenic courtesy?" she asked far too sweetly.

He wasn't schizophrenic, but she was definitely driving him crazy. "Let me take you home. If it will make you feel any better, you can pretend I'm a taxi driver."

To his immense relief she agreed. "Don't expect a tip, though. I already wasted forty dollars to-night."

Alex had been totally silent since tucking Isabel into the passenger seat of his car.

She had tried valiantly to focus her attention out the window. She wanted to ignore him. To pretend that the whole evening had never happened, but she kept stealing glances at him out of the corner of her eye.

It just wasn't fair. She'd been attracted to him from the moment he'd entered her office, and it hurt to find out that the only thing about her that interested him was her client list, or rather the name of one client in particular.

He pulled into a parking spot in front of her condo and killed the engine.

"I could have lied." His voice startled her, coming as it did after so many minutes of silence.

She opened her car door. "What would be the point? You must have already figured out that you weren't going to get what you wanted from me."

She stepped out of the car, proud of her exit line.

Alex followed her to the door, standing motionless as she searched for her key. "What exactly is that, Isabel?"

Her head snapped up and she stared at him. The question, asked in far too soft a voice, sent a sensual thrill skittering down her spine that had absolutely no business being there after what she'd learned about him.

The man was definitely acting dangerous again.

"We've been all through this. You want my client's name."

He reached behind her and she went motionless, unable to function with his nearness.

He started pulling out her hairpins. "Are you sure that's all I want from you?"

She wanted to yell at him not to do this to her but refused to give him the satisfaction. "Of course. It's not as if you're attracted to me or anything."

The way he was looking at her belied that comment, and the feel of her hair falling from its French twist set off alarms inside her. "Even if you were," she said in a breathy voice, "you must realize that after the way you attempted to use me, I couldn't trust you."

He shook his head and moved closer. "I didn't lie

about my reasons for taking you out when you asked about them. Why would I lie about being attracted to you now?"

She found herself crowded against her front door and had to fight the urge to pull him the final few inches until their bodies touched. Her skin felt hot and tight, while a heavy sensation pooled in her belly.

"Maybe you are somewhat attracted to me, but we both know that isn't why you asked me to dinner." She'd tried to sound firm and cool this time, but once again managed only to reveal her physical reaction to him through a voice way too soft and inviting.

He put his hands against the door, one on either side of her head, enfolding her in his presence, overwhelming her with his male scent and the heat emanating from his big body so close to her own. "Is that so important?"

She swallowed. "Yes."

His eyes devoured her while he brushed one finger down her cheek. "I don't agree."

Warm, firm lips drowned her protest as he moved his hands from the door to cradle her head.

His mouth slanted over hers in a sensual assault. She told herself that she should not respond to his kiss, but his mouth was so hungry. His passion fed her own.

Her body started to melt as he sucked her lower lip into his mouth and nibbled on it.

Had she ever kissed before? Really kissed? If this conflagration of her senses was a kiss, then nothing she'd shared with her former dates counted as such because this was unique. This was passion. It felt too good to even think about stopping. She heard a moan and realized that it was hers.

Her defenses were completely helpless in the face of such sensual mastery and her reaction to his kiss.

Her moan acted like a catalyst for him and his hard-muscled body squashed her into the door, the evidence of his arousal pressing against her as they made contact from chest to tangled legs. The rough passion-filled movement—at odds with the tender way he cradled her head and the now gently nipping kisses he was giving her lips—affected her body in an unexpected way.

She felt warm everywhere, particularly in her most feminine place. Not only was she hot there, but she felt empty and swollen at the same time. She tipped her pelvis toward him, seeking some sort of connection that would assuage the ache growing in her innermost being.

He made a harsh sound and his mouth moved over hers, demanding that she open her lips to his invasion. Unable and unwilling to deny him, she let her lips part. He swept inside with his tongue and she tasted tiramisu and masculine ardor. The combination was both erotic and overwhelming.

Her new favorite dessert. Even chocolate didn't taste this good.

Running her hands over the raw silk of his shirt, she gloried in the textured fabric and the hard muscles underneath. She wanted to touch him everywhere, to have him touch her.

She had the first half of his shirt buttons undone and one spaghetti strap was perilously low on her arm when he tore his mouth away from hers. "Key."

Key? Her mind was lost in an unprecedented sexual frenzy. Nothing made sense except the feel of his body against hers.

Since he wouldn't kiss her, she kissed him—along his jaw, down his neck. She had made it to his chest when he shoved himself away from her.

"Baby, you are killing me."

The chilly evening air buffeted her with the loss of the heat generated by Alex's body. She shivered with unsatisfied desire and cold, trying to understand why he'd pulled away.

"Your key. Isabel, give me the key to your door."

She was so disoriented that she did just that.

Alex rammed the key into the lock and shoved open the door. He turned and lifted her in his arms and carried her into the hallway, pushing the door shut with his foot.

"Lock it," he ordered.

She did.

"Where's your bedroom?"

The flat question finally broke through the passion dulling her brain's activity.

She vehemently shook her head, fear slicing through her. And not fear that this man would take more than she willingly offered but rather fear that she would offer too much. If she'd ever had this volatile a reaction to a man before, she would not be such an inexperienced twenty-eight-year-old woman.

She was sure of it.

That inexperienced status was not going to end tonight, however. She had allowed herself to get carried away on the porch, but she wasn't about to make love with a man who had tried to use her.

"No, Alex. You can't take me to bed."

He acted like he hadn't heard her and started heading down the hallway.

She struggled against his arms, but it was useless. He was much too strong, but still she wasn't afraid of *him*.

"Let me down. I'm not ready to make love to you. I don't trust you."

Why had she said it like that, as if there was a chance that someday she might? She wouldn't. She couldn't. She wanted commitment. He wanted a warm body.

He stopped. His eyes burned into her. "Don't say that, baby."

"Please, Alex."

His jaw tensed and his now almost black eyes narrowed. Long seconds passed before he nodded with a jerky movement. Turning, he headed into her living room, where he gently set her on the overstuffed white leather chair that matched her sofa.

Then he stepped back, his uneven breathing testimony to the desire he barely had in check.

He ran his fingers through the black silk of his hair. "Okay. You're right. This is moving too fast."

She nodded. Never would be too fast. "I don't trust y—"

"Stop saying that," he demanded, interrupting her midword.

His body tensed in an emulation of battle readiness. Did he think he could force her to trust him?

"Okay, but it's true," she couldn't help adding.

His eyes pinned her with intense frustration, the soft light from the lamp she had left on earlier casting his face in disturbing shadows.

"Why, damn it?" he demanded.

She stared at him, unable to believe that he could be so dense. "You tried to use me. Of course I'm not going to have much faith in you. You admitted it, for goodness' sake. It's no use trying to deny it now that you've decided you want something else from me. Namely, my body."

"I'm not ready to give up on this attraction between us," he bit out.

My, my, my, the man was angry, but he had no one to blame but himself.

He could have asked her out because he *liked* her, instead of trying to pump information out of me. "I'm sure you'll easily get over whatever small attraction you feel for me."

His glare would have melted kryptonite and she was just a mere woman.

"There's nothing small about the way I respond to you or the way you respond to me, for that matter. Do you think I didn't notice the way your nipples stood up and saluted at the restaurant just because I was looking at you? I wanted to touch them so badly, it was all I could do to let you finish your dinner. And I let you order dessert," he added, as if expecting a medal for that forbearance.

When she didn't say anything, he looked at her fiercely. "And don't tell me that you make a habit of trying to undress your dates on your front porch."

Heat stole into her cheeks, but she tried to brazen it out, keeping her eyes averted from the evidence of an open shirt and exposed male flesh. "I did not try to undress you."

"Really? Then I guess it was somebody else who did this to my shirt."

Her baser nature got the better of her and she looked where he was pointing. The dark raw silk outlined the hard planes of his chest and the sexy black hair sprinkled across his golden skin.

"Okay, so I got a little carried away."

His smile could only be described as feral. "If this is a little carried away, I can't wait to experience a lot carried away with you, sweetheart."

If she'd unbuttoned one more button she'd be able to see the V of hair disappearing into the top of his slacks. Her mind pretended that she had and insisted on casting up the sexy image for her to mentally drool over.

Her own weakness was responsible for her attention moving south, and she felt her whole body tighten with desire. He was still hard, the ridge of a very large penis pressing against the front placket of his pants. She stared, absolutely fascinated by this evidence of his desire.

"Isabel, if you keep looking at me like that, I'm going to do something about it."

Heat radiated from her cheeks like a woodstove burning wrapping paper, and she turned her head away so fast she just about gave herself a whiplash. "Sorry."

"Don't apologize, honey. I like having you look at me, but I don't think you're ready for the consequences."

"I never will be," she mumbled, forcing herself to look him in the eye.

His expression said he didn't believe her. "We'll see."

He turned and walked to the small cabinet she used to store her music collection. He opened the door, gave the cabinet's contents a cursory glance, and flipped the door shut again. He headed toward the large entertainment center against the wall opposite the couch.

She didn't know if anger or sexual frustration was responsible for the ferocity of his movements. Either way, she felt as if a caged beast was on the prowl in her living room. He opened a door and shut it again with barely controlled savagery.

"What are you looking for?"

He opened another door on the entertainment center. "The drink you offered me earlier."

In his present mood, there would be no point in refusing. Besides, she could use a glass of wine herself. She had a bottle in the fridge that she had intended to serve him before they left for dinner.

"Bottom right cabinet. The glasses are in the dining room." She stood. "Do you want ice?"

He pulled out the bottle of twelve-year-old scotch she kept for the rare visits from her father. "No."

"Fine. I'll be right back."

She poured her wine and returned to the living room with a rock glass for Alex. He poured himself two fingers of the smoky liquid while she went back to her seat, kicking off her pumps and tucking her feet under her in the oversized chair. She took a sip of wine and watched Alex.

He drank about half of his scotch before turning to face her. "I want to see you again."

"I'm not going to tell you my client's name."

He made a savage movement with his hand. "I know that."

"I thought I made it clear before, but you still tried to use me." She couldn't mask the hurt she still felt.

He didn't deny it. "I made a mistake. I didn't take your feelings into consideration."

She supposed for a man like Alex that was as close to an apology as she was going to get. She wasn't sure it was enough.

He put down his unfinished drink. "I'll call you tomorrow."

"Is there any point in my telling you not to bother?"

"No." He looked at her until she met his gaze. "Don't fight me on this, Isabel. The time for that is over."

Should she remind him they had met only yesterday? Perhaps he felt the same primal knowing that she did—an intimacy not reliant on length of time in a relationship.

It frightened the life out of her. "I'm not trying to fight you, Alex. I'm trying to protect myself."

"I'll protect you."

Did he have any idea how arrogant he sounded? Probably not. She had a feeling that Alex was used to people taking his statements as gospel.

Contrary to her actions on the porch, she was not a complete idiot. "I will protect myself."

He shrugged and turned to leave. She got up to follow him and lock the door. The last thing she wanted tonight was another lecture on safety.

He stopped on the threshold. "I'll talk to you tomorrow."

He leaned down and touched her lips briefly with his. It was quick and unexpected. She didn't even have time to think about stepping away, much less doing so.

Then he was gone.

The next morning, Isabel's mood could only be described as cranky. She'd spent most of the night alternating between reliving Alex's kiss and reminding herself that any sane woman would refuse to see him again. The result was that she woke up tired and disoriented. The feeling had persisted through a hot shower and a double-shot tall latte from the drive-through espresso shop on her way to work.

How could she be so attracted to a man she didn't trust? She found the answer as troubling as the question.

On some level, she *did* trust Alex Trahern.

He had tried to use her, but he had not lied to her about it when she asked. That thought had tormented her throughout the night. Was she foolish enough to pursue a relationship knowing what she did about him?

The converse ate at her. Would she be an idiot to throw away what she had discovered in his arms last night? If a simple kiss could affect her so strongly, what would it be like to make love? A lot better than merely pleasant, certainly.

He wanted to see her again. He'd made that clear in his own arrogant fashion.

Could she believe him that it was simply for her own sake, not because he wanted to know the name of her client? She'd made the mistake yesterday of assuming that to be the case. Her own naïveté astonished her. She should have realized that a man like Alex, a dark and powerful man, would prefer the sleek and sophisticated type—not an optimistic dreamer like her. The kind of passion she'd experienced with him last night was probably run-of-the-mill for Alex.

It humiliated her to think of how easily she had been duped, how much she even now wanted to believe that he had been as affected by her as she had been by him.

"What's that look for? Don't tell me that *Tall, Dark, and Dangerous* didn't pass muster last night. I gotta tell ya, girlfriend, if that's the case, maybe you should let me have a look at your list." Bettina leaned her hip against Isabel's desk, taking no pains to conceal the blatant curiosity burning in her dark eyes.

Isabel gave her friend's empty hands an accusing glare. "The least you could have done if you wanted to grill me is to bring me sustenance."

"We interrogators know our stuff. If I made the mistake of bringing you coffee, the caffeine might give you the edge you need to avoid my carefully worded questions. You'll notice I didn't sit down, either. This is my intimidating, on-the-edge-of-your-desk stance." Bettina grinned. "Is it working? You ready to spill your guts yet?"

"I spent yesterday evening with Alex. I'm immune to your amateurish techniques."

Bettina grimaced. "That bad, huh? I was looking forward to some juicy girl-talk this morning."

Bettina radiated disappointment and Isabel felt like laughing, albeit somewhat bitterly.

If only her friend knew.

"I guess that was just wishful thinking, anyway. It's not like you'd let him get physical on the first date, after all." Bettina slid off the desk and sat in the chair in front of it. "You are the woman who made your last boyfriend wait until the third date before you lip-locked with him."

Isabel could feel the skin of her face heat. With any luck, the blush wouldn't be obvious to Bettina. From the look in her friend's black eyes, Isabel could tell that her luck had gone south with her mood that morning.

Bettina's eyes widened and so did her grin. "Don't tell me he kissed you?"

Isabel glared.

Bettina slapped her thigh and hooted in victory. "Even better, you let him."

Isabel wanted to deny the truth but knew she couldn't. Bettina would know the second the words were out of her mouth. Darn it, anyway.

"Yes. He kissed me. Yes. I let him. It won't happen again. End of story."

"He didn't pass the test? Come on, now." Bettina crossed her long legs, the short neon-green leather skirt she wore hiking up her thigh. "Spill to Aunt Betty. I want every last detail."

It wouldn't do any good to try hedging. *Aunt Betty* could give a terrier with a bone a run for his money when she was on the scent of *girl-talk*.

"He did pass the test, sort of. I think I discovered a new psychological phenomenon."

Bettina's pencil-thin black brows rose.

"I couldn't decide last night if Alex is courteous or an inconsiderate toad."

Leaning forward in her chair, Bettina said, "Now this is getting interesting. Was the toad part when he kissed you?"

"No. That was the Isabel has lost her mind part. The toad part was when he told me—not once but twice—that my dress was inappropriate for the elements. The other toad part was when he lectured me about living in an unsecured building. The final, culminating, not-to-be-denied, purely toad part was when he admitted that he only asked me out so that he could find out the name of the client that wanted to hire Marcus Danvers."

The sound of distress that emanated from her friend so matched Isabel's own feelings that she said, "Exactly."

Bettina got up and came around Isabel's desk to hug her. "Aw, girlfriend, men can be such jerks."

Isabel nodded as she accepted the quick hug.

Her friend straightened and after a full minute of silence spent scrutinizing her, she finally asked, "Did you let him kiss you before or after the final toad part?"

Isabel sighed and frowned in consternation. "After. Which means I'm a complete idiot. Not that he asked my permission. He just did it," she added in her own defense.

"Was it good?"

"I came close to undressing him on my front porch."

Bettina gave out a long, low whistle, going back to her chair and sitting down. She didn't say anything. She just sat there and stared at Isabel. As interrogating techniques went, it was pretty effective.

"What?" Isabel demanded after several seconds of silence.

"Tell me something."

Isabel sighed. "What do you want to know?"

"How many of your requirements did he meet before you found out that he had an ulterior motive in asking you out?"

"He passed the whole first level and some of the second, if you count schizophrenic courtesy," Isabel grudgingly admitted.

Bettina's head slowly bobbed up and down and she brought her fingers together steeple fashion, considering Isabel with a look that would have done a psychologist proud. "I see."

"I'm glad somebody does," muttered Isabel. "What exactly is it that you do see?"

"You're going out with him again, aren't you?"

Isabel felt like pulling her hair out. "I don't know. I'd be a fool if I did, knowing he's probably trying to use me."

She wanted Bettina to deny the plain truth that Isabel would be one egg shy of a soufflé to go out with Alex again. She wanted her gutsy friend to talk her into taking the risk.

"He kissed you. From your description, it was a pretty hot kiss," Bettina mused. "Information isn't *all* that he wants."

Feeling goaded, Isabel replied sarcastically, "No. I suppose he'd take some nice, casual sex to go along with it."

"I promise you, sex between us isn't going to be *nice* and I'm not a casual kind of guy, Isabel."

Alex stood framed in Isabel's open doorway, wearing his customary dark attire and a brooding expression.

Isabel lost the battle against the headache that had been flirting at the edges of her consciousness all morning.

"Hello, Alex. You said you'd call."

Chapter Four

Alex flicked a cursory glance over at the woman Isabel had been talking to when he came in, the one who had said Isabel described his kiss as *hot*. He blinked at her flamboyant green skirt and day-glow orange T-shirt, and then turned his attention back to Isabel.

She looked like she'd gotten less sleep the night before than he had.

"You said not to bother."

She rubbed both sides of her temple in a circular motion. "I didn't mean for you to come by my office instead."

She could use sustenance and a couple of pain relievers. "Would you like to go somewhere for breakfast?"

The woman standing next to Isabel said, "Mmmm. Mmmm. Mmmm. There's nothing hesitant about him, is there?"

Isabel didn't answer her right away. She stopped rubbing her temples to focus her attention on Alex. He felt exposed, although her look was filled with more irritation than perception.

"No, Bettina, he's not subtle. He's more like a Mack truck, but then again the two of you might have something in common there."

Bettina considered that while looking Alex up and down, like he was a piece of abstract art on display at Saturday Market.

"If we have something in common, he must be more harmless than he looks," she finally said.

"In a pig's eye," Isabel said. "This guy is dangerous with a capital D. He goes after *information* and he doesn't care how he gets it."

Alex had had his fill of being talked about as though he wasn't there.

He pulled the bottle of pain relievers—which he'd grabbed that morning for his own headache—out of his pocket and dangled it in front of Isabel's eyes. "The only information I want is an answer to my invitation. Do you want to go to breakfast with me, or not?"

Isabel's gaze set greedily on the bottle in his hand. "Bettina, do you have anything for my headache?"

"Sorry, girlfriend. You know how I feel about over-the-counter meds. I visit my chiropractor when I get a headache."

Isabel sighed and lifted her gaze from the white plastic bottle swinging loosely in Alex's hand to his eyes. "I suppose you're going to refuse to share unless I come with you."

"Yep."

She frowned. "I could buy my own, you know."

"This is easier."

"I can't just drop everything and go to breakfast with you. I have clients to call and obligations to fulfill."

Bettina snorted. "Right. When you skip breakfast, you're as cranky as Tyrone when he's not getting any. Do your clients a favor and eat, already."

Isabel whipped her head around to glare at her friend,

only to regret the hasty movement when the pounding increased. "You're supposed to be on my side."

"I didn't say go to bed with the guy. I said get breakfast," Bettina replied, radiating innocence.

Isabel pushed away from her desk and stood.

She put out her hand. "Painkillers first, breakfast second. Just so there will be no confusion, this time you're buying, right?"

"I paid last night, too." He wasn't going to let her reference to last night ruin his mood. "It was your choice to leave a forty dollar tip for the waiter."

He handed her the bottle of pills.

"My head hurts too much to argue." She popped open the bottle and shook two tablets into the palm of her hand.

Handing it back to Alex, she said, "Excuse me for a minute," and left the office.

"Forty dollar tip?" Bettina asked.

Alex nodded but he didn't explain.

"I don't think she should, you know."

Alex shifted his concentration from the doorway, waiting for Isabel's return, to Bettina. "Should what?"

"Have sex with you. It's too soon for her."

"Apparently, I'm not the only one that lacks subtlety."

Bettina ignored the warning in his tone. "I mean it. I'm glad you said you aren't the casual type because she's not either, and I don't want to see her hurt again."

"Don't you think your warning is a bit premature?" Who the hell had hurt Isabel before? "I just met her and I'm taking her to breakfast, not a hotel."

Bettina shook her head. "No, you're a dangerous man and you want Isabel. It's in your eyes. Besides, you said *when* you two had sex, not *if*, when you walked in here. Your intentions are clear. I just want to know if they're also honorable."

Since walking into Isabel's office two days ago, Alex's world had felt tipped on its axis. Bettina's demand to know his intentions didn't seem nearly as bizarre as it should have under the circumstances. Still, he wasn't about to make promises after knowing Isabel for such a short time.

"You want to know if I plan to marry her?" He used a tone that had served him well in intimidating others in the past.

Bettina was not fazed. "Yes."

"I don't know."

Bettina smiled and patted his shoulder. "You'll figure it out. Until then, keep the kisses this side of incendiary."

"There aren't going to be any more kisses," Isabel informed them from behind him.

Alex turned around, more than happy to escape her lunatic friend. Later would be soon enough to disabuse Isabel of the notion that they wouldn't be kissing again.

He took her by the elbow. "Let's go."

Alex had Isabel ensconced in the passenger side of his car before he spoke again. "Your friend has an overweening sense of responsibility toward you."

"She has three children." Isabel shifted the seatbelt away from her neck. "Mothering comes naturally to her."

"So does interfering in other people's business."

Isabel grimaced. "She calls it a gift."

"More like an irritation. Does she grill all the men you date about their intentions?"

Isabel's grimace turned to a look of alarm. "She questioned your intentions?"

"Yes."

"Darn." Isabel started rubbing her temples again.

That wasn't the reaction he had been expecting. "What do you mean, 'darn'?"

"If she's already playing the role of mother hen, she must approve of you. That's about the last thing I need." Isabel blew out an exasperated breath and glared at Alex. "Thanks a lot. You could have just called."

Alex gripped his steering wheel, wishing he could do the same to the conversation spiraling out of control. "You would have hung up."

The look on her face told him that he was right. She crossed her arms across her chest. "That's no reason for getting me into this mess with Bettina."

Feeling as if he'd entered an alternate reality, he asked, "What mess have I gotten you into with Bettina?"

"She's going to hound me about you, that's all. She'll push and push until I finally convince her that you're the wrong man for me. Even then, she'll throw your name in my face every time I say I want a ba . . . never mind, every time I don't have a date on Friday night. I've got months of irritating little comments ahead, all because you couldn't pick up the telephone."

"You really are cranky when you haven't eaten, aren't you?"

That seemed to deflate her. "Yes." Pinching the bridge of her nose, she closed her eyes and leaned back against the seat. "This headache isn't helping any, either."

She didn't look in any condition to choose where they ate, so he headed his car toward a small restaurant that he favored for conferences with clients. Its quiet atmosphere was conducive to talking, something he and Isabel needed to do. That could wait until after she'd been fed and the pain relievers got rid of her headache.

Somehow they had to get past the fiasco of last night.

Because he'd meant it when he said the time for fighting the attraction between them was past. He'd spent two years trying to ignore his reaction to her photograph. There was no way he'd succeed against the far stronger instincts provoked by the woman in person.

She was all softness and light; a crusader, trying to better employment conditions, one client at a time. He would have disdained such naïveté in anyone else but found it irresistible in her.

Her freshness permeated his being and warmed the cold places, places that had been cold for a very long time.

And he wanted her, so much so that despite the scotch last night, he'd gone home shaking. He had to have her. No information in the matrix of his relationship with Isabel could dispute that fact. Even before Bettina had said anything, he knew that Isabel wasn't the type for a casual sexual fling, but he did plan to have sex with Isabel.

That meant a commitment. He had avoided serious involvement of any kind with other women. First, because he had been too busy building his company, and then because he had been too focused on revenge against Hypertron and Isabel's father.

The fact that the woman who had breezed in past his defenses was John Harrison's daughter had ceased to matter about halfway through dinner last night. He would have Isabel, but he wasn't going to give up his revenge.

It had nothing to do with her. She didn't even like the way her father ran his company. She would not be devastated by its demise.

The fact that Alex planned to be part of her life when it happened would necessitate some alterations to his revenge. He wouldn't be able to tell John Harrison of his part in the destruction of Hypertron. Isabel would not understand. She was too tenderhearted to grasp Alex's need for justice regarding his father's death.

Losing that satisfaction was the price he had to pay to have Isabel. He would pay it, but first he had to get past the defenses Isabel had erected last night. From the stubborn set of her jaw, he assumed that wasn't going to be easy.

Isabel finished her breakfast in silence. Alex had been quiet on the drive to the restaurant and then successfully squelched any attempts she made at conversation over breakfast. Of course, since those attempts had to do with her not seeing him again, she couldn't really blame him.

The waitress came by and took away their empty plates, and Isabel turned down a second cup of coffee, figuring she'd had enough caffeine already that morning to jump-start an engine. She fiddled with her half-empty mug and checked her watch. It was only nine-fifteen. She didn't have an appointment for nearly an hour.

Alex pushed his coffee cup away and focused all of his attention on her.

Isabel forced herself not to squirm under his close scrutiny, but she wanted to. Man, did she want to. No wonder his kiss had rocked her senses. Having his undivided attention was enough to cause her heart rate to accelerate and that thing was happening with her breasts again—like they were growing fuller. And her nipples strained against her bra. But at least today Alex wouldn't be able to tell that. Her emerald green sweater set would hide the evidence.

She moved in her seat, trying unobtrusively to ease the ache of her flesh against the lace of her bra.

He pushed his coffee away. "If you don't want to talk now, we can meet later."

Like that would help. She didn't want to meet him again. She didn't want to talk things out or give him the chance to talk her into seeing him again.

Last night had been a blunder, one she didn't plan to repeat. "Last night was a mistake."

He surprised her by nodding in agreement. "Yes, it was. I shouldn't have used the excuse that I wanted information from you to ask you out."

What on earth was he talking about? "You've got that backwards. You used a date with me to try to get confidential information from me about one of my clients."

"If I'd really been motivated by a desire to find out who had hired you to approach Marcus, I would have."

The quiet way he said the words and the absolute conviction in them gave Isabel pause. She took a hasty sip of what remained of her lukewarm coffee. As much as she didn't want to, she half-believed that Alex was right. She could not imagine anyone, herself included, stopping him from his chosen course.

She carefully set the coffee cup back on the table. "I don't understand."

"I didn't, either. Not last night, anyway. But I did a lot of thinking when I should have been sleeping."

"Are you saying that you asked me out for some reason other than to get the information you wanted?" Confusion and hope warred in her head and heart.

"Yes."

Sudden illumination hit and her hope sank like a lead balloon. "I'm not going to have sex with you," she blurted out.

He didn't look shocked or even particularly bothered by her outburst. In fact, he smiled. His dimple flashed at her and Isabel's heart skipped a beat.

"I want us to get past last night. I need to know if you'll try."

"I don't know. I still don't understand why you asked me out. You've implied that it wasn't to get information . . ." she let her voice trail off, not knowing where to go from there.

"I convinced myself that was why I wanted to see

you." He didn't sound particularly happy about the fact.

"But it wasn't?"

"No. After I left your office yesterday, I shouldn't have wanted to see you again, but I did."

"Why not?" Did he also have a policy against getting involved with business associates?

He shrugged, his masculine grace highlighted in the fluid movement of his body. "That isn't important now. What is important is that I've accepted my desire to spend time with you."

"And if I don't want to spend time with you?" she asked, more for academic reasons than because it was true.

Alex let his fingers trail over her hands curled together on the table in front of her. Their warmth sent sensation crashing through her.

"I will have to convince you otherwise."

"What if you're saying all of this to convince me that you aren't trying to use me, but you really are?"

Alex gently pried her hands apart and took each one in one of his own. "I haven't lied to you yet, have I? Even when I knew you would get angry, I told you the truth."

She had to give him that. It wouldn't have taken much for him to convince her last night that he'd had no ulterior motives in spending time with her. It was, after all, what she had wanted to believe. Now that she knew the truth, she didn't want to take the risk of being hurt again.

Opening her mouth to answer, she was interrupted by the sound of a familiar voice.

"Isabel, what a fortuitous circumstance."

She hastily pulled her hands from Alex's grasp and turned to face the speaker. "Hello, Lawrence."

Lawrence Redding was about the same age as Isabel's father, but no two men could be more different. Although on the surface Lawrence gave the impression of a typical corporate manager, he was in fact nothing of the sort. He worked in the corporate world, but he didn't allow that world to control his life. He was at heart a bohemian.

Lawrence extended his hand to Alex. "Lawrence Redding. Are you one of Isabel's clients as well?"

Alex briefly shook the other man's hand. "No, our relationship is personal."

At Alex's slight emphasis on the word personal, Lawrence's expression turned apologetic. "Terribly sorry. Didn't mean to interrupt." He turned a charming smile on Isabel. "I'll call your office, shall I?"

"Don't tell me you're looking to change jobs again. I thought we found the perfect match for you at Benning Systems."

"An intelligent man is always open to options."

She stifled a sigh. What Lawrence meant was that he wanted her to find him some options. "Give me a call tomorrow morning. I'll see what I have on the books."

Lawrence nodded. "Wonderful." He turned to Alex. "Nice to meet you. It's good to see Isabel taking time for her social life. Sometimes I think she forgets that she's young and life is to be enjoyed."

Before Alex could reopen their earlier discussion, Isabel checked her watch and said, "I'm sorry, but I've got to go."

Alex nodded and stood.

When they were in the car, she was surprised he didn't take the opportunity to press his advantage and go back to their earlier discussion. The drive back to A.A. Placement was a silent one.

"My mother says the same thing about me," he said, as he parked his car in front of Isabel's office building.

"Excuse me?"

Alex turned to face her. In the small confines of the car, his gaze had the same impact his touch had had in the restaurant. "She thinks I've forgotten how to enjoy life."

The personal admission stunned Isabel.

She wasn't sure how to respond. "What about your dad?"

Alex's face went blank. "He died two years ago."

"I'm sorry," she said, feeling inadequate, but not knowing him well enough to add anything else.

"Thank you."

"So your mom thinks you work too hard?" Maybe he had bad work habits. For some reason the thought depressed her. It was almost as if she *wanted* Alex to meet her requirements.

"Mom thinks I spend too much time alone."

"Maybe she's right."

He reached out and cupped the back of Isabel's head, pulling her closer and closer until their lips almost touched. "All the more reason for you to see me again."

"Oh, Alex."

His lips touched hers in a brief but soul-stirring kiss.

Alex contemplated the latest information report he had compiled for Guy St. Clair on Hypertron with grim satisfaction. John Harrison's company was skating on the edge of financial disaster. One bad quarter and their stock would drop like a skydiver whose parachute wouldn't open.

There were rumors that the next quarter's report would be even worse and the one Alex had been waiting for. The new technology for Hypertron's expansion might be as much as sixty days late getting to market. Not an unusual circumstance for an electronic com-

pany to face, but Hypertron had made the mistake of putting all available resources toward this one venture. They couldn't afford the delay.

Once the stock dropped, the company would be vulnerable to Guy St. Clair's takeover bid. Extremely vulnerable.

What should have been bone-deep contentment that he was so close to his quarry felt more like wary anticipation.

Too many things could still go wrong. His information could be incorrect. Hypertron could surprise him and get their technology to market on time. St. Clair could change his mind and look for another investment opportunity. John Harrison could find out what was going on and protect himself.

Harrison was more than a savvy businessman. He was brilliant in investment and finance. The most appealing aspect to the deal right now was how completely unexpected the takeover bid would be. Although the industry knew that Hypertron had gone into debt again for expansion, very few people were aware of the precarious balancing act that Harrison had perpetrated to get the capital he needed.

Alex had made it his business to know. He had gone one step further and done research into the financial institutions that held Hypertron's debt.

Harrison had strayed outside the normal venues to get his cash. He'd gone to a venture capitalist, who had just realized a major loss on one of his other investments and who wasn't in a position to extend more credit to prevent a hostile takeover. Alex suspected that the venture capitalist would be happy to sell the loan to St. Clair, thus giving the corporate raider a more secure position. Almost everything was in place for the demise of the company that had destroyed Alex's father.

"So, did you find out who hired Isabel to contact me?" Marcus asked as he strolled into Alex's office.

Alex slid the papers he'd been studying back into the manila file folder. "No."

"No? You're kidding. The best in the business couldn't talk a headhunter into dropping a little information?"

Marcus's surprise grated against Alex's nerves. "She's not a headhunter. She's a career guidance specialist."

Marcus's brows rose into his hairline. "A *career guidance specialist?* Where did you come up with that?"

"It's how Isabel sees herself."

Marcus shook his head. "She must be one hot female if she got to you. Man, I wish now that I'd agreed to meet with her."

Alex pinned Marcus with a look. "She's off limits."

"It just figures she's married. Most of the really hot ones are." Marcus let out an exaggerated sigh.

"She's not married."

Marcus's eyes widened. "She engaged?" he asked.

"No." Alex's irritation had started showing in his voice.

"Boyfriend?"

"Not that I know of," Alex grated out.

He should ask her but he doubted it. His instincts told him that there was no way Isabel would have let him kiss her as she had last night if she was involved with someone else.

"But she's off limits?" Marcus asked the question very slowly as if he couldn't quite grasp the meaning of the words.

"Yes. She's off limits," Alex repeated.

"She did get to you. I don't believe it." Marcus sat down and stared at Alex with a dazed expression.

"She won't give out the name of her clients. It's an issue of confidentiality. We'll have to approach this from a different angle."

Marcus nodded. "Yeah. One that includes you staying the hell away from her."

"That's not going to happen."

"Alex, I don't think it's a good idea for you to try to get the information. She's obviously affected you in a way no other woman has since I met you. She's hazardous." Marcus spoke as if he couldn't believe what he was saying.

"I'm not going to get the information. You are."

Marcus smiled. "That's more like it. You had me worried there for a minute. I thought you might be interested in her."

"My relationship with Isabel has nothing to do with her father's company or what he did to my dad two years ago."

Marcus's smile turned to a look of disbelief. "*Relationship?* You *are* interested in her."

"Yes." So interested that he had ordered flowers delivered to her office with a card that invited her to dinner again.

He was waiting for her to call. He hoped she wasn't going to make things too difficult. She had been very clear that morning that she didn't feel she could trust him. He would have to convince her otherwise. He wasn't a threat to Isabel, just to her father's company, and she never had to know that.

"Alex, I didn't think I'd ever have to ask you this, but do you know what you're doing?" Marcus's concern was evident in the fact that the man's ready smile was nowhere to be found.

"Yes. Don't worry about my relationship with Isabel. If she did call you for Harrison, she doesn't have a clue what he wants. She's nothing like him."

Marcus leaned back in his chair and considered Alex's words. "How can you be so sure? You just met her two days ago."

"Once you've met her, you'll understand my certainty. She's too damned innocent to be playing any deep-level games."

"Or that's what she wants you to believe," Marcus argued.

"Call her this afternoon and tell her that you've changed your mind. You want to meet with the person who is interested in hiring you. You want to know all your options."

Marcus stood. "Okay, but I can't help wishing we'd decided to go this route before. I have a feeling you should never have met Isabel Harrison."

Chapter Five

The scent of roses tantalized Isabel's senses.

Focusing on her work was impossible with the gorgeous bouquet of yellow blooms distracting her. Even more distracting than their heady fragrance was the dinner invitation that had accompanied them and the quandary it represented.

Common courtesy dictated she thank Alex for the flowers, but she didn't know how she wanted to respond to the invitation. Even if Alex's motives were pure, she knew with feminine intuition that he would demand all that she had to give. In her previous relationships, Isabel had always been able to hold something back, to protect her emotions. She had never fallen head over heels in love.

She'd never fallen in love, period.

That had been important to her. Her father had taught her something important, along with Nanny Number One through Nanny Number Three.

Loving someone made you vulnerable to pain.

By the time Nanny Number Three left, Isabel had

figured out that she couldn't allow herself to get too attached to the people in her life. It hurt too much when they went away.

Sometimes even when they stayed. She'd tried to tell herself that she didn't need her dad's attention, that he loved her but just didn't know how to show it. It didn't work. His emotional distance and neglect had hurt, still hurt when she let herself think about it.

She had studied the photos of her family when she was a baby. Her mother and father had gazed at each other and at her with undisguised love in too many of the photos for it to be anything but real.

She hadn't seen that look on her dad's face for as long as she could remember, not for his daughter or anyone else. Not that she hadn't tried, but eventually even a child realizes when a person is beyond reach and gives up. At least she had.

She clung to one special memory from when she was very small. Her mother had been reading her a bedtime story, and her dad came in to kiss her good night. She'd gone to sleep feeling safe. She had no other memories of him tucking her in. Nanny Number Two had read bedtime stories. By the time Nanny Number Three came along, Isabel had learned to read to herself.

The phone rang and Isabel picked it up, grateful for the interruption of her tumultuous thoughts. "This is Isabel."

"Miss Harrison? This is Marcus Danvers. We spoke a couple of days ago."

Sometimes employees would call her to reconsider after an initial negative response, but Isabel truly hadn't expected Marcus Danvers to be one of them. "Yes, of course. What can I do for you, Mr. Danvers?"

"I think I responded too hastily to your offer."

"Technically, no offer was extended," she reminded him.

"Right, but you did call me because you have a client interested in hiring me. Isn't that true?"

"Yes, but you made it clear that you are very happy in your position at CIS."

Sometimes the knowledge that other employers were interested in the employee made a manager react strangely. They took out their frustration or fear on the employee, making their own situation more precarious, in as much as they wanted to keep their employee.

However, she had not expected such a reaction from Alex. "Has something happened to change that?"

"No, I won't lie to you, Isabel. I like my job, but I want to explore all my options."

Marcus's reply made sense, but she couldn't help feeling guilty. If he liked his job, she didn't want to counsel him toward a position that would take him away from Alex.

Squelching the overpersonalized reaction, she said, "Would you like to come in and discuss the position with me?"

"I'd rather talk directly to the person who wants to hire me. The fit depends on a lot more than the job description."

How right he was. Isabel had seen far too many clients unhappy in what should have been ideal jobs because of who they had to work under. However, she couldn't help wondering if Mr. Danvers's insistence on speaking to the potential employer was just another ploy by Alex to find out who it was.

She was a little dismayed by the prospect. She'd been approached by irate employers before, but none quite as determined to find out who else wanted to hire their employee.

On the chance that Marcus's interest was genuine, Isabel felt the need to respond to him as if Alex had never stormed into her office demanding answers.

"You're very wise to realize that," she said in response to his assertion that the employer was the ultimate decider, "but my policy is to interview the employee first and then refer him or her to the employer if there appears to be a match. I try to provide both employer and employee with the best possible customer service."

"I appreciate that. When would you like me to come in?"

They set up a time for the interview and Isabel hung up.

Her attention swung back and forth between the phone and the yellow roses. How could she go out with Alex now?

This was why she kept a firm demarcation between business associates and her personal life. She didn't like the feeling that she might be betraying someone. It didn't affect her rapport with her father, but then she wouldn't call their association all that personal, either. To Dad, business was business. He would never hold the fact against her that she hired one of his employees away from him.

She didn't think Alex would be quite so sanguine.

Alex stared at the thank you note in his hand with a mixture of irritation and disbelief.

She had said no.

After waiting all day yesterday for Isabel to call, the pithy little note thanking him for the flowers but declining the invitation dissolved the last remnants of Alex's patience. He picked up the phone and dialed Isabel's office number.

When she picked up at the other end, he didn't waste time with pleasantries. "What do you mean that you don't think it's a good idea to see each other again due to our business association?"

"Alex?" Isabel's voice was breathless and a little wary.

"Yes." Who the hell did she think it was? "Do you turn down so many men when they ask you out that you have a hard time keeping track when one of them calls?" He knew he was being unreasonable, but he couldn't make himself care. She had said *no*, damn it.

"No. Of course not. Alex, are you okay?"

Her concern only annoyed him more. "Explain."

There was a pause on the other end of the line and then she spoke. "I explained my policy about not mixing my business and my personal life to you the first time you asked me out."

He gripped the phone receiver more tightly in his hand. "We agreed that we don't have a business association."

"Actually, you made that assertion and I made the mistake of agreeing. I was wrong though, wasn't I? Business was the primary reason for our date."

Was she ever going to forgive him for that? "I thought we worked through this. What's going on, Isabel?"

"Nothing's going on. It's simply a matter of business ethics." Her words came out in an unconvincing rush.

She was lying to him. Why? Then it hit him. Marcus had called her. Marcus's appointment to interview with Isabel was set for that very afternoon. She probably thought her relationship with Marcus would be compromised if she went out with Alex.

He should have anticipated this complication, but when it came to her, he hadn't been operating with his customary clearheadedness.

He couldn't tell her that there was no conflict of interest. She would probably think he was trying to use her again if she found out that he had encouraged Marcus to call her to set up the interview. They could wait to see each other again until after Marcus had interviewed with her client and turned down the job. That would solve her problem with her perceived conflict of interest. It would even give her some time to get over her anger about their disastrous first date.

Looking at things logically, waiting to see Isabel was the most rational course of action.

"Alex, are you there?"

"I'm here."

"You got silent all of a sudden." She sounded nervous.

"I'm glad you liked the flowers, sweetheart."

"Oh, I did. They're beautiful, but Alex . . ." she hesitated, "I don't think you should call me 'sweetheart.' "

"I'll be at your condo to pick you up at seven tonight." The words shocked him, but they tasted right on his tongue.

"I've explained that I can't see you."

She didn't sound happy about it and that pleased him. "Our relationship has nothing to do with your business."

"We don't have a relationship," she insisted. "We had one date, a date which was very much about business, when all was said and done."

"We've had more than one date, sweetheart."

"That breakfast doesn't count. I was coerced."

Irritated that she refused to acknowledge the personal attraction between them, he said, "Do you make it a habit to kiss your business associates until it's all they can do not to make love to you standing against your front door?"

She gasped and her indignation shimmered across

the phone line. "We were never in danger of making love on my porch."

"That's not the way it felt to me. I barely had enough self-control left after your kiss to get the front door open. From where I stood," which had been darn close to her, "you were in pretty much the same condition, if not worse."

"I . . . that's ridiculous," she stammered out.

"In fact, *when all was said and done*, that date had a hell of a lot more to do with mutual attraction than any small attempt on my part to get information."

"E . . . even if we are attracted to each other, I can't date you right now, Alex. I just can't."

Alex stifled his retort. He reminded himself that it wasn't Isabel's fault that she was in a difficult position. It was his. He swore.

Isabel's sharp intake of breath let him know that she had heard. "I'm sorry," she said and he knew she meant it.

He wanted this woman. The fact that she was John Harrison's daughter was complicating the hell out of Alex's life, but it didn't alter the facts. Alex needed Isabel on a level that had nothing to do with logic, nothing to do with his desire for vengeance. His need for her was elemental and primitive.

He had always scoffed at the concept of love at first sight. He still did, but something had happened the day he met her, something he refused to ignore.

He would have to find another way to get the information he needed. He wasn't going to use Isabel, even indirectly. He would not allow her to be part of his revenge. He had to keep the two separate, even if it meant taking some risks.

"I told Marcus to call you."

"*What?*"

"Marcus set up an interview with you because it

seemed like the most expedient means of finding the information I wanted."

"You had Mr. Danvers call me just so that he could find out my client's name?" she demanded.

"Yes." He waited uneasily for Isabel's reaction. She hadn't gotten past her initial anger over finding out that he had planned to get the information himself on their date. Would she go ballistic again now?

"Why are you telling me this?" she asked, sounding a little dazed.

"Because I want to see you."

"You're arrogant, but I hadn't thought you were stupid."

Here was the explosion he'd been waiting for.

"You cannot possibly expect that telling me you planned to use me again would change my mind about going out with you." Incredulity and temper laced her voice, but at least she hadn't hung up on him.

"Isabel—"

The phone clicked in his ear.

Slamming the phone in its cradle, Isabel almost choked on her frustration.

How could a man be so incredibly compelling and idiotic at the same time? Did Alex have any idea what she had gone through knowing that she could not both see him again and give Marcus Danvers the kind of service as a career guidance specialist that he deserved? Finding out that it was all part of one of Alex's plots to gather information was enough to make her want to scream. Or go shoe shopping.

Okay, so she'd suspected something of the sort when Marcus had called, but that didn't make it any more pleasant to have her suspicions confirmed.

She pushed back from her desk and walked rapidly

to Bettina's office across the hall. *Yes.* Bettina's door stood ajar, indicating that she was not with a client. Isabel rapped a quick tattoo on the door before walking inside.

Bettina put down her phone and smiled at Isabel. "Hi, girlfriend. You look like you want to shoot someone. Been talking to your dad?"

"I wish." Isabel flopped down onto a red love seat.

As Isabel had allowed the romantic side of her nature to exhibit itself in her office's floral décor, so had Bettina's flamboyant personality come out in hers. Startlingly bright watercolors graced the walls while her furniture was glass, chrome, and vibrant primary colors.

Bettina leaned down and opened one of the drawers in her glass-and-chrome desk. When she stood up, she had a bag of plain M&Ms in her hand.

Sitting down in a cobalt blue chair positioned kitty-corner to the love seat, she tossed the candy into Isabel's lap. "Talk."

Isabel opened the bag but didn't eat any. "Alex just called."

Bettina's eyes rounded in understanding. "He didn't like the fact that you won't see him again."

"No, but I didn't like what he had to say even more." The smell of chocolate finally broke through her irritation and she popped a small handful of M&Ms into her mouth. "You aren't going to believe this. I swear."

Bettina took a handful of the candy as well. Her eyes gleamed with interest. "Try me."

"Alex told his assistant to contact me so that he could find out the name of my client."

Bettina almost choked on her candy. She coughed and Isabel leaned over to pat her back.

Bettina took a deep breath, let it out, and then asked, "He told you that?"

"Yes."

"Why?"

"He wanted the information. He assumed Mr. Danvers's contacting me would be a surefire way of getting it. The man is very focused."

Bettina rolled her eyes. "I'm surprised you weren't already wondering about that possibility. I know I was. What I want to know is why Alex told you what he'd done. He must have realized it would mess up his plans."

"You knew Alex was behind his assistant's calling me?" Outrage at her friend's secretiveness poured over Isabel. "Why didn't you tell me?"

"Don't be dumb. I didn't *know* anything. I had a hunch."

"You didn't share your hunch with me."

Bettina shrugged. "I guess I should have. I forget sometimes how trusting you are of your clients. You always assume the best."

"Well, actually I suspected something along those lines, too, but suspecting something and knowing it are two very different animals." One caused worry, the other pain.

"So, Alex is a little ruthless. Don't tell me you didn't already know that, not after your first date. And let's be honest here, you still let him kiss you. You still went to breakfast with him. You like him. Ruthlessness and all." Leaning back in her chair, Bettina tapped her long, hot pink nails against the blue armrest. "The real issue is why Alex would tell you his plans."

"That's easy. He wants to see me again." Isabel didn't want to go into her friend's other assertions.

Bettina put her hand out and Isabel poured a pile of chocolate pieces into it. Bettina popped the candy into her mouth and chewed, her eyes indicating she was deep in thought.

After several more M&Ms, Bettina finally spoke. "Why didn't he just wait until Mr. Danvers got the information? He must have realized that once you no longer were conducting business with his assistant, you'd be willing to see him again."

Isabel hadn't thought of that. "Maybe. Then again, I might not have."

Bettina laughed. "Girlfriend, you can lie to Alex. You can even lie to yourself, but you can't lie to Aunt Betty. You would have seen Alex again and I'm betting he knew it."

While considering Bettina's words, a small tendril of hope entered Isabel's heart. Hope that he had told her because he really *wanted* to see her again. She didn't like the feeling of hope. It meant that she cared much more than was safe about Alex's reasons for doing what he did.

"Then why tell me now?"

"Alex obviously wants to see you more than he wants the name of your client." Bettina smiled expectantly.

Isabel frowned in return. "That, or he has some deep reason that I can't begin to guess at."

"Do you think Alex is lying to you? Maybe he over-heard Mr. Danvers calling you to make an appointment and decided to circumvent his leaving the company by making it appear that he wasn't truly interested in changing jobs."

Instinct told Isabel that Bettina's reasoning was flawed. "I don't think so. He was pretty brutal in his honesty the night we went out. I can't see him lying now."

Bettina's teeth flashed white against her dark skin in a big smile. "Then I guess that leaves the obvious. Mr. Tall, Dark, and Dangerous wants you . . . bad."

"Believe it or not, that does not set my mind at ease."

"Come on, Isabel. You aren't going to tell me that having a guy like that after you isn't turning your in-sides to melted Godiva chocolate."

That was the problem. Isabel was afraid that not only were her insides turning into melted chocolate but her brain was having a meltdown as well. What else could explain the fact that she was entertaining thoughts of seeing Alex again?

"Bettina, I've got a huge favor to ask you."

Alex hadn't expected this turn of events. After Isabel had hung up on him, he'd assumed that she would cancel her appointment with Marcus. She hadn't. In fact, according to Marcus, she had called him to confirm that he still intended to come in for the interview.

What was she planning? Alex had been sitting at his desk for the past twenty minutes trying to figure it out. He didn't like mysteries, particularly when they surrounded something he wanted as much as he wanted Isabel. Had she figured out who he was? Did she plan to help her father?

Neither of those scenarios made sense. She had been apologetic and genuinely disappointed that she could not see him again until he told her that he was responsible for Marcus's contacting her. Then she had been angry. It made no sense that she would still want to see Marcus.

Unless she was so angry with Alex that she was trying to perpetrate a little vengeance of her own by luring away his right-hand man to another position. Somehow, he couldn't see Isabel plotting revenge of any kind. He reminded himself that he didn't know her that well, and that there was only one way to find out. He needed to see her eyes when they talked.

Besides, he didn't want to give her the option of hanging up again.

Isabel's pleasant, welcoming office looked just as it had the day he'd first met her, with two exceptions.

Isabel wasn't in it and the roses he had sent were. She had placed them on a small table next to the pink sofa.

Other than a few papers lying on her desk, the room was tidy. Where had she gone? She couldn't be very far. Her meeting with Marcus was in fifteen minutes. Alex strolled over to the desk to check her calendar, looking for a clue as to where to find her.

According to Isabel's schedule, she was supposed to be at her desk making phone calls right now. He let the papers fall back in place before idly glancing at them. He sighed over the fact that she would leave work out on her desk for anyone to read and her office door unlocked. She was too trusting.

It slowly dawned on him that he wasn't looking at work related to Isabel's job. It was some kind of list.

What the hell? Isabel had written "Character Traits Necessary for a Potential Husband and Father" across the top of the paper. Everything inside of Alex froze. Isabel was planning to get married? Why had she accepted his invitation to dinner and then breakfast?

He took a closer look at her list and realized that the word *potential* said it all. Isabel was looking for a husband, someone to father her children, if the words she'd written were to be believed. He could not believe it.

What woman went husband-hunting in this day and age? Even more unbelievable than Isabel's actions was the surge of possessiveness that coursed through him. No one was going to marry Isabel and make babies with her. No one, except him.

"Alex. What are you doing here?"

Stepping away from the desk and her list, he looked up. "I'm here to talk to you."

Isabel stood across the room, a look of resigned irritation on her face. Her short jacket and ankle-length skirt the color of green heather emphasized her small waist and feminine curves, the same curves that had haunted his dreams last night.

She frowned. "You could have called."

"A man's ego can only take getting hung up on so many times."

Her brows rose at that. "I would have thought that your ego could take a hit from the reigning heavyweight champion without a noticeable bump."

He let the barb slide. "Marcus said that you're still planning to meet with him."

She came farther into the room, taking time to put her purse in a cupboard and her coffee cup down on the desk before answering. "Yes."

"Why?"

She sat down at her desk and raised her head to meet his gaze. "Unlike you, I do not have devious motives for everything I do. I confirmed Mr. Danvers's appointment because under the circumstances, I thought it was best to do so."

Alex sat on the edge of her desk, only a few inches from her list. She darted a look to the papers on her desk and then back to his face. It was obvious she was trying to gauge whether he'd noticed them or not. He waited to see if she would ask. She didn't.

He didn't feel like enlightening her. "*Under the circumstances*, it would seem that meeting with Marcus would be a waste of your time."

"On the contrary, it is never a waste of time to do my best for my clients."

Disappointment swirled through him. She was after revenge after all. He couldn't blame her, but that didn't mean he had to like it. "Don't be too disappointed when it doesn't work."

"When what doesn't work?" she asked.

"Your little revenge plot. Marcus isn't going to leave CIS."

Her eyes widened. "You think I'm doing this to get revenge? For what?"

"For what you think I've done to you."

"Just what is it that I think you've done to me?" The saccharine sweetness of her voice did not reach her eyes. They had narrowed, their emerald depths brilliant with anger.

He wanted to reach out and brush her hands, which were clenched in a stranglehold on top of her desk. "You think I used you. You think I put my desire for information above my attraction to you."

"I don't just think those things. That's exactly what happened," she said between clenched teeth, "and now you are accusing me of using my position to get revenge for it. I can't believe this. If you came over to work things out between us, you're doing a very poor job of it."

He gave in to the urge and reached out to touch her.

She jerked her hands away, hiding them under her desk in her lap. "What about you?" she demanded. "I have only your word that Mr. Danvers called me in order to obtain information for you. For all I know, he's interested in leaving your company and you're trying to prevent it by making me distrust my client."

Anger that she could believe him capable of acting so dishonestly welled up inside. He had no problem keeping employees. He didn't need to resort to trickery to do so.

"You're accusing me of lying?"

She shook her head. "No, I'm pointing out that both our motives are suspect."

"I did not lie to you."

She angled her chin proudly. "I didn't lie to you, either, and I'm not interested in petty revenge games."

He brushed his finger down her cheek. This time she did not flinch. "Where does that leave us?"

She sighed and looked away. "There is no *us*."

"There could be."

Chapter Six

Isabel tried to ignore the sensations pooling inside from Alex's touch.

She reached up, intending to remove his hand, but ended up placing hers over it instead. "What are we going to do, Alex?"

His eyes turned dark with the desire that seemed just under the surface whenever they were together. "Right now, I'm going to kiss you," he said, as he lowered his mouth to do just that.

She wanted his kiss. She needed the feel of his lips pressed firmly against hers. She didn't care if it made sense. She didn't care if he thought she was capable of petty revenge. Right now, all she cared about was the taste and texture of his mouth against hers.

She moaned, allowing her lips to part. He didn't hesitate to take advantage. His tongue swept inside to mate with hers and everything in her coalesced into one thought.

She wanted more.

She stood, plastering her body against his. Gripping his shirt, she pulled him closer yet. He groaned and fit her body to his. Proof that the rapid-fire desire plaguing her affected him, too, rubbed against her stomach. His mouth went from hot and demanding to volcanic in the space of a second, and she went under like the trees on Mt. St. Helens when it erupted.

She didn't know how long the kiss lasted, but the laughter of a coworker drifting in through the open door brought her back to the present, where they were and what they were doing.

She tore her mouth from Alex's and he let her go, looking as dazed as she felt. His mouth wore a pink tint from her lipstick and she touched her own lips, wondering if they looked as bruised and swollen as they felt.

She leaned across her desk and pulled a tissue from the box on the corner and handed it to Alex. "Pink's really not your color."

"Thank you." He swiped at his lips, wiping away the evidence of her kiss.

She sat back down at her desk. "You're welcome."

Needing a moment to focus, she averted her gaze from Alex to the papers on her desk and felt her cheeks grow hot with embarrassment rather than with passion. Had he seen the list? What must he be thinking? It made her look like a desperate Victorian spinster. He couldn't possibly understand her desire for a baby when she was hard-pressed to do so herself. Before she could begin to formulate an explanation she was far from having, a discreet knock sounded on her open door.

Marcus Danvers had arrived on time.

"Hello. I'm Marcus. I see you've already met my boss."

She forced a smile and stood, extending her hand. "Good afternoon, Mr. Danvers. It's a pleasure to meet you."

The wiry blond giant walked forward and shook her hand, and then gave his boss a questioning look.

Alex shrugged. "I don't know why she wants to meet with you. I told her why you called, but apparently she needs to hear it from your lips. She thinks I might have made it all up in order to ruin your chances of leaving CIS."

Isabel let out an indignant gasp. "I did not say I believed that. I said that I *could* have believed that."

Marcus smiled, blue eyes twinkling. "I see."

Alex said nothing. She wished she knew what he was thinking. Unfortunately, she'd have to wait to find out. She had work to do right now.

Isabel put her list in a drawer and then walked around her desk. "Please follow me, Mr. Danvers. My coworker Bettina Fry will be conducting your evaluation."

"What's going on, Isabel?" Alex's voice demanded an answer. Now.

She took a deep breath and let it out before turning around. "I asked Bettina to take Mr. Danvers's case because I didn't feel that I could give him unbiased service."

It had been hard to admit, but whatever was going on between her and Alex, it would affect how she handled his assistant's situation. Marcus seemed to ask Alex another silent question.

Again, Alex's shoulders rose and fell in a gesture of acceptance. "You might as well meet with her as long as you're here."

Marcus mimicked his employer's shrug. "Guess so." He turned to Isabel, his mouth curved in amusement. "Lead the way."

Isabel nodded with what she hoped gave the appearance of professional efficiency. She took Marcus to Bettina's office and left him in the hands of her very capable friend. If Marcus was there only to glean information, Bettina would figure it out. If he matched the job, she'd be able to discern that as well. Regardless, a confusing mixture of emotions centered on Mr. Danvers's current employer wouldn't hamper Bettina.

Isabel walked back into her office, not sure whether she hoped that Alex had left or stayed. When she saw him sitting at her desk, reading her list, the list she had put away before leaving the room, she made up her mind.

She really, really wished that he had gone. "What do you think you are doing?"

Alex looked up from the papers. "I stack up pretty well against these requirements, honey. Maybe you shouldn't be so quick to tell me you don't want to see me again."

Since she had no intention of saying anything of the sort, she didn't bother to argue. Why did he think she had asked Bettina to take on Marcus Danvers?

"I put that away in my desk before I left." She pointed accusingly at the papers on the desk in front of Alex. "You took it out."

He didn't look in the least repentant. "Yes."

"That's an invasion of privacy."

"You should have locked your desk."

"I should have realized I had left an information shark in my office. Silly me." The words came out in a sarcastic drawl that hid her inner turmoil. What was he thinking? That she was crazy or merely desperate?

He looked down at the papers and then back up at her, his almost-black eyes giving nothing away of his thoughts. "Is this why you were so worried about what you called my 'schizophrenic courtesy' the other night?"

"I don't know what you mean," she hedged, instilling her voice with a haughty edge. Which was easy, considering how mad she was.

"You were sizing me up, weren't you? Trying to decide if I'd make good husband and father material according to your little list of requirements."

The list was three pages long. "It's not little."

He held her gaze captive. "No, it isn't. Damn it, Isabel. What do you think you're doing? You can't go looking for a husband like you would a job applicant."

She didn't see why not. It beat dating jerks. "It's really none of your business, Alex."

"Everything you do now is my business. Why did you make the list? Are you pregnant? Do you need a husband?"

She stared at him, appalled. "Of course not. I made the list because I want a *baby. I want a family.*" Once the words were out, she realized the truth of them. She didn't just want a baby. She wanted it all, the family she'd never had.

He looked skeptical. "You're too young for your hormone alarms to have gone off."

She'd heard it all before from Bettina. She wasn't going to listen to it from him. "How would you know? Are you some kind of expert on women's biological urges?"

"I don't have to be an expert to know that most women don't plan this kind of attack on the males of their acquaintance because their biological clock starts ticking at the age of twenty-eight."

Of course he knew how old she was. Alex knew everything, darn him. Except what it felt like to have a biological clock that sounded like Big Ben, telling her it was time to have a family. "I'm not planning an attack against the men in my life. That's a ridiculous thing to say."

And she wasn't the first twenty-eight-year-old woman in history to want a baby, either.

He lifted the papers and waved them. "What would you call this?"

"I would call that insurance against another poor choice!"

Alex's eyes went from enigmatic to interested in a heartbeat. "What poor choice?"

She didn't want to have such a personal discussion in her office in the middle of the day. "Do we have to do this now?"

He studied her and she felt like he could see into her soul. "What time are you finished here?" he finally asked.

"Four-thirty. Why?"

"I'll meet you at your place at five. We'll go to dinner."

"Make it six and I'll feed you." If they had another argument—which seemed likely, based on the amount of stuff left unsettled between them—she didn't want to have it in front of witnesses.

He stood up and walked around the desk, stopping in front of her. "I'll be there."

She had no doubt. The man was tenacious.

He leaned down and brushed his lips across hers. "See you then, sweetheart."

By the time she'd gathered her wits enough to turn around and face the door, he had already left. She didn't realize that he had taken the list with him until she sat down at her desk and saw that the papers were gone.

Alex cradled the phone to his ear. "Yes, Mom, I remember I promised to come for lunch on Sunday. You had Miss Richards put it on my calendar."

He had barely walked into his office when his secretary put through the call from his mother.

"She's a very efficient secretary, Alex, but even she can't make you remember a social obligation on her day off."

His mother said something else, which he missed as he looked down at the pile of papers he'd taken from Isabel's office. He bet she'd been furious when she realized he'd taken them. He wanted time to study them, time to fit them into the information matrix surrounding her.

"Alex?"

"I'm here."

"Is something the matter?"

Genuine concern tinged her voice. Since his father's death two years ago, Alex had seen a marked change in his mother. She expressed emotion more freely and she worried about Alex. At first the worry had disconcerted him. Then, he had learned to deal with it, just as any son dealt with his mother's concern—with as much patience as possible.

"No."

"You weren't listening to me. Did I call at a bad time?"

He looked again at the papers before him. "No."

She met his one-word response with silence. Motherly silence. He still wasn't accustomed to how she could pack an entire conversation or a string of questions into well-placed silence. He stifled a sigh. "Would it be all right if I brought a guest to lunch on Sunday?"

"What kind of a guest?" Her voice held undisguised curiosity.

"Does it matter?"

Her laughter, another aspect of her nature he was getting used to, floated across the phone line. "No. It does not matter, but that isn't going to prevent you from answering me. Is this an old college friend, a date . . . what?"

"A date."

The silence that greeted this statement could only be described as expectant.

"Her name is Isabel," he finally offered.

"That's a lovely name. Where did you meet her?"

"She works for A.A. Placement Agency. She tried to hire Marcus for one of her clients."

"She's a headhunter?" The shocked tones of his mother's voice almost made him smile.

"She considers herself a career guidance specialist."

"You say she tried to hire Marcus away from your company?"

"Yes."

"And you want to bring her to lunch on Sunday?"

"Yes."

"Didn't I teach you that 'yes' and 'no' are not always appropriate responses, Alex?"

"She's John Harrison's daughter."

Alex winced at his mother's shocked gasp. "You're seeing John Harrison's daughter? Why?"

"Why do men usually date women?"

"Don't." Her voice came out strained and she took an audible breath before continuing in a softer tone. "Do not give me that flippant answer. I know you, Alex. You blame Mr. Harrison for what happened to your father. I will not stand by while you hurt an innocent woman in order to exact revenge."

"Isabel has nothing to do with Hypertron or what happened to Dad. She doesn't even know who I am."

"But you know who she is, Alex."

Alex heard the concern that tinged his mother's voice, but this time it wasn't for him. Her worry about what he planned to do with Isabel came across the phone lines loud and clear.

"Isabel is the woman I'm seeing. That's it."

"You said she has nothing to do with what her father's company did two years ago," his mother probed.

"Right. She's nothing like her father." Isabel would

never have made the choices John Harrison had made
in dealing with Ray Trahern.

"You're really dating her?"

He would be once he had talked Isabel through her
current irritation with him. "Yes."

"Is it serious?"

Letting his hand rest on Isabel's list, he made a decision. "Yes, very."

Isabel tossed the pasta and fresh green beans in the
light pesto sauce. The stuffed chicken breasts she'd prepared earlier were warming in the oven while the white
wine she'd bought to go with dinner chilled in the
fridge. Everything was ready for Alex's arrival, everything but her.

Well, technically that wasn't true. She was dressed ap-
propriately for a casual evening at home in an oversized, leopard-pattern silk tunic, black denim leggings,
and a pair of soft leather shoes with a short heel.

However, mentally she was not yet ready to face Alex.
She had almost called and cancelled twice this afternoon. The knowledge that he had her list made her go
hot all over with embarrassment. She had no illusions
that he would politely pretend to have forgotten their
discussion in her office this afternoon.

It was no wonder that her nerves were stretched to
the limit at the thought of spending the whole evening
cooped up in her condo with Alex. Whose bright idea
had it been for them to have dinner here, anyway? The
answer, of course, was hers, which only went to show
that her brain had gone past the meltdown stage to
evaporation.

The doorbell rang. Tucking her hair behind her ear,
she headed for the front door. The chimes rang out a
second and third time before she reached it. Her ner-

vousness turned to annoyance. She swung open the door ready to chastise Alex for his impatience and the words died unuttered.

The man on the other side of the door was not Alex. She really didn't need this. Not right now. Not minutes before Alex was scheduled to show up on her doorstep.

"Brad, what are you doing here?"

Brad gave her his signature smile. All teeth and no sincerity. "Hey, babe. Long time no see."

"Not long enough," she replied, making no attempt to be civil. The jerk did not deserve polite reserve.

He deserved to be dipped into a swamp in southern Florida, one full of alligators, just like him.

He didn't even blink. "I'm sorry about what happened, babe. I still had some growing up to do."

They had broken up a little over a month ago and she didn't think he could have done any significant growing up since then. "I'm supposed to care because why?"

His face twisted into a fair imitation of sadness and regret. She wondered how long he'd practiced in front of the mirror to perfect the look.

"I can't blame you for being hurt, but I thought you'd be ready to talk about it by now."

The white-haired old lady who lived with her husband in the condo to the right of Isabel's peeked out her door and waved. Isabel stifled a groan. After kissing Alex on her front porch the other night, she didn't want to give her neighbors any more fodder for gossip. Brad didn't look ready to leave. He could be very persistent. Alligators usually were when stalking their prey.

Stepping back from the door, she waved Brad inside. They had nothing to discuss, but she would tell him that away from prying eyes. Brad's eyes filled with triumph and he followed Isabel into the living room. She couldn't help comparing his insincere charm to Alex's brooding presence. Where Alex had filled the room just by being there, Brad had no more impact on Isabel's senses than if she'd had the television on.

"Say what you need to and leave. I'm expecting someone."

"Bettina coming over for some girl-chat?" he asked with a condescending smile.

"No, I've got a date." One that would not appreciate finding another man in her living room when he arrived.

Brad's brows rose, but he didn't appear impressed. "Trying to make me jealous, cupcake?"

Had she truly ever thought his patronizing endearments anything but drivel? She couldn't remember. All she knew was that right now they grated on her like nails scoring a chalkboard. "I'm trying to get you to leave."

He attempted to look hurt. "Is that any way to act when I've taken my pride and my heart in my hands to show up here and beg your forgiveness?"

He stepped forward and took her hand in his. She tried to pull away, but he didn't let go.

"Don't get melodramatic. I know it's one of your fortes, but it does nothing for my mood." She yanked on her captive hand again, to no avail.

"Isabel, babe, we were good together. Don't let one unfortunate incident ruin our future. She meant nothing to me." He leaned closer, and she had the awful suspicion that he meant to kiss her. "I know what you want and I can give it to you. Marriage. A baby. All of it."

She cursed her own naïveté in sharing her dreams with the philandering jerk. "I don't want any of those things with you."

Ignoring her, he leaned down. He really was going to

try to kiss her. The idiot. She pulled her free arm back in order to gain leverage for the blow that would break Brad's hold on her arm. It was unnecessary. Brad released her wrist and went flying backward in one fluid movement. He landed against the wall and slid down to sit like a puppet whose strings had been cut.

"Keep your hands off my fiancée or they're going to end up broken. The only man giving her a baby will be me." Alex towered over Brad, fury reverberating in his voice and body.

Brad pushed himself up from the floor. He looked at Alex and then at Isabel, his expression honest for once. He looked baffled and worried. "You're engaged to him?" he asked, pointing to Alex.

"No," she said.

"Yes," Alex replied at the same time.

She turned to frown at Alex. He didn't spare her a glance; he was too busy glaring at Brad.

Brad edged toward the door. "I'll call you later."

"I'd rather you didn't," she said, not believing for a second that Brad would take her feelings into account. He certainly hadn't when he started sleeping with his voluptuous boss. Isabel would have to inform the receptionist at her office that she didn't want to accept calls from him.

Alex grabbed Brad by the shirtfront and pinned him against the wall. "If you call or come by to see Isabel again, you'll be dealing with me."

The menace in Alex's voice made Isabel shiver and must have had a similar affect on Brad because he left without another word.

Hiding her secret satisfaction at seeing the alligator detoothed so very easily and thoroughly, she rounded on Alex. "There was absolutely no need for you to go caveman here or make false claims, Alex."

He was all over her like sand on a windy day at the beach. "Who the hell was that guy, and why did he think he could give you babies?"

She didn't bother to mention that Brad had said one baby. She didn't think Alex would care about the distinction, but she did. She had no doubt Brad would be willing to humor her with having one child so that he could marry the only heir of the man who owned the lion's share of Hypertron. However, she did doubt Brad would agree to more children. He was much too self-involved for that.

"Brad is an ex-boyfriend, one I made the mistake of telling about my desire for a family."

"Did you show him your list?" Alex asked the question like an accusation.

Isabel crossed her arms under her chest. "No. I did not show him the list. I didn't show it to you, either, if you remember correctly."

He nodded. "Is he the reason why you made it, the mistake you're trying to avoid making again?"

"Yes."

"What happened?"

"We broke up."

"Why?"

The thought that Bettina and Alex must have gone to the same school of interrogation flitted through Isabel's mind. "Because we weren't compatible."

"Evidently he thinks you are."

"He thinks he would like to marry the daughter of the president of Hypertron. It's his idea of the fast track to upper-upper management."

Alex frowned. "I'm not interested in your position as John Harrison's daughter."

She didn't doubt the veracity of his words. There was an absolute certainty to them that almost made her shiver.

"Then you and Brad have very little in common."

Alex stepped forward until he was within inches of touching her. He reached out and curled his forefinger under her chin, tipping her face up until their eyes met. "On the contrary, we have one very important thing in common."

"What is that?" The question came out breathless, but then, Alex's touch affected her that way.

"We both want to marry you."

He drowned her gasp of surprise and protest with his lips.

Chapter Seven

Alex had spent his entire life waiting to kiss this one woman. He needed to show her that she belonged to him, that he was the only man who had the right to give her babies.

She tasted like the first bite of a hot fudge sundae on a warm summer's day, so damn sweet and utterly irresistible. He wrapped his hands around her waist and pulled her closer. Her muffled protests died as her body went pliant against his.

Digging her fingers into his shoulders, she opened her mouth under his. Her generous passion almost sent him to his knees. He moaned as her hips rocked against the bulge in his jeans. He wanted to rip off their clothes and rub his hardened flesh against the nest of curls between her thighs before plunging into her wet and welcoming heat. He wanted to make her his.

His hands roamed up her back, pressing her body into contact with his. He could feel the stiff nubs of her nipples through the layers of clothes that separated them. He cupped her breast through the silky fabric of her shirt and almost lost control completely.

Isabel wasn't wearing a bra. The only thing between him and the fullness of her creamy flesh was a thin layer of leopard-print silk. Scorching heat shot through him. She felt so damn good against him. So right. He kneaded her pliant flesh, allowing his thumb to graze her nipple.

Isabel tore her mouth from his and let out a sharp cry. "Oh, Alex. This is incredible."

He wasn't going to argue. The way he felt when he touched Isabel was incredible. It was also dangerous.

Dangerous because she didn't trust him yet.

As much as he wanted to make love to Isabel right now, he knew she wouldn't understand what it meant. She wouldn't understand the seriousness of it, the implacable permanence it would herald. He wanted her so much that his body was rigid with the need, but he had to control himself if he wanted his plans to succeed. He wanted more than an evening of pleasure. He wanted forever. Drawing on the last vestiges of his willpower, he pulled away from her.

She stared at him, her eyes unfocused in her passion.

He stepped back. "Is that terrific smell dinner?"

He couldn't actually smell anything but her unique and highly arousing scent. He was making a guess about dinner. She took a deep breath, and he almost yanked her back into his arms as her hardened nipples pressed against the silk of her shirt.

"You want dinner?" she asked, clearly dazed.

No, damn it. He wanted her. "I'd rather make love to you, sweetheart, but it's too soon for you."

The hazy expression faded from her eyes and they narrowed. She crossed her arms under her breasts and he longed to reach out and cup the soft, feminine curves. "Too soon for *me*?"

Yes, damn it. If it wasn't he would have their clothes off and her against the wall before she could draw her next breath. "Yes. Now, can we have dinner?"

Being chivalrous wasn't all it was cracked up to be, not when his body was begging for release.

She glared at him. "Let me get this straight. It's too soon for *me* to make love, but you plan to at some point in the future. Only right now, you want dinner?"

She didn't sound impressed with his chivalry.

And that made him angry. He hadn't stopped because he wanted to. He was doing this for her. Maybe a little blunt speaking would make her see the light.

"Sweetheart, if we don't leave this room right now I'm going to slip your blouse up your body, letting the silk brush against those hard little buds that have been teasing me since our first date, and then pull it off you. Then I'm going to taste you, all of you. That will require you losing the rest of your clothes. Once you are naked, I'm going to bury a certain extremely hard portion of my anatomy so deeply inside you that you aren't going to be able to tell where you end and I begin."

Isabel's eyes had slowly lost their angry sparkle, to be filled once again with unfocused passion. She swayed where she stood. Her tongue darted out and wet her lower lip. "I see."

"Do you?" His voice came out harsher than he intended. Controlling his desire for Isabel was getting more difficult by the second.

She swallowed. "I'm not ready to make love with you."

Hadn't he said that? "Dinner?"

She nodded. "Right. Dinner."

Isabel leaned her forehead against the smooth, cool surface of the refrigerator. She wished she'd worn a bra tonight. Her nipples were so tight that they actually hurt as her blouse brushed against them. She didn't want dinner. She wanted Alex, but she didn't trust him. It would be really, really stupid to make love to a man she didn't trust.

That didn't stop her breasts from aching for more of his touch or her mouth for the taste of him. Her thighs involuntarily pressed together trying to assuage the throbbing there. Alex's words spun through her mind like a tornado, leaving sensual devastation in their wake. He wanted her more than any man ever had. Even though he had stopped and even though she didn't have much experience in these things, she didn't doubt the desire she had sensed in him. That kind of need demanded a response, a response her *body* was willing to give.

But as much as she wanted him, his attitude really, really irritated her mind. And her pride.

"I admit that I don't know much about cooking, but I don't think you can prepare food by trying to mind-meld with the refrigerator, sweetheart."

His voice skated across her taut nerves. Willing herself to play it cool, she drew away from the appliance and turned to face him. She almost wished she hadn't. Barely controlled passion swirled in his eyes.

"Dinner is already made," she forced the mundane words out through tingling lips. "Would you like to open the wine?"

"Where's your corkscrew?"

She pointed to a kitchen drawer. "There."

They went about the routine of putting dinner on the table. Alex helped with natural ease. Isabel chose to eat in the dining room, not trusting the cozy closeness the small table in the kitchen would provide. After she and Alex sat down, she looked down at her plate and gave a silent moment of thanks. Nanny Number Six had insisted Isabel develop that particular habit. When she looked up, she found Alex studying her.

She forced a smile. "I hope you like dinner. It's pretty simple."

"Why did you invite me to dinner, Isabel?"

"You invited yourself," she reminded him.

"You offered to cook."

"It's less expensive than shoe shopping."

He didn't smile at her little joke. "Is that what you were going to do tonight? Go shoe shopping?"

She shrugged and took a fortifying sip of her wine. She went shoe shopping when she was stressed. "Maybe."

"You didn't have plans with Brad tonight?"

"Of course not. I wouldn't have invited you over if I had. His arrival was completely unexpected."

Why had she thought eating in here would be an improvement over the close confines of her cheery kitchen? The soft lighting and dark wood in the dining room lent an all-too-romantic setting to the meal she was sharing with Alex to maintain her peace of mind.

"Why did he come?"

If his parents had taught him that it was rude to pry, Alex hadn't taken to the lesson.

She picked up her knife and cut a small piece off of the stuffed chicken breast on her plate. "He said he wanted to apologize."

"Did he?"

She ran the conversation she'd had with Brad through her mind. "Sort of. I guess. In an offhand way."

"Did he do something that requires more than an offhand admission of guilt?" Alex asked the question casually, but his tense posture indicated he wanted the answer for more than curiosity's sake.

"If I cared and if he really wanted to renew our relationship, then I'd have to say yes. It would take a lot more than a token 'I'm sorry' to make it better."

He mulled over her answer for a moment. "You said he's an ex-boyfriend."

"Yes." She wondered if the government realized what

it had missed when Alex Trahern opted for the corporate world rather than training to be a spy or interrogator.

"How recent was your relationship?" His face became more expressionless with each question.

"We broke up about six weeks ago."

"It was serious, then? You were thinking about marriage and babies with him."

She didn't like the direction their conversation was taking. "Don't you think your questions are a little personal for our short acquaintance, Alex?"

"What we did in the living room was a whole lot more personal. Answer the question, sweetheart."

When he used the endearment it did something funny to her heart. She liked it. Was Alex the type of man to call all the women he knew names like that? Somehow, she doubted it.

"I never seriously considered marriage with Brad."

"Why not? Didn't he fit your list of requirements?"

She felt her cheeks heat at the mention of her list. The list that made her appear desperate and crazy. "I didn't have them then. It was simpler than that."

"What was it?"

"I thought about my work when he kissed me." She thought about other things, too, things like what kind of flowers to buy the office receptionist for secretary's day, stuff that had absolutely nothing to do with passion and commitment.

Satisfaction radiated off Alex. "What do you think about when I kiss you?" he asked in a husky tone that made her thighs clamp together again.

She wasn't about to answer that loaded question.

Alex didn't seem to expect her to because he asked another one almost immediately. "Is that why you stopped seeing him?"

She shook her head. "I found him in bed with his oh-so-lovely, oh-so-married boss when he was supposed to be at work."

After hearing about how she responded to Brad's kisses, would Alex believe it was Isabel's fault that Brad had cheated on her? Brad certainly had. He'd made it clear that if Isabel had been more passionate, he would never have gone to bed with the other woman. Isabel had told herself it was just an excuse and a poor one at that, but part of her had been afraid Brad was right. She'd feared that she lacked the passionate nature to maintain the long-term interest of a man.

"Brad is a jackass."

She smiled in response to Alex's words. "Yes, he is."

After dinner, they moved into the living room. Alex poured himself some scotch while Isabel sipped on her wine leftover from the meal. She put on a Bach harpsichord CD before sitting down on the sofa. Curling her feet under her, she leaned against the overstuffed leather arm of the couch. She had lit vanilla candles earlier, and their fragrance filled the room now.

Alex prowled restlessly around the room. It reminded her of the first night they met, but there was no sense of controlled fury, just curiosity. She felt as if he were studying everything in the room and weighing her in the balance.

"Do you always do this?"

He turned abruptly when she asked the question. "What?"

"Study your date's home so intently."

He walked over to the sofa. Although he sat at the other end, she felt as if he'd invaded her space.

He regarded her, his eyes giving away none of his thoughts. "No. I don't date often and when I do, I don't usually spend this much time compiling data on my date's home."

"Compiling data?"

His smile was self-deprecatory. That didn't make the dimple any less devastating. It was a good thing for her peace of mind that Alex did not smile often.

He took a sip of his whiskey and then answered. "Gathering information is what I do. When I look around your home I notice things about you."

"Data that you store away for future reference?" she asked, trying to understand how his mind worked and wondering if it was an impossible task.

This time his smile was approving. She could get addicted to that dimple.

"Yes. The data fits into your information matrix."

Information matrix? She was definitely getting in over her head. "So what have you learned?"

"You have an eclectic taste in music, everything from country to classical."

"That's pretty obvious to anyone who looks at the CD's I have in my cabinet."

He shrugged. "I didn't say the data was top-secret stuff."

She cocked her head to the side and studied him. "I would have expected a man with your talents at gathering information could have observed something more subtle and equally more important than the fact that I like a lot of different types of music."

"You don't think your taste in music is important?" Before she could answer, he went on. "Everything about you is important to me, Isabel."

Warmth spread through her at his words.

"Your relationship with your father isn't close."

She frowned at the satisfaction in Alex's voice. Surely he couldn't be happy about her near-estrangement from her dad. "I told you I do not approve of his work habits. I didn't say we aren't close."

He laid his arm across the back of the sofa, and she wanted to move over enough to curl into his side.

"You didn't have to." He waved his hand toward the photo display on her bookshelves. "The pictures you keep out say it all. There are casual shots of you with Bettina and other friends, but the only picture you have of your father is a formal studio shot."

"Maybe he doesn't like having his picture taken." She didn't know why she was arguing with Alex. He was right. Her only somewhat recent photo of her father was one he had professionally done for a Hypertron annual report.

"Well?" he asked, not giving her an out.

"My father and I are practically strangers." The stark truth hurt, but she couldn't pretend otherwise. She had tried, but her father had no interest in sharing her life in more than the most superficial of ways.

"I wasn't very close to my dad, either." Alex looked as if the admission surprised him as much as it had surprised her.

"I'm sorry. It hurts, doesn't it?" she asked.

"His dying hurt more."

She didn't doubt it, so she nodded. At least with her dad, there was always the hope that one day he would realize he needed her and want a bigger role in her life.

"I'm going to my mother's for lunch this Sunday. I want you to come with me."

The change in topic wasn't nearly as disconcerting as the subject of that change. "You want me to meet your mother?"

"Yes."

"Why?"

"It's traditional for a man to introduce his mother to the woman he intends to marry."

Alex watched the cascade of emotions cross Isabel's face. First shock, then confusion, and finally anger.

"This is about the list, isn't it?" she demanded.

"This is about you and me, sweetheart."

She shook her head vehemently. "No. It isn't. You think I'm some kind of desperate fruitcake who will marry any man that comes along." She jumped up from the couch and started pacing. "Well, you're wrong. I'm not desperate. I want a baby and a family, but that doesn't make me crazy." She stopped in front of him. "Do you hear me?"

"I hear you just fine." Hell, her neighbors probably heard her. "Sit down, sweetheart. We can talk this out rationally."

"There's nothing rational about informing a woman you've only known a matter of days that you intend to marry her!" Her voice had risen until the panicked tones were almost at screeching level.

"Calm down, Isabel. I'm not proposing we elope tonight."

She glowered down at him. "You aren't proposing at all. You informed me I was going to marry you, told Brad I was your fiancée, but unless I'm the crazy woman you think and have forgotten something important, you haven't asked me anything!"

Hell. He hadn't expected her to be looking for moonlight and romance, not when she'd made a shopping list of requirements for her future husband. "You didn't put 'romantic' on your list, and for the record, I don't think you're crazy."

"Leave my list out of this. You didn't have any right to look at it in the first place, even less right to take it from my office, and you aren't going to use it as an excuse to insult me now." Her breasts heaved as she gulped in air.

Setting his drink on the table next to the couch, he stood up. She backed up a step, but he reached out and snagged her arm. Taking the almost-empty wineglass from her hand, he placed it next to his glass on the small table.

Gently pulling her toward him, he said, "I did not realize that my wanting to marry you would be so offensive to you."

She stared at him. Her mouth opened, then closed. She swallowed. "I didn't mean to imply that marriage to you would be an insult."

He nodded. "Good." Then he lowered his lips to hers.

He kept a tight leash on his desire. He wanted to calm her down, not overwhelm them both with the sensations that erupted whenever they touched. He waited until she softened against him, and then tugged her toward the couch. Sitting down, he pulled her with him. She landed on his lap, her hands locked at the back of his neck. He allowed himself the pleasure of kissing her for another full minute before pulling his mouth away.

"You like kissing me." He knew without her admitting it that she didn't think about work when she kissed him.

She sighed and opened her eyes, allowing her hands to slip down to rest against his chest. "Yes, but that doesn't mean I'm going to marry you after knowing you such a short time."

He thought about that. "How long do you think you'll have to know me before you agree to marriage?" He couldn't afford to wait too long. He wanted Isabel tied to him before St. Clair went after Hypertron.

She bit her lip. "I don't know."

"I fit your requirements," he reminded her.

She frowned. "So you say, but I don't know that."

He didn't like the implication in her words. "We're compatible, Isabel. I even have decent work habits."

Her chin angled up. "Just what do you consider decent work habits? Taking some poor schmuck on a date to worm information out of her?"

Frowning, he rubbed her arm in what he hoped was a soothing gesture. "I keep a lot better hours than your dad, and you won't ever have to worry about walking in on me and my sex-starved boss."

"Because you own your own company?"

"Because you can trust me to be faithful."

Her fingers traced a pattern on his chest, wreaking havoc with his control. He reached up and covered her hand with one of his.

Her eyes widened, but she didn't pull her hands away. "Work habits are something you have to observe over time."

He didn't know how much time he had, but he could see her point. He went on another tack. "There's enough attraction between us to cause lightening storms. That's better than the minimal passion requirement you put on your list."

Her face turned a soft shade of pink. "That's true, but marriage is more than sex."

"Right. It's about family, too. I'll give you babies, Isabel. As many as you want." It had surprised him when he'd realized how much he wanted to do just that. He hadn't liked being an only child, and he didn't want any child of his to grow up without siblings.

Her lips parted with a soft, "Oh," and her cheeks went a deeper shade of pink.

He smiled. "That is what you want, isn't it? You want a family and I'll give you one."

"Why?"

"Because I want you."

She gripped his shirt. "That doesn't make sense. If you want me, you should be trying to seduce me, not marry me."

"Do you want me to seduce you, honey?" The thought was a tantalizing one, especially with her sweet derriere cuddled against his thighs.

She released his shirt and jumped off his lap in one swift motion. She tripped as she stepped backward and he reached out to steady her. "No. I don't want you to seduce me. I want to understand why you want to marry me."

He didn't know if he could explain. He was accustomed to moving once he'd made a decision, and he had decided that he wanted Isabel . . . permanently.

He stood and she hastily stepped farther away. He frowned. "I'm not going to attack you, sweetheart. Relax."

She made an obvious effort to do so, taking in several deep breaths and letting them out. "I know that. It's just that this is all so confusing. I haven't even had one normal, uneventful date with you."

"You know you won't be bored with me. That was on your second-level list," he said, in case she'd forgotten.

She eyed him with interest. "You figured out the different levels?"

He didn't think she would appreciate it if he told her they were so obvious a small child could have done so. "Yes."

She chewed on her lower lip and then finally said, "I'll go to meet your mother."

Triumph rolled over him. "Great."

She crossed her arms. "It doesn't mean I'm going to marry you. It's just that I like to meet new people."

"Whatever you say, sweetheart."

Chapter Eight

Alex read the online news announcement a second time. Hypertron reported low earnings for the last quarter. Unsurprised, Alex made a notation for the file. With this news, which confirmed Alex's initial findings, St. Clair would begin preparation for the first steps in the hostile takeover.

Tapping his fingers on his desk, Alex considered how this information would impact his relationship with Isabel Harrison. He'd spent two years mooning over a photograph. After meeting Isabel and discovering the woman fulfilled every fantasy the photo had inspired, it had not taken him long to determine that if she was set on getting married, he was the man she'd get married to. They were compatible, even if she did not yet see it that way. And physically they were more than compatible, they were combustible.

He was thirty-two years old. The prospect of settling down to marriage and family appealed to him. His mother would make a wonderful grandmother, and for the past four years she'd been pressing him to start dating "seriously." With his company well established and his financial picture secure, he was ready to take her advice. With Isabel.

He wanted Isabel. Isabel wanted marriage and a family. So, they would get married and he'd give her a baby. The thought of what it would take to get her in that condition played havoc with his mind and his flesh. Having the beautiful, spirited, and slightly innocent woman share his bed on a nightly basis would be no hardship.

No other woman had affected him as she did. When he was with her, he wanted to touch her. All of her. And the more time they spent together, the stronger the attraction grew.

Ideally, the marriage should take place before St. Clair's takeover of Hypertron. Although Alex no longer planned for his role in Hypertron's destruction to become public, there was no guarantee it wouldn't. He knew better than anyone how easily buried information could be brought to the light, and he didn't want Isabel in a place where she might walk away from him without a backward glance when she found out.

If finding out about his revenge against her dad's company upset her, his instincts told him that as his wife, she'd try to work it out. If they were just dating, she might say good-bye—and mean it. He couldn't take that chance.

Every detail except one that he had managed to plug into the matrix surrounding Isabel pointed to a single truth: She belonged with him.

The one circumstance that had given Alex pause—the fact that she was Harrison's daughter—had ceased to matter.

Isabel might not think she'd known Alex long enough to make a commitment, but he would just have to prove to her that she was wrong.

Snatching the phone from its cradle, he dialed St.

Clair's number and ended up leaving a message. He needed to tell Marcus about the latest development.

Walking into the outer office a moment later, he found Marcus leaning on Veronica Richards's desk, in what appeared to be a wholly flirtatious conversation. Alex stopped short. He hadn't realized that his secretary was capable of something so basically human as flirting.

Marcus was a different matter. Alex's assistant had no trouble attracting women. However, Marcus had never shown interest in women like Veronica. He tended to go for women who could only be described as big and brassy.

It took a moment, but Veronica became aware of Alex standing a few feet from her and Marcus's little tête-à-tête. She looked up and blushed guiltily. "Mr. Trahern. What can I do for you?"

"Actually, I was looking for Marcus."

Marcus pushed away from Veronica's desk and walked toward Alex. "Sure thing, boss."

Marcus winked at Veronica as he passed her. After a hasty glance at Alex, she pretended interest in something on her desk.

Alex led Marcus back into the office and sat at his desk. "I wouldn't have said that she was your type."

Marcus's mouth tipped up at one corner in a sardonic smile. "People aren't always what they appear on the surface."

"In the years that I've known you, the women you've dated have been all surface. Are you saying you're looking for something different with Veronica?"

An expression that looked entirely too familiar crossed Marcus's features. It contained confusion and irritation. Both feelings were all too frequent for Alex since he had met Isabel for him not to recognize a fellow sufferer. Marcus had it bad, but from the way he wiped his face free of expression, Alex figured he wasn't going to acknowledge it.

"So, what's up?" Marcus asked.

"Heard any word from Bettina on the employer who wanted to hire you?" Better to get that out of the way first.

Marcus had told Bettina that he'd called Isabel only to find out the name of the prospective employer. Evidently, the news had not surprised Bettina, and she'd still offered to set up the interview, provided the employer still wanted to after being told the truth of the situation.

Marcus had agreed and they hadn't heard anything since.

He grinned. "Don't you know that's supposed to be confidential? How am I supposed to make the best decision for my career with my current boss breathing down my neck?"

Alex frowned. Was Marcus seriously considering leaving CIS?

"Relax, Alex. That was a joke. Bettina called this morning and told me she'd spoken to the prospective employer, and he's deciding whether or not to go ahead with the interview."

"I don't believe it's Isabel's father."

Marcus nodded. "That's what my gut's telling me, too."

Whoever it was would have an opportunity to try to convince Marcus to leave CIS. Alex didn't like it, but the plan was set in motion, and he had no choice but to trust his right-hand man.

Alex moved on to the principal reason for this meeting. "Hypertron just announced low earnings for last quarter."

Marcus let out a low whistle. "The game's afoot, eh?"

"The stock should see a dip tomorrow," Alex agreed.

"When Hypertron announces that the new technology is going to be late to market, that dip is going to become a steady decline."

"Are you sure the technology is going to be late to market?"

Alex knew Marcus wasn't asking for guarantees. He was wondering if Alex had heard from their informant at Hypertron since the last report a week ago. "Bart called yesterday. It's still touch and go. The design team is scrambling, but it looks good for a late entrance."

Marcus shifted in his chair and studied Alex. "You don't sound as excited as you should be, considering that the revenge you've waited two years to get is at hand."

"I'm not an excitable man."

Marcus chuckled. "You're telling me, but don't you think your lack of reaction is pretty remarkable? Even for you."

"There are still too many unknown variables in the matrix." Like what adding Isabel to the equation would do to the outcome.

Isabel picked up the soft, flexible shoe and examined it. The fluorescent lights of the mall reflected off the sage green pump. She didn't recognize the maker, although it appeared well made and had the stamp on the sole proclaiming it to be genuine leather. It smelled good. She inhaled the fragrance of new leather and smiled.

For her, the smell was more compelling than flowers or expensive perfume. Perhaps she should try on a pair. She caught the attention of the store clerk and asked him to find a pair in her size. Darn Alex, anyway. She didn't need another pair of shoes, but here she was trying on some anyway. The pumps weren't even on sale.

She'd come shopping to escape her apartment and the telephone that would ring any moment with Alex on the other end of the line. He had phoned every night since their date, ending each call with one or more things he fulfilled on her list.

So far he'd informed her that he was gainfully employed, liked her favorite country singer, and agreed that families should vacation together. Last night he'd had the nerve to inform her that she found him attractive. She hadn't been able to deny his words and had ended up demanding to know if the feeling was mutual. He'd laughed and reminded her what happened every time they kissed. Alex laughing was one of those rare pleasures in life a woman couldn't take for granted.

"Here you are, miss."

She slipped off her own shoes and tried on the pumps. They fit perfectly. She stood up and admired the way they shaped her feet. Taking an experimental step, she considered her problem.

Alex.

He wanted to marry her, but why? The question gnawed at her. He said he wanted her, but that wasn't enough reason to marry a woman. Not in today's age. Never mind that Isabel wouldn't have an affair with him. He hadn't even tried, and the way she responded to his touch should have led him to believe it was at least a possibility.

And maybe, just maybe . . . it was.

He hadn't said anything about love. She had to admit that if he had, she would have thought he was even more insane. The problem was, she didn't think that particular emotion was in his plans for the future, either. He had been appalled that she might expect a little romance like a genuine proposal. She might be looking for a husband with something as pragmatic as a list of job requirements, but that didn't mean she wanted him to treat marriage like a business deal.

She hadn't thought of that potential pitfall when contemplating the brilliant idea of making her list, but then she'd never expected one of her dates to read it and claim it as an implied contract, either.

"Are you all right, miss?" the shoe salesman asked.

Her attention snapped back to him, the shoes, and what she was doing in the mall. She smiled. "Yes, I'm fine. I don't think I'll take the shoes, though."

Even a pair of perfectly fitting, absolutely gorgeous shoes could not dispel the melancholy her situation had elicited in her. Not when she very much feared that she was falling in love with Alex, a man too hard to be affected by such a soft emotion. A man, moreover, who had decided he wanted to marry her for reasons she couldn't even begin to understand.

A lovely woman, Priscilla Trahern lived in a beautiful home. Isabel hadn't missed the fact that the single-story white house with neatly manicured flowerbeds was in a gated community. Alex's influence, no doubt. Isabel had liked Alex's mother the moment he introduced them. Priscilla had a kind smile and a motherly air, though she dressed and held herself with elegant aplomb. She reminded Isabel of Nancy Reagan in pastel.

Lunch could have been awkward. In fact, Isabel had been more than mildly concerned about it. She feared that at the first gentle probe from his mother regarding the state of their relationship, Alex would announce a forthcoming marriage. Thankfully, the probe never came.

Priscilla guided the conversation along interesting but hardly intimate channels throughout the meal. When it was over, she surprised Isabel by instructing Alex to clear the table and inviting Isabel to join her in the living room.

As they left the dining room, Priscilla said, "Just leave the dishes in the sink, Alex."

Priscilla turned to Isabel as they entered a graceful room done in shades of seafoam green and cream. "My housekeeper prefers that I don't attempt to load the dishwasher. She's got her own method and she doesn't want my interference."

"I understand." Isabel sat down on a Queen Anne-style chair with moiré upholstery, crossing her ankles. "Nanny Number Seven was the same way. She said that when I tried to help by loading the dishwasher for her, I ended up making more work because she had to unload it, start all over, and load it again."

Priscilla's soft gray eyes widened. "Nanny Number Seven? What an unusual way to refer to someone."

Isabel felt her face heat. She probably sounded terribly rude, referring to the woman that way. She usually only did so in her head. It was a measure of how comfortable Priscilla had made Isabel feel that she had slipped and made the comment out loud. "Her name was Anne. She wasn't really my nanny."

Isabel had referred to her as a nanny with a number to protect herself from getting too emotionally involved with Anne, who had been both kind and caring to Isabel.

"Dad said that I no longer needed a caregiver when I turned twelve. I guess he was trying to make me feel more grown up." Only she hadn't felt grown up. She'd felt abandoned. Until her dad hired Anne. "She was our housekeeper."

"I see." Priscilla's face mirrored sympathetic understanding.

"I started referring to the nannies by a number in my head after the second one left. It was my way of keeping them at a distance so it wouldn't hurt so much when they were gone. It wasn't easy for them working for my father," she said by way of explanation.

In a gesture that both startled and comforted her, Priscilla reached out and touched Isabel's hand. "We do what we can to protect our hearts when they've been hurt too much."

Remembering that Alex had said his father died, Isabel believed Priscilla truly did understand. She wondered what the older woman had done to protect her heart.

"It doesn't always work," Isabel said, remembering the wrenching pain when her dad had replaced Anne.

The housekeeper had argued with him one too many times over his neglect of Isabel. Rather than spend more time with his daughter and shut Anne up, he had replaced her with someone else.

Unable to cope with another loss, Isabel had held herself at a complete emotional distance from the next housekeeper, Bonnie. In a twist of fate that Isabel had never understood, that housekeeper still worked for her father. Isabel had often wondered if it was simply her destiny to lose the people she allowed herself to love.

"No, it doesn't," replied Priscilla, a wealth of understanding and residual pain in her eyes. "Loving others is always a risk."

Isabel agreed. A risk she hadn't meant to take when it came to marriage. Her list of requirements had seemed safer than an emotional entanglement. There were so many ways a marriage could end. Priscilla was the living example that it didn't always have to be in divorce.

But now that her emotions were getting more and more entangled with Alex, she wanted him to respond on the same level, not to keep quoting her list like each item was a point in a negotiation toward settlement.

Priscilla must have read something on Isabel's face because she leaned forward and squeezed Isabel's hand again. "Loving *can* bring pain, a great deal of pain, but it can also bring joy that outweighs that pain. Don't be afraid to love."

Isabel couldn't believe that she and Alex's coolly elegant mother were having such a personal conversation, and yet she was glad in a way. Since Anne, Isabel had not confided the hidden parts of her heart to anyone, not even Bettina.

"Was loving your husband worth the pain of losing him?"

Priscilla leaned back and sighed. "Yes, but I didn't accept that until very recently. I was so angry with Ray for neglecting me and Alex for his work that when he died that anger grew into bitterness."

"What changed?"

"Me. I changed inside. I finally forgave Ray for his neglect and for dying before we could fix our marriage."

Looking at the peace that now filled Priscilla's expression, Isabel didn't doubt the veracity of her words. Hadn't Isabel realized long ago that the only answer to the pain of her dad's neglect was forgiveness? But would that work for the future? Could she risk loving a husband, knowing that he might hurt her as her father had done?

"What's going on in here? You two look like you're solving the crisis in the Middle East."

Alex's voice jolted Isabel from her emotional thoughts.

"Your young lady and I were just getting to know each other better, Alex. It is a mother's prerogative," Priscilla replied.

Alex smiled, genuine warmth lighting his eyes as he looked down at his mother. "And you like what you've gotten to know?"

Isabel couldn't believe he would put his mother on the spot like that. "She's hardly had enough time to make a judgment about me one way or the other," she inserted before Priscilla could answer.

Priscilla laughed. It was a gentle sound, in perfect accord with Priscilla's proper behavior and yet genuine. "On the contrary, Isabel. I believe I can answer my son's question without reservation. You are a lovely young woman, and I would like nothing more than to know that my son was seeing a great deal of you."

Touched, Isabel said quietly, "Thank you."

Priscilla smiled and nodded, seeming to comprehend the wealth of emotion behind the simple words.

Isabel turned to see Alex's reaction to his mother's words and was not surprised at the look of complacent satisfaction on his face. He knew what he wanted. She just wished she understood why he was so sure it was her.

Isabel had been silent for most of the drive home from his mother's house. What was she thinking? He'd like to know what she and his mother had been talking about while he cleared the table. They had been so somber when he joined them in the living room. At first, he'd been afraid that his mother had told Isabel about Hypertron's role in his dad's death. But Isabel hadn't seemed angry or accusatory, just thoughtful.

Alex hoped she didn't have any plans this evening. They needed to spend more time together. She wasn't going to agree to marry him until she trusted him. The only way he could think of to cement that trust was to spend time together. Besides, visiting with his mom had been very nice, but each casual touch from Isabel sent his hormones into overdrive.

He wanted to touch her.

He wanted to hold her.

He wanted more, but he didn't think she was ready.

Then again, maybe that was the key to getting her trust. Would she continue to withhold her trust from a man to whom she had given her body?

Pulling into the parking spot in front of Isabel's condo, he turned off the Aston Martin and waited. Would she invite him in, or would he have to come up with an excuse to follow her inside?

She unbuckled her seatbelt and opened the door but didn't get out. Her silky honey-brown hair swung against her shoulders as she turned toward him and fixed him with her emerald gaze. "Would you like to come in for a while?"

He'd like to come in for all night, but he would settle for what he could get. "Yes."

She nodded and slid out of the car. Following her into her apartment, he enjoyed the feminine sway of her hips in the long sarong-style skirt she wore. Her top molded the soft curves of her upper body, and he wanted to reach out and brush the gentle indentation of her waist.

She stopped to light some sweet-smelling candles on her way into the living room. The action was so automatic, he didn't think she was attempting to set the mood. Too bad. She then turned on the stereo and the soft chords of Tim McGraw singing a love song with his wife, Faith Hill, filled the room. The song was about a man and his woman making love.

He doubted Isabel was even aware of the lyrics. She seemed preoccupied. He wished she'd chosen a different CD because the lyrics were all too real to him. The husky tones in the singers' voices, combined with the words they sang, were a powerful reminder of the night he'd had dinner here with Isabel and the way she'd come apart in his arms.

He'd felt like a real knight in pulling back from taking her so soon, but now he was starting to think he'd just been an idiot. Women didn't want chivalrous men anymore. They wanted to make up their own minds about things like whether they got swept away by passion. Remembering the grateful look in her beautiful green eyes when she'd realized what he'd stopped them from doing didn't sit well with his new theory, so he tried to squelch it.

He watched her flutter aimlessly about the room and considered helping her to find a place to light. Preferably him. That white leather sofa had distinct possibilities.

"I guess it's my turn."

They weren't the words he was hoping for, so it took Alex a minute to realize what she'd said. When he tried, he still didn't get her meaning, so he asked, "What's your turn?"

She shifted her shoulders and sighed before turning to face him. She looked even more somber than she had while talking to his mom earlier. He wanted to fix whatever was bothering her.

"It's my turn to invite you to meet my father, only I can't promise he'll show up for dinner or anything else, for that matter. He has deplorable work habits."

Alex wasn't ready to explain to Isabel yet about what had happened between his father and Hypertron. He hadn't been all that surprised that she'd shown no awareness of it. The lawsuit had never made it to the papers. Her dad was as fanatical about secrecy as Alex was. Alex had wondered why John Harrison hadn't told his daughter about it. Learning about the distance in their relationship had cleared that up for him.

And Alex couldn't say he was sorry. If Isabel had known about his father's relationship to Hypertron and what had happened because of it, she would never have gone on that first date, much less let herself melt in his arms. "Don't sweat it."

She frowned, cute little creases forming between her eyes. "That's easy for you to say. You didn't have to worry about your mother calling at the last minute to cancel today, or worse—not bothering to call *or* show up."

Suddenly, disconcertingly, tears stood out in her eyes, and Alex wanted more than anything to prevent them from falling.

He took a step toward her. "It's not important, honey. What we have together is all that matters."

She blinked back her tears, but her eyes and long lashes remained moist. "Then why bother having me meet your mother?"

"Because I knew you two would like each other and she's a big part of my life." He could have bitten his tongue after uttering the last part of that sentence. He didn't mean to remind her of Harrison's lack of interest in her life.

"I guess you think that it isn't important to me for you to meet my dad because we aren't that close, but you're wrong. It's very important to me." This time the tears spilled over.

Alex groaned. "Don't cry. Please, Isabel. I can't stand it." He reached out and drew her into the circle of his arms. He held her, not because he wanted her, although he did. He held her because she needed comfort and he needed to comfort her. The last time he'd felt this way was with his mom on the day his father died. "We'll make it work, sweetheart."

She shook her head against his chest. "No, we won't. We can't do anything. No matter what we plan he'll put the company first. I knew Bettina almost two years before she ever met my dad," Isabel said, her voice filled with misery.

Damn. What was he supposed to do now? Alex had very little experience with tears, and he felt completely out of his depth. "Stop crying, sweetheart. We'll find a way."

Why the hell was he promising to try to do something he wanted less than a root canal?

"Your mother is wonderful." Isabel took a shuddering, tear-filled breath. "She's kind and I liked meeting her."

Alex could pretty much guarantee he would not enjoy meeting Isabel's father. "I'll meet your dad at the wedding."

He'd meant to make a joke out of it, to maybe even shock Isabel into an angry retort about how she hadn't promised to marry him yet. Anything to stop her crying. Only it didn't work that way. Her tears increased and she tried to pull out of his arms, but he wasn't letting go.

"Haven't you been listening to me?" She pounded against his chest as if her father's inconsistency was Alex's fault. He didn't mind because at least she wasn't crying so heavily now. She was just mad. "I've been planning on walking myself down the aisle since I was thirteen years old, and my dad missed my eighth grade graduation."

Alex swore out loud. John Harrison was a bastard and deserved to lose his company for more than what he'd done to Ray Trahern. For Harrison, Hypertron had always come first—even over his only daughter. No wonder Isabel was so worried about work habits in her potential husband.

"I don't care if I ever meet your father." Life would be a lot simpler if he never had to come face-to-face with John Harrison in Isabel's presence.

Taking a deep breath, Isabel pushed against Alex's restraining hold. He reluctantly let her go. Her face was set in lines of determination. She wiped the tears from her cheeks and tucked her hair behind her ears.

"I'm not promising a wedding here, Alex, but you're an important person in my life, and I care whether you meet my dad. This time I'm going to see to it."

Alex doubted even Harrison's selfish work habits could stand against the determination in Isabel's eyes. How long did he have before he would be forced to tell her about his father's experience with Hypertron? Could he tell her without her suspecting his need for vengeance?

She walked over to the phone, picked it up, and dialed.

Who was she calling?

"Bonnie, this is Isabel. Is Dad home?" She waited a moment while Bonnie responded. "May I speak to him, please?"

Alex felt emotions swirl through him as he faced the reality of what Isabel was doing. Maybe her father wouldn't be available. His hope died a quick death when she spoke again.

"Hello, Dad. I've got someone I'd like you to meet. Are you going to be home for a little while?"

The look of disappointment on Isabel's face should have made Alex feel guilty, but his relief didn't leave any room.

She narrowed her eyes and squared her shoulders. "It will have to wait. Alex and I will be there in twenty minutes."

Isabel shook her head at whatever her dad was saying on the other end. "Let me put it to you this way. If you aren't home when I get there with Alex, I'm going to find an irresistible new job for the senior design engineer on the Borland Project."

Isabel hung up the phone, cutting off a tirade that Alex could hear across the room. She smiled at Alex.

"The Borland Project is very important to Hypertron right now."

Alex knew that. It was the project he and his associates hoped would be late coming to market, the final piece in the matrix surrounding his vengeance against Harrison. "So you threatened him with it."

Isabel's eyes sparkled, and Alex could tell she was pleased with herself. "I've never taken that approach before. Shall we see if it works? It might be fun to find my dad waiting docilely for our arrival."

Alex could think of a lot of amusing ways to spend time with Isabel. None of them included meeting John Harrison.

Chapter Nine

Isabel had been wrong.

Harrison wasn't waiting docilely for them to arrive. He paced the floor, irritation coming off him in waves. Alex let her go ahead of him into the room and noticed that her father's attention focused on her with cold precision. Alex knew that as soon as Harrison realized who had accompanied her, his anger would shift to a new target. Alex didn't mind facing Harrison's anger.

He did mind the prospect that Isabel might share her father's fury.

"What the hell do you think you're doing threatening me?" Harrison demanded. "I thought you'd grown out of these petty little emotional displays, Isabel."

Isabel, who had been smiling happily at her father, clearly intent on giving him an affectionate hug, stopped midstep in her progress across the room. Her face lost the telltale signs of happiness. It lost expression altogether, and her hands fluttered to her sides like deflating balloons.

Alex's body tensed with battle readiness. He knew that Harrison was a bastard, but how could he be such a stupid one? He must realize that his words had hurt her, and yet the man's entire focus seemed to be on how she had put a cramp in his schedule.

Certainty welled up inside of Alex. One more cruel word and he would take a much more personal sort of vengeance against Hypertron's president. Coming up behind Isabel, he rested his hand on her shoulder and squeezed.

The tension he felt there was reflected in her voice when she spoke. "It's nice to see you too, Dad. It's been a long time."

Harrison's face registered chagrin. "Not that long."

He didn't sound sure of the statement.

Isabel sighed and Alex rubbed the side of her neck with the pad of his thumb. Her shoulders relaxed slightly and she shifted closer to him. He transferred his focus to her father. The signs of stress were all there: exhaustion lines around eyes the same color as Isabel's, tense jaw, gray hair that looked as if he'd been running his fingers through it, skin pale from spending too much time under fluorescent lights.

John Harrison knew his company was in trouble.

Alex searched inside himself for satisfaction at the signs of the other man's troubles, but all he could feel right now was apprehension that his plans with Isabel were going to end up just as wasted as Hypertron.

"Alex, I'd like you to meet my father, John Harrison." Isabel spoke quietly, her voice practically begging him to not be offended by her dad's behavior. "Dad, this is my friend Alex Trahern."

Alex waited for the words to sink in. It was a sign of Harrison's preoccupation and obvious tiredness that he got all the way through extending his arm and shaking Alex's hand while meeting Alex's gaze before the shock of recognition widened his eyes. He'd never actually met John Harrison, but Trahern was an uncommon name, and Alex looked enough like his father for someone who had worked so many years with his dad to guess at the connection.

The explosion didn't come.

Harrison turned to Isabel and the look in his eyes could be read only as disappointment. What the hell?

The older man actually looked defeated. "Why did you bring him here, Isabel?"

Her shoulder rose and fell under Alex's hand. "Because I wanted you to meet him."

John Harrison nodded, the aggression draining out of him and making him appear even more worn out than before. "You wanted me to meet the son of the man I supposedly ruined, is that it?"

"What are you talking about, Dad? Alex's father is dead."

Harrison rubbed his hands over his eyes. "Don't play games with me, Isabel. You're on one of your crusades, aren't you?"

Apparently giving up on getting a straight answer from her father, she turned to face Alex. "What's he talking about?" Her soft green eyes were filled with confusion.

He squeezed her shoulder again and answered her father. "The only crusade your daughter is on right now is to have her father meet the man she's going to marry."

Father and daughter exclaimed in unison.

"Like hell!"

"Alex!"

"Is this true?" Harrison demanded of Isabel.

She gave Alex a withering look before turning to face her father. Alex waited for her to deny it. Once she found out about his dad's connection to Hypertron, the chances of a marriage taking place would go to nothing anyway.

"I wanted you to meet him. After all, I met his mother.

It only seemed appropriate that we keep things even," she said, sidestepping the marriage issue altogether.

Harrison looked stunned. Alex didn't blame him. Isabel hadn't denied the engagement.

She wasn't finished. "Now, would one of you kindly explain what else I'm missing here?" she asked, fixing them with a glittery emerald stare that dared them to refuse.

Alex caught Harrison's gaze and challenged him with his own to answer Isabel's question.

The older man cleared his throat. Surprisingly, he looked less than willing to discuss the past. Alex would have thought he would use the first opportunity available to poison Isabel against him. "It's a long story, Isabel. I don't have time to go into it right now."

Isabel shook her head. "Not good enough. You've been telling me all my life that you don't have time for what's important to me. It's not going to fly this time. Start talking."

The emotions vibrating in Isabel's voice struck a chord deep in Alex. He could hear the pain of a woman who had always taken a back seat to her father's company in his affections and priorities. Alex wanted to protect her from the pain of her father's rejection and from the upset that learning the story about Ray Trahern was going to cause her.

He couldn't do either.

This might be the only chance Alex would ever have to hear Harrison's excuse for stealing Ray Trahern's discovery and causing his death, but he didn't care. All that mattered right now was that Isabel was going to be hurt, and Alex couldn't stop it. He reached out and cupped her shoulder again, trying to communicate with his touch that what her father was going to say had nothing to do with them. He almost sighed aloud with relief when she didn't pull away.

Harrison ran his fingers through the silver streaks of his hair, leaving it more disheveled than before. He looked just like what he was, a man on the edge of disaster. "Ray Trahern worked for me at Hypertron. He was one of the best design engineers I've ever had, one of my best friends."

Alex was shocked by Harrison's claim to friendship with his father. It made what had happened even more obscene. But he wasn't surprised by the compliment to Ray Trahern's abilities. Alex already knew his dad had been the best. Only the best could have discovered the technology that had done so much for Hypertron's bottom line.

When her dad stopped speaking, Isabel prompted him. "What happened?"

"He developed a new technology and he wanted to patent it, then sell it to Hypertron."

"I don't understand." Confusion laced Isabel's voice. "Did he do the developing at home?"

Alex answered for her father. "No, my dad did his work in his office, using Hypertron's equipment."

Isabel turned her head and let her confused eyes focus on Alex. "If he used the company's equipment, how could he patent the technology? Didn't it already belong to Hypertron?"

"That's what your father argued, but Dad did all the developmental work after hours."

Isabel's expression was troubled. "Didn't he sign an intellectual property rights agreement? I thought Hypertron required that of all their employees."

"We did and he did, but Ray felt that he had the right to his development." Harrison's voice sounded weary rather than argumentative.

"He did have a right to that technology, damn it," Alex said. "He worked long hours for Hypertron, gave your company everything that he had. It was common knowledge that employees could use the equipment after work hours for their own pursuits."

"The arbitration board found in Hypertron's favor," Harrison replied.

Alex didn't argue that point. He didn't have to because it didn't matter. It wasn't the loss of the patent or the money his father could have made from it that drove Alex's revenge. It was the death of his father.

He looked Harrison right in the eye. "You're right. They found in your favor and my father died the night he lost the case."

Isabel's gasp of dismay broke the tension arcing between Alex and her father.

Harrison reached out to touch his daughter, but she moved away from both him and Alex, her arms crossed over her body in a defensive gesture, the look in her eyes disturbing.

"It wasn't like that," Harrison said. "I'm not responsible for Ray's death. Damn it, he was my friend. I offered a damn good discovery bonus, but he turned me down. He wanted his day in court."

Alex couldn't let that pass. "A limited bonus was hardly a fair offer for something that was already making Hypertron money hand over fist."

Harrison expressed anger for the first time since his initial irritation with Isabel. "It was already making money for my company because Ray had incorporated his design into three lines of our products without my approval. He had me over a barrel and he knew it. I couldn't let him have the patent. It would have meant the end of my company."

"And your company is all that ever really mattered to you, isn't it, Dad? At least since Mom died." Isabel's broken whisper tore at Alex's insides.

Harrison looked as if Isabel had used a knife rather than words to slay him, but he didn't deny her accusation. In an action that Alex could have sworn was reflex, the other man looked down at his watch.

Isabel noticed the action as well. "We've taken up enough of your time. I'm sure you'll want to get to the office now." She turned to Alex. "Are you ready to go?"

He nodded. He didn't dare speak. He felt as if he and Isabel were on a precipice, and he didn't want to go over.

"Isabel." Harrison's voice arrested her and Alex at the door. "I haven't been a good father, but I do care. Don't let him use you to get revenge against me. Don't let him hurt you like that."

Isabel's response was to lead the way outside.

Alex looked out the window at the rain-washed fields sloping away from his farmhouse. He wanted to break the unnatural silence that had gripped Isabel since leaving her father's house, but he didn't know how.

She hadn't even protested when he'd brought her here rather than to her apartment, and she had gotten out of the car and followed him inside without a murmur. She sat on his couch sipping a glass of wine he'd forced on her when they first came in, her expression remote.

"He wasn't always like this."

Coming after such a long stretch of silence into the stillness of the room, Isabel's words acted like a sonic boom to his senses. He pivoted away from the window to face her.

"Isabel—" He didn't know what he would have said because she interrupted him.

"I have memories of the time before my mother died. We were a happy family. He cared. He really did. The pictures in our family photo albums are almost scary, they were so happy. *We* were so happy."

He walked over and squatted down in front of her until their eyes were level. "That's why you want to get married and have a baby, isn't it? You want to recreate that happiness. You've got guts, sweetheart. Probably more guts than anyone I've ever known."

Her eyes widened. "I'm not—"

He wouldn't let her deny it. "Most people would run from family and commitment after the pain you've been through, but you're willing to take a risk, to try to make your own happiness. I admire you."

She squeezed her eyes shut and inhaled. "Why didn't you tell me about your dad and Hypertron?"

He'd been waiting for this question, but unfortunately he still didn't know if he had an answer that she could live with.

He brushed her cheek and she opened her eyes.

"You didn't trust me after the fiasco with Marcus. If I told you about my dad and Hypertron, you would have run as far and as fast as you could in the other direction."

She acknowledged the truth of that with a nod. "But I should have known. Why didn't I know? Isn't that something a father would tell his daughter? I mean I wasn't a kid. I know the industry. We could have talked about it." Her bewildered and wounded words made him wince.

Alex couldn't explain why her dad hadn't bothered to tell her, but he could speculate. And he figured so could she. That's probably why she sounded so wounded.

"It wasn't in the papers. You know how obsessed with secrecy the hi-tech industry is. Your dad and mine agreed to arbitration so the dispute would stay out of the media. Neither one of them wanted Hypertron's stock to dip, and my dad had to consider finding future employment. Even if he'd won the case, the earning potential on technology is limited. In the computer industry some new technologies are obsolete within two years."

"I know."

Of course she did, but talking about it gave him time to marshal his thoughts in other areas, not that it was doing a whole lot of good. Failure and fear stared him in the face.

"My dad said they were friends . . ." her voice trailed off as if the thought she'd been about to voice had evaporated.

"Yes." It still shocked him. "I guess it makes sense. My dad was in charge of one of the design teams. He would have worked pretty closely with your father. They both spent enough time at Hypertron to develop a relationship outside of business."

He was thinking out loud, but she seemed to agree.

"I guess," she said. "I know Dad spends more time at Hypertron than anywhere else. Did you notice how overworked he looked? He needs a vacation."

He'd be getting one. Soon. After St. Clair took over Hypertron, John Harrison would have all the time in the world to devote to his relationship with his daughter and to regaining his health.

"Alex?" She was biting her bottom lip.

He reached out and gently nudged it from between her teeth with his fingertip. "Yes?"

"Why did your dad put the technology in three product lines without getting my father's approval?"

Alex shot to his feet and paced back to the window. The scene outside was no more inspiring than his thoughts. "I don't know. It's not totally uncommon in the hi-tech world for a design team lead to make such a decision."

"But three products?"

Alex's hands clenched. "Would it have mattered if it were ten? The truth is, he made a boatload of money for your dad and brought Hypertron to the next level of competition in the computer industry. That kind of thing deserved a lot more than a bonus and a pat on the head. My dad wanted the recognition that owning the patent would give him."

"Did my father know that?"

Again, Alex didn't know. He spun back to face her. "Does it matter?"

She shrugged. "You tell me."

"None of it matters to us."

Her expression closed. "My dad was right about one thing. You're the kind of man who would want revenge."

He couldn't deny it. He'd never lied to her and he never would. He might not always tell her everything because it could hurt her, but he wouldn't lie. He squatted down next to her again. "Yes."

She looked pained. "I really thought you were different, that my connection to Hypertron didn't matter to you."

Different from whom, he wanted to demand, but right now he had to deal with the matter at hand. "It doesn't. You have nothing to do with your dad's company in the present and you sure as hell had nothing to do with what happened two years ago."

She surveyed him with an expression so vulnerable his heart ached. "Am I part of some revenge plan against Hypertron?"

"No." He gently cupped her cheek and met her gaze, his own as compelling as he could make it. She had to believe him. Their future depended on it. "What we have together has nothing to do with Hypertron, your father, or my father. It's between us, sweetheart."

He brushed his lips lightly across hers and then leaned back, keeping their gazes locked. Would she believe him?

She took a deep breath and let it out slowly. "I want to believe you."

"Then do. I'm not using you, sweetheart. From the

first time I saw you, it's been about you, not your connection to your dad's company." He didn't think that now was the time to tell her about the picture in his investigative file on her and how long he'd fought the attraction. "In fact, that was the one thing holding me back from getting involved with you."

"You mean because I'm John Harrison's daughter?"

"Yes."

"And now?"

"I told you, what we have is between us." He'd told her he wanted to marry her; she had to know he wasn't fighting the attraction any longer.

"You should hate me along with my father."

Hate her? He didn't even hate her father. Not anymore. He still wanted revenge, but he was more interested in seeing the company—which had been built up on his dad's development—dismantled than he was in the man who owned it.

And the feelings he had for Isabel did not resemble hate in any shape or form. He desired her. He needed her. Being with her made him feel content, complete. If he believed in love, he might even think he loved her. He was sure that he was as close as he would ever get to that emotion.

"I don't hate you." The words were inadequate. "I need you."

She reached up and wrapped her fingers around the hand that held her face. "I'm not just a cog in the wheel of your vengeance?"

"You're the woman I want to marry."

Her eyes widened and she bit her lip again.

"Marry me, Isabel. You want a family. I'll give you one."

"My list . . ."

He didn't know what she was going to say about it because she let her voice trail off.

"I meet your requirements. You know I do."

"What about love?" she asked quietly.

"You didn't say anything about love on your list." If he sounded accusatory, it was because he didn't know anything about the kind of love she was talking about.

"The list is not some sort of contract, Alex. It's a guide. My guide!" The anger seemed to come out of nowhere after her silence and stillness.

Realizing that words were inadequate and that he didn't have the ones she wanted to hear anyway, he locked his mouth over hers. She didn't respond, nor did she pull away. She maintained the almost complete motionlessness that had marked her since leaving Harrison's house.

Despair gripped Alex's insides. He couldn't lose her, not now. Not when he had finally accepted just how much he needed her. Driven by a desperate longing to make Isabel return his kiss, he opened his mouth and ruthlessly pushed against the seam of her lips with his tongue. He had to show her that the passion they shared was real. He needed to know that her desire for him had not vanished after the day's revelations.

Isabel felt the ice that had surrounded her emotions since going to her father's house shatter under the impact of Alex's kiss. Need buffeted her. It was more than a physical reaction to Alex's kisses; it was a gut-level emotional response. And it wasn't just hers. Alex's desire for her came off of him in waves of sensual heat and desperation. Desperation that had finally broken through her apathy. The fear in his eyes, eyes that always held such self-assurance, had been her undoing.

She opened her mouth to his questing and he growled low in his throat in approval. Then he swept inside and she forgot to think. Tongue sliding warmly against tongue, teeth clashing, lips crushed together in relentless craving. No words could describe his taste, the sensation of intimate sharing their kiss elicited. The air became trapped in her chest as she forgot to breathe, only to rush out in one big shuddering whoosh when her lungs could take no more.

But the kiss did not stop, Alex's heat reaching out to warm the places chilled by the visit with her father. She fumbled for a place to set her wineglass and dimly heard a clunk when she missed the table and the glass fell to the floor. Then she locked her fingers onto his shoulders, dragging him as close as she could get him. Her tongue sparred with his as the urgency of the kiss consumed them both.

Frantic to feel his skin, she unbuttoned his shirt and slid her hands inside. Alex's entire body shook at the contact.

"Yes, baby, just like that. Touch me. I need to feel your hands on me." His guttural demands against her lips sent delight zinging along her nerve endings.

He settled his palms under her bottom and she couldn't help squirming into those big hard palms. He groaned and stood. At first, her legs just hung there, her feet not touching the floor as his male arousal rubbed against her lower belly. Then he hitched her higher and she instinctively wrapped her legs around him, locking her ankles behind his back. Her sarong-style skirt opened and the sensation of her bare thighs rubbing against his sides sent blood rushing through her veins.

She felt light-headed and very, very desperate. Alex pressed against her bottom, forcing her femininity against the bulge of his hardness, and she moaned, rocking against him. He carried her out of the room without breaking contact with her mouth. She didn't know where he got the strength to do it. She couldn't have stood on her own two feet right now, much less walked. Each step increased the erotic stimulation of his arousal pressed against her and the fabric of his clothes rubbing against the smooth skin of her thighs.

The sensation of disorientation and shifting told her he was taking her upstairs. She hoped they got wherever they were going soon. She was greedy for him to assuage the ache between her legs. She'd never wanted anything so much in her entire life. The world tilted, and then she was on a bed with Alex propped above her. He'd added his rocking to hers and she felt pressure building, building, building.

She tore her mouth from his. "Alex."

He kissed her neck, under her ear, making a sucking motion, and the pressure in her feminine center grew almost unbearable. She moved her head from side to side on the bed. "Alex, please. Do something. I can't stand it."

Hot breath in her ear sent more shivers down her spine. "I'll do whatever you want, sweetheart."

The promise was every bit as erotic as his hands kneading her backside, but she didn't know how to ask for what she wanted. She only knew if she didn't get it, she was going to die—or go insane. "Please," she whispered.

He stopped kneading her backside and pushed himself up and away from her.

"No, Alex. I need—"

He silenced her protest with a finger against her lips and pulled her into a sitting position. "I want to see you, Isabel. Let me see you." The aching need in his voice so matched her own right then, she could not have denied him anything.

Speech was beyond her, so she kicked off her shoes in answer. He smiled, his brown eyes turning even darker with desire, and she could not stop herself from leaning forward to kiss the sexy dimple in his cheek. Then she just had to taste the skin she had kissed. The saltiness of his skin tantalized her, and she ran her tongue down his jawline. Alex used the time to slip off her bolero jacket, then pulled the amber-colored silk tank top she wore under it out of her skirt. His hands slipped under her top and caressed the heated flesh of her midriff, the touch searing her skin.

She wanted to feel all of her skin pressed against his.

When he took too long to remove her tank top, she did it for him. Tossing it to the side of the bed, she looked at him uncertainly. She wanted her bra off, too. Skin against skin. Her nipples were puckered and pressed against the thin silky cups. She wanted to feel them against his chest, wanted to rub them across the hair that grew in a triangle over the rippling muscles.

Was it possible to actually catch fire from excitement? She didn't know, but she was certainly burning up.

But she didn't know if she could take off her bra and follow through on her brazen desires. Alex had stopped moving and stared at her, his eyes intense, and that intensity paralyzed her. She licked her lips, waiting to see what he would do next.

For a full five seconds the answer was—nothing. Then he slowly reached out and cupped her breasts, as if he thought moving too fast would make them disappear. He squeezed gently, and her erect nipples began to throb for more direct stimulation. He seemed to know just what she needed because his thumbs began rubbing those aching little peaks in tantalizing circles, and still she wanted more.

The unbearably sweet ache between her legs grew stronger.

With one deft movement, he unclasped the front closure on her bra. Slipping her straps off over her shoulders he removed the lingerie slowly, teasing her skin with the feel of the fabric sliding against it. Gooseflesh broke out on her arms as her lips parted and her breath came in shorter and shorter pants.

"You're so damn hot, baby. I'm going to incinerate before we even finish getting you undressed." His sexy growl sent shivers of lascivious longing prickling through her.

And then he was standing up, pulling her with him. When she was on her feet, he undid the tie on her sarong skirt and let the garment fall to the floor. She stood in front of him, naked now except the high-cut French briefs that she'd bought on a whim to match her bra. They were made of the same almost-sheer stretchy material, and she felt his gaze burning through them to the heated center of her feminine core. She wondered at her lack of embarrassment, so unlike that other time.

Alex made her feel things she would never have believed herself capable of experiencing, things that made it impossible for her own nudity to embarrass her.

He didn't speak. He didn't move. He simply looked.

"Alex?"

"You're so beautiful, Isabel. It hurts to look at you."

She didn't doubt his words. She couldn't. He *looked* like a man in pain. He didn't stop looking at her, although he started removing his own clothes, and she let her eyes feast on him like a dieting woman faced with a buffet table of chocolate desserts. First his shirt went, landing on the floor at his feet. Smooth, slightly tanned skin over taut muscle certainly looked good enough to eat. Then he toed off his shoes and socks, revealing masculine feet, the sight of which turned her temperature up a notch.

Sexy feet? Alex had them.

She watched in fascination as he unzipped his pants and then slid them carefully off. As the bulging muscles of his upper thighs and well-sculpted calves came into view, the breath caught in her throat in appreciation.

He stopped when he got to his briefs, and the obvious bulge in them made her suck in that caught breath. She couldn't help it. She reached out and touched him with one fingertip, allowing it to slide down the length of his penis, so blatantly hard and yet mysterious behind its dark cotton covering.

Making a feral noise, he pulled her into his arms and she got her wish—her breasts pressed against his chest. She moved side to side and felt the roughness of his hair against her nipples. The sensation was so incredible that her knees almost buckled, so she did it again.

Alex's hands were inside her panties in the back pressing her intimately against him. "Isabel, honey, you are unbelievable. You're so damn passionate."

"It feels so good," she tried to explain as she made another side to side movement against his chest.

"You sound surprised. Doesn't it usually feel this good?" His voice echoed with masculine pride.

The words dissipated some of the passionate haze around her. "No, but I don't have a lot of experience," she admitted. Though she doubted that if even if she did, what she was experiencing with Alex could have been duplicated with anyone else. Her response to him in every other way was unique.

He tipped her chin up and forced eye contact with his own dark pools that hid his thoughts. "Are you trying to tell me that you're a virgin, sweetheart?" He sounded disbelieving while he looked like the idea both worried and excited him.

She shook her head. She might as well be, for all the practical experience she had had, but she wasn't. Not quite anyway. "At twenty-eight? I don't think so."

She hoped she sounded more blasé than she felt.

Interpersonal relationships were just not her strong suit and making love fell under that category. Though she had to believe that judging by her response to Alex so far, she wasn't going to fail so miserably at it this time.

His eyes glowed with dangerous lights and an atavistic thrill went through her.

Chapter Ten

Alex refused to feel guilty for the primitive satisfaction that coursed through him at the knowledge that Isabel didn't have a lot of experience. She was unique in every other way, why not this one, too?

Her passion belonged to him.

He could tell that her own responses were surprising her and that added an excitement all its own to their lovemaking. What man did not want to be *the one* to bring out his woman's sensuous nature? But for all her passion, she was also nervous, and he didn't want her nervous. He wanted her hot.

Leaning down, he kissed the corner of her mouth, teasing the edge of her lips with his tongue. She sighed and her body melted into him. He kept up the tender kisses until he felt the fires that had been banked by their little discussion rekindle in her. Her breathing grew ragged once again, and she was making those sexy little noises that had been driving him wild since the first kiss.

The firm round cheeks of her backside beckoned his hands and he cupped her there, pulling her farther into the heat of his body. Isabel moaned, her head falling back on her neck, and did that thing where she brushed her nipples against his chest again, only this time slowly, voluptuously, and he almost lost it right there.

Changing tactics, he moved one hand to her back and pressed her against him in a way that didn't allow movement. "Baby, you're doing bad things to my control."

She laughed with wholly feminine satisfaction. "I don't want you controlled." She nipped his earlobe. "I want you to feel as amazing as I do."

And she thought he didn't? "If I felt any more amazing, I'd embarrass myself."

"Mmmm."

He couldn't help but smile. That little hum could mean anything, but he was pretty sure it wasn't an agreement to his ending the party early. Temptation to tumble her back on the bed and bury himself inside her roared through him with the power of a rocket launching, but he couldn't do it.

The beautifully passionate creature in his arms deserved more than slam, bam, thank you ma'am, and he was determined to give it to her. He maneuvered her back toward the bed, pushing her gently down onto it when her legs hit the extra-high mattress. He pulled back from her, stepping away to take in the sight before him. Her hips were almost on the edge of the bed while her legs dangled over, her toes barely touching the floor.

Pleasure so acute that it was pain shot through his groin. Her panties practically begged him to tear them off, the way they didn't quite cover the soft curls of her femininity.

"Alex?" Her eyes were heavy-lidded with desire and a soft pink flush covered her creamy skin.

"Yes, baby?"

"Are we done?"

He knew she was teasing him. He almost laughed,

but he didn't have it in him. "No, we are a long way from done, but I want to see you. Do you mind?"

She shook her head, her honey-brown tresses fanning out across the pewter-colored comforter. "I like looking at you, too."

The admission had the same affect that her gentle caress to his penis had earlier. It rocked him. He knelt down at the end of the bed between Isabel's knees. Taking one dainty foot into his hands, he lifted it for his kiss and then nuzzled the instep. A sound of feminine need came from the bed and he smiled.

"I want to kiss you all over."

He didn't wait for her to agree but moved his lips along her ankle and up her calf, placing baby kisses on the silky skin as he went. By the time he reached her inner thighs, she was moving restlessly on the bed, her hips rotating sexily.

"Please, Alex. I need you now."

He nuzzled the apex of her thighs, inhaling the unique scent of her passion. She went completely still. The triangle of lace still covering her was damp and her musky fragrance attested to her readiness. He flicked his tongue out and gently caressed the skin along the elastic line of her panties. Isabel arched off the bed, and he couldn't resist sliding one finger under the small piece of fabric. Wet and swollen flesh closed around his finger and he damn near came in his briefs.

Unwilling to give up his kissing expedition along her body or the incredible pleasure of touching her sultry flesh, he kept one finger inside her while lowering his head to kiss the soft round mound of her belly. She shuddered and cried out. Her hands came away from where they were gripping the comforter to lock onto his hair. She tugged.

"I want you," she cried out.

"I want you, too, honey. All of you."

He let her tug him as far as her breasts and then he stopped. Using his one free hand, he squeezed first one beautiful mound and then the other. Taking one nipple between his thumb and forefinger, he gently tugged.

She cried out.

He locked his mouth around the other nipple and sucked. Hard. The wet flesh surrounding his finger grew more swollen until he could barely move his finger back and forth. Using his thumb, he rubbed her clitoris. Her entire body tensed.

"Marry me, Isabel."

Sensation trembled through Isabel. She felt as if her entire body were going to detonate, and she both craved and feared the explosion. She wanted to demand that Alex stop teasing her and finish it, but her throat would not work except to make keening cries. She couldn't think, much less beg, with his fingers and mouth doing such amazing things. She bucked her lower body against his hand.

She felt more than helpless with her legs dangling off the bed and his hard male body tormenting her own.

How could he expect her to answer a marriage proposal in this condition?

She felt each of the muscles in her body tense but most especially those surrounding Alex's finger. Her world shattered into a million pieces of sensation as wave after wave of pleasure shook her body. She screamed so loudly that when she stopped, she felt waves of vague embarrassment wash over her. Alex continued the ministrations with his fingers, softening the caresses until her body relaxed against him. He kept touching her, though, and her body jerked in response to the renewed pleasure.

She reached down with one leaden arm and touched his forearm. "Stop," her mouth clumsily formed words, "too much."

He seemed to understand because he slowly withdrew his hand and released her nipple from his mouth, giving it one final kiss before he moved her completely onto the big bed. He curved himself around her, cuddling her sweaty body close to his. She felt his erection, hard against her thigh, and realized that it wasn't yet over for Alex.

"Was that just round one?" she asked, not sure her body or her heart could survive another intimate encounter with Alex.

He brushed his hand down her arm. "Round two comes after we're married, sweetheart."

She digested his statement before lifting her head so she could see his still-passion-filled features. "Are you saying that you won't go any further unless I agree to marry you?"

He smiled, his expression so primitive he belonged in a museum exhibit with Cro-Magnon man. "No marriage, no baby, Isabel."

She rolled her eyes. "There are ways to prevent conception, Alex. I'm not asking you to give me a baby." She wasn't sure she was asking for anything, but she didn't like the idea that he thought he could call the shots like this.

"I don't have anything." The frustration in his voice allayed some of her pique. "I wasn't expecting this."

The admission made her feel even better. As arrogant as Alex was, he wasn't prepared for the eventuality of her falling into his arms. Besides, if he didn't have anything on hand, that implied he hadn't needed anything for a while, didn't it?

She did some quick mental calculations in her head. "It's a safe time for me right now."

His smile was rueful. "No such thing. Not one hundred

percent anyway, sweetheart, and remember, no marriage, no baby."

She glared at him, her lower lip protruding into the first sensual pout of her life.

He gave a husky chuckle. "It can wait until we're married."

The hard male flesh, which continued to pulse unabated against her outer thigh, said otherwise. She reached over and brushed it, feeling satisfaction as his body jerked against hers.

"Cut it out, honey. We aren't going any further until my ring is on your finger."

The boneless lethargy left her limbs in a flash and she sat up. "That's not a decision for you to make, Alex." Okay, so maybe they couldn't go all the way, and maybe, just maybe, she didn't mind that fact, but that did not mean everything else was off limits.

He sat up, too, reaching out to hold her shoulders. "It's time you admitted that you belong to me. You won't meet another man who fits your requirements the way I do."

His sheer arrogance should have astounded her, but she was starting to take it in stride. "And if I say 'no'? What then? Do you plan to blackmail me into marriage by withholding your body from me?"

His mouth tipped in a lazy grin and that darn dimple teased her again. "Would it work?"

She wouldn't answer that question for stock in an Italian shoe company. "Answer me. Is that what you're trying to do?"

Alex shook his head. "No, sweetheart. No blackmail. You *are* going to marry me and we *are* going to wait to finish making love until that happens."

He really believed that. He also apparently believed that she had nothing to say in the matter. "What if I don't *want* to marry you?"

His thumbs caressed her neck. "You do."

She let that go for now because she wasn't entirely sure he was wrong. The idea had been growing on her since the night they'd come close to making love on her couch. "What if I don't want to wait?"

"You said that you planned to walk yourself down the aisle because you couldn't count on having your dad show up to do it."

What did that have to do with making love? "So?"

"So, if we flew to Vegas and got married down there, you wouldn't have to worry about him showing up at all."

She took a deep breath, ready to let loose on him for thinking she'd get married in some tacky wedding chapel in Nevada. His gaze shifted from her face to her breasts and the words died on her lips. "Don't look at me like that."

"I can't help it."

Pleasure thrilled through her at his words. "I'm not getting married in Vegas. My dad may not show up, but Bettina will." Just in case he hadn't gotten it, she said, "I want her there, and I want to get married in a church, like normal people."

He nodded. "We'll get married here, then. Next week."

"I never said I'd marry you." She couldn't believe she was having the conversation one scrap of lace away from being naked.

Alex pinned her with his gaze. "Say it."

She would be a fool to agree to marry him now. Something in his gaze stopped her from telling him so. He'd already admitted to needing her. She didn't think such an admission had been an easy one for a man like Alex to make. He definitely wanted her, regardless of his dumb dictates about what was or was not going to happen before their marriage.

Zebra Contemporary

Whatever your taste in contemporary romance — Romantic Suspense … Character-Driven … Light and Whimsical … Heartwarming … Humorous — we have it at Zebra!

And now Zebra has created a Book Club for readers like yourself who enjoy fine Contemporary Romance written by today's best-selling authors.

Authors like Fern Michaels…Lori Foster… Janet Dailey…Lisa Jackson…Janelle Taylor… Kasey Michaels… Shannon Drake… Kat Martin… to name but a few!

These are the finest contemporary romances available anywhere today!

But don't take our word for it! Accept our gift of FREE Zebra Contemporary Romances — and see for yourself. You only pay $1.99 for shipping and handling.

Once you've read them, we're sure you'll want to continue receiving the newest Zebra Contemporaries as soon as they're published each month! And you can by becoming a member of the Zebra Contemporary Romance Book Club!

As a member of Zebra Contemporary Romance Book Club,

- You'll receive four books every month. Each book will be by one of Zebra's best-selling authors.

- You'll have variety — you'll never receive two of the same kind of story in one month.

- You'll get your books hot off the press, usually before they appear in bookstores.

- You'll ALWAYS save up to 30% off the cover price.

SEND FOR YOUR FREE BOOKS TODAY!

Be sure to visit our website at www.kensingtonbooks.com.

To start your membership, simply complete and return the Free Book Certificate. You'll receive your Introductory Shipment of FREE Zebra Contemporary Romances, you only pay $1.99 for shipping and handling. Then, each month you will receive the 4 newest Zebra Contemporary Romances. Each shipment will be yours to examine FREE for 10 days. If you decide to keep the books, you'll pay the preferred subscriber price (a savings of up to 30% off the cover price), plus shipping and handling. If you want us to stop sending books, just say the word... it's that simple.

FREE BOOK CERTIFICATE

Yes! Please send me FREE Zebra Contemporary romance novels. I only pay $1.99 for shipping and handling. I understand that each month thereafter I will be able to preview 4 brand-new Contemporary Romances FREE for 10 days. Then, if I should decide to keep them, I will pay the money-saving preferred subscriber's price (that's a savings of up to 30% off the retail price), plus shipping and handling. I understand I am under no obligation to purchase any books, as explained on this card.

Name _____

Address _____ Apt. ____

City _____ State _____ Zip _____

Telephone (____) _____

Signature _____

(If under 18, parent or guardian must sign)

Thank You!

Offer limited to one per household and not to current subscribers. Terms, offer and prices subject to change. Orders subject to acceptance by Zebra Contemporary Book Club. Offer Valid in the U.S. only.

CN055A

llı.ı.l.llı...ıll.ıl.l.ıl.ıl...lı..ll.l.ı.ll.ı.lll..l

Zebra Contemporary Romance Book Club
Zebra Home Subscription Service, Inc.
P.O. Box 5214
Clifton , NJ 07015-5214

PLACE
STAMP
HERE

But he didn't love her.

And that shouldn't matter. He'd been right when he said it wasn't on her list of requirements. Love scared her, so she'd left it out of the equation. At least her mind had. Her heart was another matter. And her heart was telling her something she really did not want to hear right now.

She felt like groaning in agony at her sheer stupidity. She'd gone and done it.

She loved Alex. Was in love with him. Head over heels. Top over tail and drowning in it.

She hadn't planned to fall in love with Alex. She hadn't planned to fall in love with anyone, but her response to his touch had torn away the last of her defenses. She wanted to spend the rest of her life going up in flames in his arms. And she wanted him to be the father of her babies.

The risk of loving him was great. She could lose him like she'd lost almost everyone else she'd let herself love. Yet, if she rejected his proposal and let him walk away, her loss would be assured. Either way, she had to take a risk. At least if she married him, she had a chance at a life with him—a *chance* at happiness.

"Okay, I'll marry you." Maybe Alex was right. Maybe she was a risk taker by nature.

His smile took her breath away. "Next week."

She let out an exasperated sigh. "That's too soon."

His fingers started a gentle but insistent caress on her collarbone. Bending his head, he brushed her lips with his own. "You want to wait for more of this?"

His tongue caressed her bottom lip before he gently pulled it between his teeth and sucked.

"Or this?"

He let one hand slide down to caress her breast, and renewed passion zinged along her senses.

"This *is* blackmail," she said, panting.

"Think of it as persuasion," he said, as he pushed her back onto the bed.

"You're getting married?" Bettina's voice rose in incredulity. "*In two weeks?*" Several customers at the small coffee shop in the mall turned to look. Bettina shook her head decisively. "No way, girlfriend. This can't be happening."

That's exactly what Isabel had told herself when she woke up this morning in her bed. Alone. Alex had brought her home after some very satisfying *persuasion*. Both physical and mental. They both knew what they wanted, so why wait? Or so he'd argued. Such skewed logic would undoubtedly have had no effect on her if she had not been reeling from the aftereffects of not one but two more mind-blowing orgasms. Neither of which had been accompanied by the final act of making love.

Alex was adamant about waiting to make babies until they were married. The way he kept using the plural for that word also had its effect on her. His dreams for the future so closely matched her own. It made sense to pursue them together. Her decision to marry him was a logical one, based on how well he fit the requirements of her list. At least that's what she told herself. It beat the alternative, hands down . . . that she'd lost her mind.

"We're going for the wedding license today."

Bettina's black brows rose almost to her hairline. "You're serious, aren't you?"

"Yes." And scared. The fact that she had convinced Alex to wait two weeks instead of one didn't seem the comforting concession it had last night.

"Then I guess we better start shopping for a dress.

The good Lord knows that it will take you long enough to find a pair of shoes to go with it once we do."

Laughter tinged with a bit of hysteria at what she was doing and relief that Bettina had given such ready support exploded out of Isabel. She leaned forward to hug her friend. "I want you to be there. You, Tyrone, and the children."

Bettina returned Isabel's hug with a big squeeze. "Of course I'll be there. I might even splurge on a new dress myself. I saw a little hot pink number in a shop window downtown. It'll set my budget back and my husband's heart rate forward. That makes it just about perfect in my opinion."

Isabel couldn't help laughing again as she stepped back from Bettina. "I can't wait to see it."

Bettina smiled, but then her expression turned serious. "Have you told your dad yet?"

"No."

Bettina reached out and squeezed her hand. "You'd better call him soon."

Isabel curled her fingers into a fist and then forced herself to relax them again. "It's complicated."

Then she told Bettina about Alex's dad and Hypertron. When she was done, Bettina just stared at her. Taking a sip of her now-cold coffee, Isabel waited for Bettina to accuse her of being every kind of fool. Maybe her best friend would succeed in doing what common sense had been incapable of: convincing her that she was making a mistake.

"Do you love him?"

The words took Isabel completely by surprise. She thought about refusing to answer, but the risk she'd taken in agreeing to marry Alex had affected her in other ways as well. She wanted to open herself up to Bettina, to share her thoughts and her feelings with her best friend. "Yes. I know it's crazy and I can't believe it's happened this quickly, but I do love him."

Bettina nodded. "I thought so."

"He doesn't love me," Isabel admitted.

"Men take longer to figure out their emotions. I knew I loved Tyrone after our second date. The fool took another three months to come to the same conclusion and ask me to marry him."

Isabel smiled. "Three months isn't all that long."

"It is when you spend it trying to keep a man you love out of your bed. I wasn't going to sleep with him until he admitted he was motivated by more than male hormones."

Isabel felt her face heat. She hadn't even tried to say no to Alex. In fact, she'd demanded more than once last night that he make love to her. He'd refused. Her only comfort came from the fact that she wasn't the only one who'd lost it last night. Alex had actually pleaded with her to touch him after the second round of persuasion. She'd watched in awe as her hand had brought his body to the breaking point.

It had been the most exciting experience of her life.

Bettina's laughter drew more curious gazes from other patrons at nearby tables. "Girlfriend, if you could see your face. It's the color of that dress I was telling you about, and your eyes are reflecting thoughts that we can't talk about in mixed company."

Isabel took a hasty sip of coffee. "It's a good thing we're getting married, because I don't have your fortitude," she admitted.

This time she joined in Bettina's laughter.

Isabel nervously paced her office. It had been three days since she had accepted Alex's proposal, and she was living on coffee and nerves as she and Bettina rushed around getting things ready for the small wedding. She did not need the additional stress she was facing today, she told herself.

Priscilla Trahern had called that morning and invited Isabel to lunch. It had taken Isabel a full five minutes after hanging up the phone to ask herself a very important question: Did Priscilla Trahern know about her son's future bride's connection to Hypertron?

Isabel felt sick at the idea that Alex's mother might hate her. She had tried to call him to find out what he had told his mother, but he'd been away from the office and hadn't called her back. Shouldn't she, his fiancée, have his cell phone number?

According to his irritatingly efficient secretary, apparently not. Not unless he'd given it to her personally.

She'd been desperate enough to ask to speak to Marcus, only to be told that he, too, was out of the office. Darn it. Where was Alex? It was completely unfair of him to expect her to meet his mother alone. The fact that he didn't yet know about the lunch did not in any way diminish her sense of being wronged. He should have made sure Priscilla knew about Isabel's connection to Hypertron. She could just see Alex assuming in his arrogance that since it did not matter to him, it would not matter to his mother, either.

Isabel feared that would not be the case.

The phone rang and she leaped across the space to answer it. "Hello?"

"Hello, my dear. Lawrence Redding here."

She stifled her disappointment that it wasn't Alex and tried to infuse her voice with welcome. "Lawrence. Still interested in moving on?"

"Yes. As a matter of fact, I had hoped you were free today for lunch so we could discuss it."

If only she was. "I'm sorry. I've got plans."

"More personal plans with the interesting gentleman I

met the other morning?" Blatant interest laced his voice.

"No." Taking a deep breath, she blurted out the truth. "I'm meeting his mother for lunch to discuss wedding plans."

"*Your* wedding plans?" He sounded as dazed as she felt.

"Yes." In for a penny, in for a pound, Nanny Number Five always used to say. "I'm getting married a week from Tuesday."

They'd had to settle for an evening midweek for the wedding, or her pastor couldn't marry them.

"Congratulations." It seemed that no one was as shocked by the imminent wedding as she was.

"Thank you, Lawrence."

Isabel glanced at her calendar and the clock. "If you can take an early lunch, I can meet you for a short planning session before Mrs. Trahern comes to pick me up."

Isabel's meeting with Lawrence turned into a nice long chat, and he was still in her office when Priscilla Trahern arrived to take her to lunch. Bettina showed Priscilla in. "Isabel, Mrs. Trahern is here to take you to lunch. Oh, hi, Lawrence. Looking for a change?"

Lawrence did not answer. His entire attention was fixed on Priscilla. He stepped forward. "You must be Isabel's future mother-in-law. I must say that it seems impossible for you to have a son old enough to marry the dear girl."

The line was as old as the hills, but Lawrence made it sound charming.

From the look on Priscilla's face, it appeared that she thought so, too. Her lovely pale cheeks bloomed with faint color. "Thank you. I'm Priscilla Trahern."

Lawrence extended his hand and she took it. Rather than shake her hand, Lawrence lifted Priscilla's to his lips and placed a chaste kiss on the back of her fingers. "Lawrence Redding. It's a pleasure to meet you, Priscilla. May I call you Priscilla? Mrs. Trahern seems so formal for a woman of your fairylike presence."

Isabel was sure that Priscilla would be offended. Fairylike presence? She expected better of her favorite client.

But Priscilla's eyes sparkled, and it was clear that Lawrence had charmed her once again. "Priscilla is fine."

Isabel transferred her bemused gaze from Lawrence and Priscilla to Bettina. Bettina winked and grinned, making it obvious she had not missed the little byplay.

Lawrence offered to walk them to the car and Priscilla accepted. The world continued its unreal dance as Isabel watched Priscilla give Lawrence her personal card and permission to call her later. Lawrence and Priscilla? Unthinkable.

Priscilla pulled her car into traffic and said, "Don't look so shocked, Isabel. Romance is not exclusive to the young."

"Yes, but . . ."

Priscilla reached across the console and patted Isabel's hand. "Don't worry. I'm not."

That gave Isabel pause. "You aren't worried?"

"I'm confident that if Lawrence were not an appropriate sort of person, you would have stepped in. Since you obviously approve of him, I'm willing to get to know him better. Besides, he makes me feel breathless, and that, my soon-to-be daughter, hasn't happened in more years than I care to count."

Isabel couldn't resist smiling. She liked the fact that Priscilla referred to her as a future daughter, rather than in-law. It filled her insides with warmth. Besides, she liked Lawrence as well. "He is a wonderful man, but he likes change," she felt compelled to warn Priscilla.

Priscilla's eyes grew troubled. "Change? Do you mean he dates a lot of women?"

Isabel shook her head vehemently. "No. In fact, I don't know of him dating anyone since his wife died a few years ago. He likes to change jobs."

Priscilla's expression cleared. "Oh. Is that all? That's really quite good news. I'm assuming that since he works with you, the job changes are voluntary."

"Yes, they're voluntary, but why is that good news?" Isabel couldn't help asking.

"It means he's not married to his work." Priscilla's eyes strayed from the road for just a moment, and Isabel saw a wealth of emotion in them. "I would rather live the rest of my life alone than marry another man who values his job above me."

Isabel understood Priscilla's feelings too well to argue.

"Alex has good work habits. He told me so." She said the words, hoping to get confirmation from Priscilla.

Alex had never once answered a page or cell phone call when they were together, but that could be lucky coincidence. She hadn't got around to asking him if he carried them in off-hours. She would have to do that when she saw him tonight.

They'd seen each other every night since she'd agreed to marry him, but he had kept their time out of the dangerous passion zone, insistent on waiting until their wedding night to make love. He kept up the refrain of no marriage . . . no babies.

She should be angry, but her old-fashioned streak had her feeling less and less blackmailed and more and more cherished by his insistence on waiting. However, she was also growing more nervous. Would she bomb out when it came to the final act as she had before? The prospect left her chilled, so she tried to ignore it as much as possible.

"Alex loves his job, but he stays balanced. He doesn't spend his nights working. He spends them renovating that old farmhouse he lives in," Priscilla said.

Isabel nodded. She loved what Alex had done with the farmhouse. It was the perfect home for a family. "I'm glad you met Lawrence. He's a very nice man."

"That was my impression as well."

Isabel fidgeted with her purse strap. How could she go about casually finding out if Priscilla knew of her future daughter-in-law's connection to the company that had caused her husband's heart attack?

"Is something the matter, Isabel? Are you having difficulty pulling the wedding together on short notice?"

Isabel shrugged. "Not really. I don't have many people to invite and Alex doesn't, either. Bettina and I found a dress on Monday. On Tuesday, I found the perfect pair of shoes to go with it, and today I'm going to order the flowers. It's going to be a very simple service."

Her evenings were busy, as was every spare moment she could steal from work, but that was to be expected, considering she was putting together a wedding in two weeks.

"Alex said you're getting married at your church."

"Yes. After Alex talked to him, my pastor agreed to forego his normal requirement of six weeks of premarital counseling in lieu of two three-hour sessions. I didn't think anyone could change Pastor Dave's mind, but Alex can be very persuasive."

"Yes. Stubborn is a word that comes to mind." There was a mixture of pride and exasperation in Priscilla's voice.

Isabel laughed. "You should have heard him with Pastor Dave."

Priscilla smiled. "I can imagine."

Isabel realized that just as she had fallen in love with Alex, she was fast coming to love his mother, which made her revelation all that more difficult to make. "There's something I need to tell you."

Priscilla patted Isabel's arm in what was becoming a familiar gesture. "What is it?"

"I'm John Harrison's daughter."

Waiting for shock, disgust, or angry denial, Isabel was unprepared for Priscilla's calm nod of agreement. "I know. It's caused me a great deal of concern."

Isabel felt her insides twist. "It has?"

"Yes. My son is very pragmatic. He thinks in terms of justice and retribution."

Could Priscilla have been concerned on Isabel's behalf? "My dad accused him of using me to get revenge."

"What did Alex say?"

"He said that I had nothing to do with what happened in the past."

Priscilla smiled. "That's what he told me, too. My son is stubborn and lamentably arrogant, but he's very honest. It appears that neither of us need worry any longer."

Isabel couldn't believe it. "You mean you don't care? I thought you would hate me."

"The only thing I care about is that you are going to be my son's wife. I certainly don't hate you." Priscilla's facial expression turned thoughtful. "Unlike Alex, I do not blame Hypertron for Ray's death. Ray gave everything he had to his job and that eventually killed him. If it hadn't been the lawsuit, it would have been something else. He cared more for his career than he cared for anything else in his life."

Isabel heard the pain in Priscilla's voice and wanted to comfort her, but the past could not be changed.

She was glad Alex apparently realized that as well, because you couldn't work on a future together when one person was still living in the past.

Chapter Eleven

Crack. The ball collided with Alex's racket, bounced off, and sailed toward the wall. It hit and took an immediate trajectory that looked like it would go straight over Marcus's head. Alex should be so lucky.

Marcus jumped at just the right moment and returned the ball with a slam. "Are you sure you know what you're doing?"

Alex dove and managed to return the ball . . . barely. Rocking back on his feet, he just managed to stay upright. "Yeah. I'm beating you at a friendly game of racquetball."

"Beating me, my ass. We're tied."

"Not for long." Alex spiked the ball so that it would land against the wall and make a nosedive for the floor. It worked, but Marcus managed to get under it and return it. Too bad he hadn't gotten up and into position before Alex hit the ball against the wall and sent it flying over Marcus's head. "My game."

Marcus walked to the back of the room and grabbed his sweat towel. He wiped his face and then took a long drink from his water bottle. "A man getting married in less than a week shouldn't be so damn focused."

Alex shrugged. If he let himself dwell on his upcoming wedding, he would have to acknowledge the nagging worry that Isabel was going to back out at the last minute. He might not have used their sexual attraction to out-and-out blackmail her, but he was aware it had played more than a small role in her decision. That shouldn't bother him. He was usually interested in the results more than the methods of getting what he wanted, and there was no denying he wanted Isabel.

So, why did it disturb him that he'd used the prospect of mind-blowing sex and motherhood to talk her into marriage? Both were very good incentives. Maybe his problem was that he didn't know which one was most important to Isabel. He wanted her desire for him to be even stronger than the one she had for the baby he would give her.

Taking a drink from his water bottle, Alex eyed Marcus. "I'm not going to let you win just because I'm getting married in a few days."

Marcus nodded. "Don't I know it? It's more like I'm going to let you win because I'm still dazed from the news."

"Unlike you, I've never made any claims to perpetual bachelorhood." There were things Alex wanted out of life that had nothing to do with CIS. "Why be shocked?"

A shadow crossed Marcus's face. "It isn't the fact that you're getting married that's got me so shaken up. It's who you're marrying."

"Isabel is perfect for me, just ask her pastor." Alex had fought against the premarital counseling sessions, but Isabel had refused to budge. She wanted to get married in a church, her church, and that meant meeting with Pastor Dave. It had turned out better than Alex had expected, though. "According to the personality tests he gave us, we're compatible."

Marcus whistled. "Since when did the clergy start using personality tests as part of premarital counseling?"

"Pastor Dave said he's been using them for over a decade. You should have seen the questionnaire he had us fill out. It was worse than getting audited by the IRS."

"And he thinks you two are a match?"

"Yes."

"You tell him about your part in St. Clair's plans for Hypertron?" Marcus took another swig from his water bottle, his blue-eyed stare expectant.

Alex's gut twisted, but he ignored it. "That has nothing to do with Isabel." Why did he have to keep telling people that?

Marcus didn't look convinced. "Are you sure she's going to see things that way, Alex?"

"She doesn't have to know about the role CIS played in the hostile takeover."

Marcus's brows rose. "You're going to try to keep it a secret? Things like that have a way of leaking out."

That's why Alex planned to be married to Isabel if and when that happened. "Once we're married, her primary loyalty will shift to me." At least that's what he hoped would happen. "She might get angry with me at first, but she'll understand. Hypertron has always been first in Harrison's affections. Isabel isn't going to mourn its demise."

Marcus didn't look convinced. "Isabel is a female."

Exasperated, Alex said, "I know that."

"They don't see things like we do."

"She'll understand," Alex insisted.

Marcus shrugged. "I hope you're right."

Alex did, too, but he didn't voice that thought. Instead, he said, "I've got a favor to ask you."

"Whatever you need, I'm your guy."

"Make sure Harrison makes it to the wedding."

Isabel had told Alex that she had tried to call her father several times that week, but he hadn't gotten back to her. She had finally left an invitation with his secretary. Alex could not believe the man's attitude. Isabel deserved better than this, and Alex intended to see her get it.

Marcus wouldn't bother appealing to Harrison's emotions. The man didn't have any. No, Alex had total confidence that Marcus would spend the next day or so determining the most effective pressure to apply and then apply it. Alex hadn't trained his blond friend for nothing on the most effective tools in information gathering and assessment.

Marcus stared in shock at Alex. "You want me to make sure your sworn enemy makes it to your wedding?"

Alex grimaced. Put like that, it sounded ridiculous, but this wasn't about him. It was about the woman he planned to marry and his commitment to making her happy. "He's also Isabel's father and it's important to her."

"What do you want me to do? Kidnap him?" Marcus laughed after asking the question.

"I don't care how you do it, just make sure he's there."

Marcus's expression turned serious. "Will do."

And Alex knew he would. Marcus could be every bit as focused and ruthless as Alex when it came to following through on a project. Now, if Alex could be just as sure the bride would show up.

The bride might very well have skipped the state with a case of mammoth prewedding jitters had not her best friend arrived at her condo just as she began imagining escape scenarios. After letting Bettina in, Isabel led her to the living room.

Crossing her arms, Isabel rubbed them up and down as if she was cold. "I thought I was going to drive myself to the church." She'd turned down both Bettina and Priscilla's offers to come over the day of the wedding. Isabel had thought she would want to be alone to prepare, but she now realized it had been the habit of facing momentous occasions in her life by herself that had made her reject the women's offers.

"Girlfriend, you didn't really think I'd stay away, did you?" Bettina's pencil-thin black brows rose in mocking disbelief.

Isabel should have known that turning down her friend's suggestion to come over and help her get ready wouldn't wash. "What about Tyrone and the children?" Isabel asked.

"They'll meet us at the church later. I brought you a present." Bettina handed Isabel a box wrapped in white foil paper with a huge iridescent bow on top.

Isabel's eyes burned. Why was she being so emotional? She forced herself to smile. "Thank you."

"Open it."

As Isabel obeyed her friend's command, Bettina said, "There wasn't time to get a bridal shower together, but I wanted to get you something special for your wedding night."

The box opened to reveal whispery white silk and lace and a pair of white fur mules, the perfect slippers to wear with a peignoir. Isabel pulled the gown out. It was the most beautiful thing she'd ever seen—and the most terrifying. It brought home more surely than anything else could have that she was going to marry Alex and spend the night in his arms.

"Thank you." She leaned forward and hugged Bettina.

"Once Alex sees you in that, the poor sucker won't remember his own name."

Isabel nodded, not really focusing on her friend's words. Her gaze skimmed the assorted packing boxes and crates now littering her living room floor. Was this really her condo? She and Alex had agreed that it made more sense for her to move into his farmhouse than for him to live here. For one thing the farmhouse was bigger, and for another it had a state-of-the-art security system. Something Alex was sure she needed. Just as he was sure she needed him.

She'd given up arguing about either.

The living room seemed to symbolize Isabel's life—a jumbled collection of confusion. Was she really getting married in less than two hours? To a man who fit her requirements but didn't love her? Pastor Dave said they were a perfect match. He'd still recommended waiting to get married until they knew each other better, but when Alex pushed him, her pastor had agreed to perform the ceremony. He even seemed happy about it. Isabel wished she could borrow some of that joy.

Right now all she felt was panic.

Plopping down on the sofa, in the one small spot not occupied by packing paper and tape, she said, "I can't do it."

Showing no consideration for the expensive hot pink creation she was wearing, Bettina dropped onto her knees in front of Isabel. "You nervous, honey?"

Isabel swallowed the hysterical laughter that tried to bubble out of her. "Terrified."

Bettina took her hand and rubbed it. "A lot of women are on their wedding day."

Isabel looked straight into Bettina's eyes. "Were you?"

Bettina didn't lie to make Isabel feel better. "No, I knew I wanted Tyrone and I was ecstatic."

Isabel took that in.

"I want Alex." She wanted him more than the air she breathed, more than she'd ever wanted her dad to notice her. "Maybe that's what scares me so much. Alex doesn't love me."

She couldn't prevent her voice from quavering on the last sentence. The fact that Alex didn't love her was the biggest factor contributing to Isabel's fear. The speedy marriage, moving from her condo, making love completely—all of it—would be easier to deal with if she knew Alex loved her.

Bettina didn't laugh. The customary mischief in her eyes was missing. Their black depths were filled with warm understanding. "Listen to me, Isabel. I know he hasn't said that he loves you, but he looks at you like you matter to him. I've seen that look in Tyrone's eyes and it's love."

Could Bettina be right? Was it possible that Alex had fallen as far and as fast as Isabel had but just didn't recognize the symptoms? "The one time I brought up the subject, he got irritated. He said it wasn't on my list."

"*You showed him your list?*"

"He found it in my office and he stole it. He acts like it's some kind of contract between us. Since love and romance aren't on the list, he thinks I shouldn't expect either."

Instead of the outraged sympathy she expected to see on Bettina's face, Isabel watched in fascination as her friend's face contorted in an attempt not to laugh. She couldn't hold it in, though, and the merriment burst out of Bettina. She laughed so hard that she had to hold her stomach.

"That's so much like a man." Bettina fell sideways on the carpet and laughed harder.

The humor in the situation finally struck Isabel and she felt laughter well up in her. Once she started, she couldn't seem to stop. She laughed and laughed, her and Bettina's amusement feeding off each other until her sides ached and her mouth hurt from smiling. Tears trickled down her face, but she barely noticed them as her nerves found an outlet in laughter.

She fell off the couch and ended up on the floor by Bettina. Isabel didn't know how long they laughed, but the hilarity finally abated enough for her to scoot herself into a sitting position against the couch.

Bettina moved to sit next to her. She looked down at her dress and smiled. "There's something to be said for wearing crushed silk. No matter how wrinkled it gets, it looks like it's supposed to be that way."

Isabel eyed Bettina's dress with a critical eye. "You're right. I'll have to remember that."

Bettina sighed. "You know, you'll probably have to show the dolt that he loves you."

"How do I do that?"

"By loving him." Bettina put up her hand when Isabel opened her mouth to protest such a simplistic statement. "It worked with Tyrone, and he's no smarter in the touchy-feely department than your Alex."

"Right." Isabel wasn't buying it. "Tyrone says he loves you all the time and he's so affectionate."

"I taught him," Bettina said with smug complacency. "Listen, girlfriend, men don't get it, usually. They think if they give you great sex, it's enough. Well, even if the sex is out of this world, it can't replace the three little words."

Isabel had her doubts about the "out of this world" part. Not that she dismissed Alex's abilities in this area, but he would be handicapped by his partner's inexperience and admittedly dismal track record. "So, how did you get that through Tyrone's head?"

"I made him realize how much he liked hearing it from me."

"What? You said it, he liked it, and so he repeated it back to you?" That sounded too easy. Besides, she'd never told Alex she loved him. She was afraid to make herself that vulnerable.

Bettina's eyes filled with mischief. "Sort of. I said it. He liked it, and then I stopped saying it. Not for long, mind you. Just a few days. Then I said it only when we were making love. After a while of that, I asked him flat out if he liked hearing it. He did. I told him that if he liked hearing it, he better learn to say it and not just when we were making love, either. I also told him that I needed to hear it, that the words gave me something even his body couldn't."

"I've never told Alex that I love him."

Bettina nodded. "I figured you hadn't. You keep your emotions pretty well guarded. It took me a while to figure that out about you. You seem so open. Always friendly, always willing to listen, but you don't share much of your inner woman, do you?"

Isabel sighed. "It's safer that way."

"It's lonely that way."

Isabel didn't deny it. She had been lonely so much of her life, but she had thought it was better than being hurt. Now she wasn't so sure. She hadn't told anyone she loved them since Anne, Nanny Number Seven, had left. Isabel had said it while hugging Anne good-bye.

"I love you, Bettina." The words came out before she had a chance to think about them and now she was glad. Bettina was the best friend she'd ever had and deserved to know what a special place she had in Isabel's heart.

Bettina hugged her. "I love you, too, Isabel. I couldn't love you any more if you were my flesh-and-blood sister."

The words touched Isabel so deeply that tears leaked out of her eyes. "Thank you."

Blowing out a heavy breath, Bettina stood up. "You

ready to get dressed? You're getting married soon, and I don't think Alex would appreciate you showing up in sweats, no matter how cool your tennis shoes are."

"Where the hell is she?" Alex demanded for the third time in ten minutes.

Pastor Dave cleared his throat and Alex mumbled an apology before resuming his pacing in the pastor's office.

Marcus shrugged. "You told me to get Harrison here, not the bride."

Alex hadn't asked anyone to make sure Isabel got there. He had thought about sending his mom over to her condo but decided against it. Isabel had to come of her own free will. He'd pushed her enough. He was determined to give her this last opportunity to say no, something he had avoided at all costs for the past two weeks. It was a risk, but he couldn't force her to marry him. He needed to know that she *wanted* to marry him.

Priscilla came into Pastor Dave's office. "She's here."

Thank you, God.

Alex, Marcus, and the pastor joined the wedding guests waiting in the main sanctuary. Neither he nor Isabel had invited many friends. With his mother and her father, the guest list numbered less than a dozen. He ignored them all in favor of looking at his bride and stopped dead in his tracks. She was so damn beautiful. She'd pulled her hair up into a twist, but honey-colored strands escaped to frame her face. Her dress, a long white sheath, covered her body from neck to toe while accentuating the curves he'd been dreaming about for several nearly sleepless nights.

She had a death grip on the bouquet of white orchids she held. Her eyes flitted from one guest to the next until they settled on her father. Harrison nodded, his mouth curved in the slightest of smiles. Isabel's eyes filled with tears. Then her gaze flew to Alex, and he could feel her gratitude across the almost-empty sanctuary. She knew he'd been responsible for her father's attendance. Holding her stare, Alex walked over to join her in front of the pastor.

Needing to touch her, Alex reached out and took one of her hands away from its death grip on the flowers. He folded it in his own, pleased when Isabel gripped his hand tighter than she had her bouquet. He caressed her palm with his thumb and he felt the tension in her ease. When it came time to speak her vows, she said them in a husky but firm voice.

Chapter Twelve

Isabel slipped the nightgown Bettina had given her over her head. The white silk brushed the floor and swirled around her ankles in voluminous, sensual folds, but it was so thin, she felt as if she was wearing nothing at all. The oversized mirror in the en suite bathroom reflected every curve and intimate detail of Isabel's body to her wary gaze.

She hastily pulled on the long lace pegnoir that had come with the nightgown. Its sleeves ended at her wrists in luxurious ruffled cuffs, making her feel alluringly feminine, but looking in the mirror of Alex's bathroom, her mouth went dry. The two thin layers did not hide the darkness of her nipples. She unpinned her hair, letting it float around her face in a honey-brown cloud. The gown was too short to hide anything, either. She sighed. That was the point, so why was she fighting it? The nightgown was *supposed* to be sexy.

She'd been ready to give Alex her body the other night. Why was she so nervous now? Probably because the other night she hadn't thought in terms of a lifetime commitment and giving away her heart as well. Tonight she would go to Alex as his wife, the woman who loved him. He would come to her as her husband, but his heart was still his own.

She'd known that going into the marriage. It was time to stop being a ninny and face him. She opened the bathroom door and entered the bedroom. Alex had transformed his . . . their room into a romantic paradise for lovers.

Her eyes took a minute to adjust to the subtle glow of light coming from a dozen candles arranged on the dresser, nightstands, and armoire. Soft, sensual music caressed her ears like a lover's touch, and the bedding had been drawn back invitingly, but even more inviting was the man sitting against the massive wood headboard of the extra-long king size bed.

Her breath whooshed out of her lungs at the sight. Alex's chest and legs were bare, his only article of clothing a pair of black silk boxers. He held a glass of champagne out to her, his hand and eyes steady. She walked forward to take it, wishing her body wasn't trembling like a kitten caught in a snowstorm.

She involuntarily jerked her hand away when their fingers touched.

"Nervous, sweetheart?"

She nodded but didn't speak. She couldn't make her vocal cords work.

"You don't need to be. I'm going to take very good care of you tonight." The sensual promise in his voice sent tremors through her senses, increasing the trembling until her champagne was at risk of sloshing over the sides of her crystal flute.

Still mute, she nodded again even though she didn't agree. Oh, she knew he'd make it good for her, but could she make it good for him? That was the sixty-four dollar question and she didn't have the answer. She'd flunked her first test in this area and since then, she'd avoided the type of circumstance that could make her feel like such a failure again.

He reached out and gently, inexorably pulled her down onto his lap. Silk whispered against skin as she settled stiffly against him. He took a sip of his champagne. What a good idea. She took a gulp of hers and wished it were whiskey.

"It was a nice wedding," he said.

"Yes." There. She'd said something.

"Your pastor is a good man."

"I agree." It was getting easier to speak.

"I liked the flowers."

It struck her that Alex wasn't going to insist they make love right this instant, and she breathed out a sigh, nestling more comfortably against him, only to draw up in another bout of nervous tension as she felt a hard ridge press against her thigh. "I was lucky to get the ones I wanted on such short notice."

"Thank you."

She raised her head to meet his gaze. Thinking he meant to thank her for putting the wedding together so quickly, she asked, "For what?"

"For marrying me."

Her throat closed, only this time it wasn't with fear. Tears burned at the back of her eyes. "Oh, Alex."

"Can I kiss you now?"

She choked out a laugh. "Yes."

This kiss held a new element, something different from the other kisses they had shared. Though his lips were gentle, she felt as if he were marking her, possessing her.

He lifted his head and stared into her eyes, his look almost frighteningly intent. "You belong to me now."

"Yes." She didn't want to deny his claim. She liked the feeling of belonging to someone.

He tipped his head down again, but she put her

hand against his lips. "You belong to me, too." He had
to know it was not a one-way street.

His tongue flicked out and licked her fingers. "Forever."

Her heart tripped. Sliding her hand up his jaw and
then down his neck to his chest, she reveled in the feel
of hard muscle and bone under hot skin. This incredible man belonged to her. She tucked the knowledge
close to her heart.

The feel of Isabel's fingers fluttering against his skin
was about to drive Alex over the edge. She'd come out
of the bathroom looking better than a fantasy in that
see-through white nightgown, but nervous enough to
bolt at his first move. He wanted to be patient. He really
did, but he also wanted to be inside of her. He'd been
thinking of little else for the past two weeks. He needed
to feel her body tighten around him, to feel her shud-
der her release.

The prospect had been driving him crazy since the
night she'd agreed to marry him.

He kissed her again, this time letting some of his desire show through. Taking her bottom lip between his
teeth, he sucked—not too hard. He didn't want to scare
her and she was still stiff against him, but he kept up the
steady pressure of his lips while rubbing her back. Just
when he thought he was going to go insane trying to
hold it all in, she relaxed and opened her mouth. He
swept inside. *Yes.* He wanted to devour her sweetness,
but he held back even though it was killing him.

It had to be right. It had to be damn perfect. He
would do anything she needed to make this unforget-
table for her. It was their wedding night and he wanted
it to be special. So special that she would never doubt
where her first priority lay. With him. He'd even lit a
whole bunch of candles in an attempt to be romantic.

He gently let his hand slide down her back until it curved around her backside. He squeezed. She moaned.

He was so hard, he ached.

"Alex?"

"Yeah?"

She kissed the underside of his chin. "I'm a little nervous."

A little? She was acting like a cat taking its first car ride. "I could tell."

"It doesn't make any sense."

She was right. It didn't. She'd been hot enough for him the other night to catch his shorts on fire, but he didn't think she'd appreciate his saying so. "So, why do you think you're so uptight?"

"Uptight doesn't cover it." Vulnerable green eyes begged him for understanding while his body demanded satisfaction. "I'm scared to death. I feel like an idiot."

He brushed her cheek. "Are you really scared to death?"

She didn't answer right away, but her eyes reflected agonized uncertainty, and his gut clenched in rejection of the message he was receiving.

What was she so afraid of? She'd said she wasn't a virgin, so it couldn't be the act of sex itself. Besides, she had responded too beautifully the other night to have a lot of hang-ups in that area. So, it had to be him. *He frightened her.* The thought was about as palatable as sushi left to sit out in the sun. So was the conclusion that accompanied it. She definitely wanted the baby more than she wanted him.

In fact, right now, he had a hard time believing she wanted him at all.

She bit her bottom lip and his libido went into overload at the thought of how those sharp little teeth would feel on his body. As yet unaffected by the revelations tearing his thoughts apart, his erection shifted against her thigh.

Her eyes grew wide and she swallowed.

How had she expected to get pregnant with the baby she wanted so badly if she didn't want him enough to consummate the marriage? What the hell had she thought she was going to do? Close her eyes and think of pink-cheeked babies while she endured him making love to her?

She smiled. "Don't look so outraged."

That smile hit him on the raw. Using every vestige of his self-control, he lifted her away from him, set her on the bed, and then stood up.

"Alex, where are you going?" She had the colossal nerve to sound surprised by his departure.

She might be willing to go forward in the face of her obvious reluctance but he was not. Part of him realized his conclusions weren't necessarily rational, but he couldn't think past the ache in his flesh to come to any others.

He stopped at the door. "I need a drink."

She hopped off the bed with more enthusiasm than she'd shown yet. "Good idea. I was just thinking whiskey might be a better before-bed drink than champagne."

Great. Now she was telling him she needed to get drunk before she wanted him to touch her. He glared at her, his jaw aching from suppressing what he wanted to say.

Too busy blowing out the candles he'd put on the nightstand, she wasn't paying any attention.

"What are you doing?"

She jumped and spun around to face him. "We don't want to leave burning candles unattended. We can re-light them when we come back up."

The whole damn room mocked him. He stormed to

the armoire and opened it. With a savage push against the power button, he turned off the stereo. Then he flipped on the light. Isabel blinked at him owlishly. He ignored her and the deceptively sexy picture she presented in her floaty nightgown and lacy robe. Using his thumb and forefinger, he pinched the flames out on the candles on top of the armoire before going to the dresser and doing the same with the candles there.

Isabel stared at him. "Doesn't that hurt?"

"No." He finished with the candles on the other nightstand and turned to face her. "Come on, I've got some brandy downstairs."

He didn't care what she said; he wasn't giving his wife whiskey on their wedding night.

Anger radiated off of her new husband in waves.

He had poured them both a brandy and moved to stand on the opposite side of the living room from her to drink his. As far away from her as he could get and still stay in the room, her mind taunted her. Not that there were many places to sit, she tried to console herself. Alex had been right when he'd told her there was plenty of space for her furniture in the farmhouse. Other than a tweed sofa and ladder-back chair, the living room was bare.

"Thank you for making sure Dad came to the wedding." She smiled tentatively at him, hoping he would accept her peace offering.

"I knew it was important to you."

She took a sip of her brandy. It burned going down. "You're right. It was. How did you manage it?"

He shrugged. "I asked Marcus to do it."

It struck her that Alex trusted Marcus a great deal. She made a mental note to thank Marcus the next time she saw him and wracked her brain for something else to say. "My living room furniture is going to look great in here."

Alex looked around the room. "I'm sure it will."

Frustration and fear gnawed at her. She knew that the tension vibrating between them was all her fault, but she didn't know how to fix it. She was much better at muddling interpersonal relationships than at making them better. She'd been afraid of messing up this night, and she'd managed to do it before Alex had barely laid a hand on her.

He swirled the brandy in his glass, his gaze focused on the amber liquid.

"Alex, are you okay?" It was a stupid question. Of course he wasn't okay. He had every reason to believe he'd married a sexually mature woman, when in fact he'd tied himself to a shivering ninny.

He looked up from the brandy, his expression almost bland. "It might surprise you to know that most men would not enjoy the knowledge that their wives needed to get drunk to face making love with them on their wedding night." He spoke in such a conversational tone of voice that at first the heavy import of what he was saying did not register.

When it did, she looked down with horror at the brandy glass in her hand. Is that what he thought? That she needed to get tipsy before letting him touch her? And why shouldn't he? She'd practically said as much.

She set the brandy glass down so fast, it rocked precariously before settling on the small table next to the sofa. "I don't need this to want your touch, Alex."

He looked at her broodingly. "Right."

"I do want you, Alex, it's just . . ." Her voice trailed off as she lost the nerve to tell him what a fool she'd been in the past and how it affected her now.

Would he lose his desire for her when he discovered

that no other man had wanted her for anything but her connection to Hypertron? The confidence she'd built up over the years living her life apart from her dad and finding success in her own career was in jeopardy of dissolving.

He raised his brow in question but didn't say anything.

Taking a deep breath, she decided that the only solution to their dilemma was honesty. Even if it made her look more of an idiot now than she had upstairs in the bedroom. "Do you remember when I told you I didn't have a lot of experience in this area?"

His gorgeous brown eyes narrowed. "What area?" He looked around the living room. "Decorating?"

All right. So, she'd messed up, but his sarcasm wasn't helping anything. "Making love," she spelled out for him.

He nonchalantly leaned back against the windowsill, his almost-nude body mocking her nerves that were strung so tight they were in danger of snapping. "You said you weren't a virgin."

He didn't sound like the conversation interested him all that much, but she refused to be daunted by that. She'd messed up their wedding night and now she was going to fix it. If he'd let her. "I'm not. I had sex once before."

His body stiffened. "Once?"

She nodded, dreading telling the rest of the story. "I didn't date a lot in high school."

"Your last experience with sex was in high school?" He couldn't have sounded more appalled if he'd shouted the words.

"No." She frowned. "Do you want me to tell you this or not?" If he did, she had to tell him her way because it all fit together, even if he couldn't see that at first.

He swept his hand out in a lazy gesture. "By all

means. I can't imagine anything I'd rather do on our wedding night than hear about your dating history since high school."

Hurt by his sarcasm, her mouth closed on the words she'd been about to say. What was the use? He'd probably think she was just as stupid now for letting her past affect her this way as she had been then to be taken in so easily. She couldn't even blame him. He wasn't the one who had behaved like a complete twit at the prospect of making love.

And it wasn't as if she didn't want to make love. She did. Desperately. If she disappointed Alex, she would deal with it then. Her fears had done enough damage for one lifetime.

She tried to give him a confident smile. "Shall we go back upstairs?"

He didn't budge. "Why? I'm not tired. Are you? Or maybe you've psyched yourself into letting me make love to you, for the greater good, of course."

His thoughts so closely matched hers that she felt a guilty blush stain her cheeks.

His brandy glass splintered against the fireplace's slate hearth, the sound shattering the nervous silence in the room and the final shred of her self-control. She screamed.

"For heaven's sake." If anything, he looked even angrier. "What do you think I'm going to do to you, Isabel? Rape you? Believe it or not, the prospect of taking a woman to bed who wants me about as much as she wants a raging case of the mumps does not appeal to me."

She stared at him, shocked by his assertion. Though why she should be, she didn't know. She'd been acting exactly as he said since walking out of the en suite a half hour earlier. "I do want you, Alex. You've got to believe me."

She knew she sounded needy, desperate, on the edge. She didn't care. She loved him and from the look on his face, she was in danger of losing him before they'd been married twenty-four hours. This had to be some record for her. It was one thing to be bad at interpersonal relationships and another entirely to go down in flames in her first attempt at making a permanent one since becoming an adult.

His jaw tightened and a look of disgust filled his features. "I'm not interested in bedding a martyr tonight, Isabel. You wanted a baby and I married you knowing that. It's my own damn fault I tricked myself into believing you wanted me at least as much."

"But I do want you," she insisted, not sure where this stuff about a baby was coming from. He had to realize she'd never have married him just to get pregnant. "If I was willing to get married just to have a baby, I would have married Brad."

"He didn't fit your requirements." Alex's derision cut through her, leaving a bloody trail of slash marks on her heart in its wake.

"This is not about my requirements!" Her entire body vibrated with the need to make him understand. "I'm scared I'll fail. I'm afraid you'll wake up tomorrow morning wondering how in the world you were stupid enough to marry a woman with *no talent for sex and even less desirability.*"

Every ounce of Alex's self-righteous anger and macho mental posturing went up in smoke at the desperate pain he heard in Isabel's voice. Why hadn't he seen it? It had been so obvious. The idea that Isabel did not want him made no sense whatsoever in the light of her earlier reaction to him.

There had to have been a different reason for her fear, but instead of looking for it, he had allowed his own insecurities about Isabel's strong desire for a baby to override his common sense. She'd never before implied she didn't want him.

He opened his arms. "Come here, baby."

She flew to him without a second's hesitation, filling him with relief that he hadn't screwed up so badly she no longer trusted him.

Once she was settled against his heart, where she belonged, he said, "Tell me about it."

He wanted to know what he was up against when he made her his tonight, what he was fighting in his effort to make her see herself as the enchantingly desirable creature he saw when he looked at her.

She started talking, her voice muffled against his chest, her warm breath fanning his bare skin. "I didn't date a lot in high school because I was shy, scared of letting people close to me. I guess it had something to do with my dad and the way I kept losing the people I loved, whatever. Anyway, I started dating this boy in my sophomore year. He was a total hunk and I couldn't believe he was interested in me, only it turns out he wasn't."

"Idiot."

She pulled back and smiled ruefully up at him. "Thanks. He wanted the lead pitching position on the summer league baseball team my dad's company sponsored. When he found out I didn't have any sway with my dad and that he wasn't going to meet the great John Harrison by hanging around the man's house with his teenage daughter, my boyfriend dumped me."

"I'm assuming you didn't have sex with the wannabe pitcher."

He watched with interest as she turned pink. "No."

"So, what exactly does he have to do with the fact we're in the living room instead of the bedroom on our wedding night?"

She grimaced. "I knew I'd get this wrong. I'm no good at relationships, Alex. You must have figured that out by now. Bettina isn't just my closest friend, she's almost my only long-term friend. I'm much more comfortable with my clients than acquaintances."

"I'm your friend, too, and I'd say you're doing just fine in our relationship." He would never have guessed a woman as warm and generous as she was would have such insecurities about how she related to others. Didn't she see the way the people around her adored her?

Hell, even Marcus felt protective toward her. He'd made his concerns for her feelings known during their last racquetball session and even in a small aside after the wedding.

She made an apologetic face. "That's why we're here in the living room instead of that incredibly romantic oasis you made of the bedroom, right?"

So his attempts at romance had not been a complete bust. "I thought you were leading up to that."

"I was. I am. The thing is, I was hesitant to date for a while after that fiasco my sophomore year. Making lasting friendships has always been hard for me, and boyfriends only added another dimension to my failures. In fact, I didn't start seeing anyone again until I was a junior in college."

"Let me guess. He wanted your dad to get him a shot at the first string football offensive team?" he teased, hoping to lighten the look of seriousness settling over her features.

It worked. A smile that actually reached her eyes lit her face and she relaxed slightly against him. "No, but you're close. He wanted an internship with the marketing department in my dad's company. The one and only time we had sex, he told me it wasn't worth going to bed with a—"

He wouldn't let her finish. "He's the one that said you were frigid and untalented at sex?"

She nodded, her teeth chewing mercilessly at her tender lower lip.

"And you believed him?"

She glared at him. "Yes, I believed him. I thought he loved me. He didn't. I felt stupid and I felt like a failure at intimacy."

"Oh yeah, you're a real failure," he said, as he pushed the pretty lace robe off her shoulders and his body instantly responded to the heated thoughts her confession had evoked.

He looked forward to showing her just how much of a nonfailure she was at making love. By morning she'd think she'd earned a degree in it. "Sweetheart, you make me so hot, I could melt rock."

Her breath hitched and she smiled, albeit a bit tremulously.

He slid his forefingers under the thin straps of her silk gown. "Do you trust me?" he asked, knowing her answer meant more to him than he would have believed possible.

She nodded and he smiled his approval for her reply as he lifted the straps and slid them over her shoulders and down, down, down until her gown caught momentarily at her hips before slithering to pool at her feet. He cupped her naked breasts with both hands. They felt so good, so soft. He kneaded them, allowing his thumbs to brush across her nipples again and again until they were hard, swollen, and red from her excitement.

Her head tipped back and she moaned.

"Do you like that, baby?"

"Yes, Alex. I like it too much." Her eyes closed.

This is how he wanted her: warm, willing, and uninhibited in her passion, like she'd been before. Moving forward until he could rock her lower body with his, he focused on giving her pleasure. Her hands dug into his shoulders as she mimicked his rocking motion. The feel of her soft curls through the silk of his boxers pushed at his control.

Sliding to his knees in front of her, he inhaled the sexy scent of her arousal.

She gasped. "Alex, what are you doing?"

He smiled as he knelt on the floor between her thighs. "Showing you just how undesirable I find you."

Then he did one of the things he'd been fantasizing about all week. He tasted her. Isabel's hands gripped his hair. "Stop. Alex. You can't do this. I'm standing up. The lights are on. Alex . . ."

Her protests ended in a moan and the hands that had been pulling his hair, started pushing him closer. He brought up one hand and caressed her clitoris with his thumb while he kissed her pouty, swollen lips. He would have congratulated himself that she'd gone nuclear so quickly, but he was too busy concentrating on not losing it before he was inside her. Her thighs tightened on either side of his head in a scissor hold. Her body convulsed and she screamed. His name.

She went limp, her thighs spreading farther apart in absolute feminine surrender as she fell forward over his shoulder. He stood up, catching her against him. "You ready to go upstairs now?"

She nodded against his chest. Cradling her in his arms, he started from the room. Her furry high heel slippers clattered to the hardwood floor, leaving her completely naked for the first time that night.

Chapter Thirteen

When they reached the bedroom, Alex went straight for the bed and dropped her onto it. Isabel looked at the extinguished candles with regret. Maybe they could make love by candlelight another night.

She watched in unashamed fascination as he slipped out of his silk boxers. He was fully, magnificently aroused. She told herself that he probably wasn't *that* big. It was just that she hadn't seen a lot of naked men. She wasn't going to go all hysterical on him again. She'd read books. She wasn't a total novice. *Of course he was going to fit.*

Men and women had been doing this for centuries. No way was Alex a virgin, which meant he'd fit before. The woman had probably been an Amazon. Almost choking on the disturbing thought, Isabel tried breathing deeply and reminding herself she had enough to worry about without hyperventilating over the size of Alex's erection.

Besides, he'd make it work. Any man who could do what he'd done to her downstairs would have no worries when it came to actually making love. As he turned away from the bed, her eyes misted happily when she realized he intended to relight the candles. He turned the stereo back on, too.

"You said you weren't any good at romance."

Incredibly, he looked uncomfortable. "I'm not, but you said you liked what I did earlier."

"I did. I do."

He nodded but didn't join her on the bed.

"Alex?" She didn't think it was a good idea to give her a lot of time to think about what was to come.

"You're so beautiful, sweetheart. I'd stand here and look at you all night if I wasn't hurting so bad to be inside you."

The words left her speechless as he finally joined her on the bed, lying down next to her with that magnificent hardness pressed against her thigh. It *felt* big, too. He caressed her body in one long stroke from her neck to her knees. She sighed with enjoyment as delight zinged along her nerve endings.

She wanted to make love.

He settled his mouth over hers with another one of those possessing, making-her-his kisses. She loved the way his lips moved and his tongue teased hers. He tasted like brandy, a surprisingly erotic flavor. She wanted to push him onto his back and have her way with him. She'd seen a woman do that in a movie once and it had looked very sensual.

He deepened the kiss while taking her nipple between his thumb and forefinger and squeezing. She almost stopped breathing it felt so good, so right. She had never considered the difference it would make to truly belong to Alex when he touched her, but it was overwhelming. The other night he had brought her more pleasure than she thought possible. Now, there was an added element to the pleasure. It felt like tenderness, permanence, and possession all rolled into one.

She moaned and reached down to touch him. The

moment her fingers closed around his hardness, he stopped moving. So did she. Her fingertips barely connected and he didn't feel like she had expected. The skin was soft, like really fine velvet, drawn tight over what felt like a rock-solid muscle. Except that she knew it wasn't muscle but rather blood-engorged tissues. Her mind knew that, but her hand felt like it had locked around a heated pipe.

Something else unexpected was how much it excited her to hold him like this. She looked up at his face, wanting to know if he liked her touching him as much as she did. His features were locked in a grimace and she snatched her hand away.

"I'm sorry."

"So am I. Put it back, Isabel. Touch me again." He didn't wait for her to comply, but reached down and grabbed her wrist, moving her hand into contact with his hardened flesh again. "Hold it, baby. Put your hand around it like before."

She uncurled her fingers and did as he said. An almighty groan was her reward. He exerted slight pressure until her hand moved up and down the length of his heated skin. She liked that. She liked it a lot. So did he. He moaned and pushed himself into her hand, lifting his pelvis off the bed.

He let her do it for only a few strokes before pulling her hand away. "I want to come inside you this time."

This time? That sounded promising.

He slipped his hand between her thighs, pushing his forefinger into the wet heat there. She bucked against that finger, wanting more of it, wanting all of him. She closed her eyes in bliss as the pleasure between her legs began to radiate outward. She felt his lips close over her nipple. He started to suckle her, and she felt herself swelling around the finger he'd pressed inside her.

He caressed her clitoris with his thumb in a beguiling circular motion and slipped a second finger inside her. "Damn, baby. You're tighter than a fist." He withdrew his fingers and then slid them in again. He repeated this motion over and over again, all the while caressing her pleasure spot with his thumb.

The sensation of being on the edge of a precipice came back, only this time she wanted her husband inside her when she went over. "Alex, please."

He knew just what she was asking for, coming over her with a burst of speed and masculine aggression. "Are you ready for me, honey?"

She spread her legs in unmistakable invitation. "Yes."

He teased her with the broad tip of his penis. "Are you sure?"

She tried to arch up under him. "Yes."

"Then bend your legs for me, sweetheart."

"Wait."

He stared down at her, his eyes reflecting frustrated desire before he closed them. He seemed to count to ten and then he opened them again. "Is something wrong?"

She took a deep breath. The words Alex had uttered downstairs were still shifting through her mind. "I'm still not on the pill."

His look grew puzzled. "Why would you be? The point of this marriage is to make babies, isn't it?"

Even now, so close to making love, he sounded slightly bothered by that assertion.

She smiled, her love reaching out to wrap around him even if he didn't know it. "You can use a condom if you like. I don't mind waiting a while to have children."

"How long?" he asked, his eyes unreadable.

"Until we're both ready."

"And if I'm not ready a year from now?"

"Then we'll wait." She may have started off this crazy business with her desire for a baby, but along the way she'd fallen in love, and Alex had become of primary importance to her. She couldn't stand his having even a lingering doubt that she was forcing herself to make love to him in order to get pregnant.

His smile warmed her insides. "Bend your legs for me."

Her insides melted at the heated promise in his voice and she obeyed him. He slid an inch inside of her. "I don't want anything between us tonight, Isabel. I've never made love with the conscious thought a baby could be the result, but I like it, sweetheart. I like it a lot."

He had stopped and was letting her adjust to his initial intrusion. He pushed forward a little more only when her inner muscles had relaxed slightly. She felt herself stretching to accommodate him, but she didn't want this slow wooing. She wanted all of him. The knowledge that he wanted to give her a baby was the strongest aphrodisiac she could ever have imagined.

"Stop playing with me, Alex, and do it," she demanded.

He shook his head. "No, baby, you might as well be a virgin, you're so tight. If I took you like you want me to, it would hurt, and I'm not going to do anything to mess up your memory of our wedding night."

As his hard flesh pushed farther inside on the next thrust, she had to accede to the wisdom of his view. Even slow and easy was becoming slightly uncomfortable. She felt like she was stretched to the limit, and he wasn't even all of the way inside yet. She moaned and shifted under him, trying to find a more comfortable position and succeeded only in forcing his penis farther inside—stretching unused, blood-engorged tissues to the point of pain.

Tears stung her eyes and she bit her lip to keep from crying out, but Alex knew. He rained kisses all over her face while keeping the lower half of their bodies completely still. "Shh, baby. Let me get inside you and everything will be all right. Just don't move again."

She shook her head from side to side on the pillow. She wasn't moving. She couldn't. She was pinned to the bed by the overwhelming male flesh in and around her. He kept up the slow rocking motion until her body suddenly relaxed and adjusted to his invasion, allowing his entire length to settle inside her.

The feelings of pleasure that had not quite abated, even with the discomfort, started to grow. "Alex?"

"Yes?" There was sweat on his brow and his muscles were taut from the effort he'd made to make their first joining special.

"I think you can move now."

He thanked God out loud and then did just that, but only one strong, slow stroke. Pleasure poured through her and she begged him to move more. He did, but he kept the pace slow and it was driving her mad.

She tried to buck against him. "Faster, Alex."

Then he was moving just like she wanted, fast and deep. Her sensitive inner flesh clasped greedily around him and the feeling of pleasure spiraled until it exploded inside her. She convulsed around Alex again and again. "I love you, Alex. I love you!"

His eyes opened and he looked at her with his fathomless dark gaze. Then his entire body went stiff. He shuddered and came inside her for the first time.

A long while later, he rolled off of her and got up to blow out the candles. He grumbled about how unromantic it was to have to leave a warm bed to do so, and she smiled. How could she help it? The man was none too steady on his feet and she'd done that to him. When he got back into bed, she scooted into his arms with brazen speed. He sighed and cuddled her close.

"I guess I'm not such a dud in this department after

all," she said, feeling not the least bit guilty over the smugness in her voice.

She was too happy that she hadn't messed it up to feel guilty.

"If you were any more of a firecracker, I'd have to get a permit for TNT to keep you in the house."

She grinned against the musky warmth of his chest. "If I'm a firecracker, you're the match that lit the fuse."

Suddenly the lazy, satiated male who had been cuddling her with sleepy relaxation was looming over her, all dominant masculinity and vibrating sexuality. "Unlike a match, baby, I never burn out."

She swallowed a startled gasp as his mouth swooped down on hers before he spent the rest of the night proving his arrogant claim.

Isabel woke up, her nose wrinkling with appreciation for the smell of bacon and coffee wafting in through the open bedroom door. She stretched, letting her legs slide luxuriously against the sheets on Alex's . . . their bed. Then she sat up and winced. Alex took his challenges seriously and he'd been seriously intent on proving the steady heat of his fire to her last night.

Her inner thigh muscles ached from their strenuous workout while places she'd been unaware of for most of her life were making themselves known. A long hot bath would be just the thing. She wondered if she could convince Alex to join her.

She smiled at the thought, while looking around her new bedroom. Alex's favorite color must be gray. A little lavender and silver to go with the solid oak furniture and pewter-colored comforter should soften the masculine décor in here enough to make her feel comfortable. Feeling domestic and content at the thought, she slipped out of bed.

The smells from downstairs were growing more tempting by the minute, so instead of running a bath, she pulled a T-shirt from Alex's drawer and slipped it over her head before padding downstairs and into the kitchen. Alex stood at the stove wearing a pair of sweats riding low on his hips and nothing else. She couldn't decide if she was hungrier for food or for him. He opened the oven and pulled out biscuits, and she decided her carnal nature could wait.

"Those smell heavenly."

He laid the pan on the tile counter and turned around to face her. His look traveled over her, stopping briefly on her bare legs and then rising to her face. "Good morning, honey."

"Good morning."

"You're wearing my shirt."

"I didn't think to pack a robe of any substance. I didn't think you'd mind."

He smiled, the possessive look she'd noticed last night in his eyes once again in evidence. "I don't."

She bit her bottom lip. Should she offer to help him with breakfast? Should she kiss him good morning? How did a bride behave the morning after her wedding night, especially after the strange one she'd had?

"Come here." It was gently spoken but a command nevertheless.

She didn't hesitate. When she got within reach, Alex pulled her into his arms and kissed her. His mouth was warm and tasted like coffee. She melted against him. When he stopped kissing her, she leaned her cheek against his bare chest.

Somehow, this touching seemed every bit as intimate as what they had done last night.

"I like having a wife." The complacent way he spoke nearly made her laugh, but she couldn't quite work up the amusement.

"I like having a husband, too," she admitted.

His hands traveled down her back. "Isabel?"

"Hmmm?" This felt so nice. She could stand here in Alex's arms all morning.

"Are you really, really hungry?"

At the unmistakable intent in his voice, she shivered. "That depends on what you're referring to, food or you."

She'd never teased a man sensually like this but she liked it. She liked it even more when he gave a low growl and made her forget all about breakfast.

The next four weeks whirled by in a happy daze for Isabel. Living with Alex was more wonderful than she could ever have imagined. He was a fantastic, generous lover and even shared the chores without a murmur of protest. He could cook and dust with the best of them, and had not raised one single complaint about the way her furniture had taken over his house.

It was their home now, he insisted, usually before taking special pains to show her in an intimate way the level of their connection to each other. A feeling of peace and belonging like she'd never known settled over her.

The only cloud in Isabel's otherwise blue sky was the fact that he'd never said he loved her. Sometimes she thought he must, the way he cherished her and made love to her at every opportunity. She hadn't repeated her avowal of love since their wedding night and wondered if, like her, he was just afraid of admitting his feelings and making himself vulnerable.

Alex pressed the intercom on his desk phone. "Miss Richards, please come in here."

His ever-efficient secretary took longer than her

usual fifteen seconds to arrive in his office. When she did arrive, she looked suspiciously vulnerable. Alex forgot about the report he meant to ask about and asked instead, "Are you okay?"

Veronica made an obvious effort to affect her usual look of dispassionate calm and failed miserably. Her eyes filled with tears. "I'm fine. I . . ."

She seemed incapable of going on yet did not go rushing from the room. He had the feeling she was as unsure about what to do with her emotions as he was. Even a month of marriage and living with an emotional woman like Isabel had not prepared Alex for this sort of display from his secretary. He grasped for something to say, feeling inadequate.

Finally, he settled on, "Would you like to take the rest of the afternoon off?"

She nodded, spun on her heel, and headed toward the door.

Marcus entered Alex's office as Veronica was leaving. He stopped and put his hand on her arm. "Ronnie, what's the matter?" Marcus looked as bewildered as Alex felt.

Silently shaking her head, she rushed from the room.

Marcus looked at Alex. "What's the matter with her?"

"Heck if I know. You're the one who calls her *Ronnie*. You tell me."

Something crossed Marcus's face that might have been guilt, but he had his easygoing mask in place so fast that Alex wondered if he'd read his friend's expression correctly the first time.

To test it, he asked, "Do you want to go after her?"

Again that look, but Marcus shook his head. "Bettina Fry called. Her client wants to go through with the interview."

"It's been six weeks," Alex said, with a certain amount of disbelief.

He'd thought that avenue of inquiry had hit a dead end.

"I know. I didn't expect to hear from the agency again," Marcus replied, echoing Alex's thoughts.

"So, who is it?"

"St. Clair."

"St. Clair? Why?" He didn't expect Marcus to know the answer to that question. It had just slipped out.

Marcus's shoulders rose and fell in a shrug. "I'm not sure, but I can guess."

That caught Alex's attention. "Guess."

"You're the best and you trained me. I can see a guy like St. Clair wanting someone with my abilities on his staff."

Damn. It made sense. "It would keep the entire takeover process in-house for him."

Marcus nodded.

"When's the interview?"

"There isn't going to be an interview."

"Why? St. Clair will probably make you a solid offer. You can't afford to ignore this kind of opportunity, Marcus."

Marcus laughed. "You sound like Ms. Fry, who, in turn, sounds an awful lot like your wife. I'll tell you what I told her. I'm content at CIS and I don't want to go to work for a corporate raider. Not enough flexibility in the job."

Alex felt his mouth crease in a smile. "That's one way to look at it."

"Besides, I've got plans for CIS."

"What kind of plans?" Alex asked.

"I think we should branch out into internal corporate investigations."

"With you heading the new department?" It was a good idea and Marcus was a natural investigator.

"Yep." Marcus smiled. "How is married life treating you?"

Alex appreciated Marcus's hit-and-run method of discussion. He'd planted an idea and was ready to move on. Alex had no doubt the issue would come up again, but Marcus had given him an opportunity to think about it and build an information matrix around the idea.

"I like it." Every day he discovered something else that enthralled him about being married to Isabel. She'd taken his farmhouse and made it a home. The rooms he'd worked so hard to restore were now warmly appealing. He smiled at Marcus. "You should give it a try."

Marcus's smile faded. "Nah. You know me. I'm not the type for long-term commitments."

Maybe that explained Veronica's tears.

"Does she know that?" he asked, indicating the doorway through which his secretary had disappeared.

Marcus's expression closed. "Ronnie knows exactly what to expect from me."

"Apparently, she doesn't like it."

Marcus raised his hands, palms facing outward. "Hey, boss. Don't blame her little display on me. I'm as in the dark about why she's so upset as you are."

Marcus, in the age-old tradition of male ignorance regarding feminine feelings, could very well be the reason for Veronica's tears and not even know it. Alex couldn't blame him. Women were incomprehensible sometimes. Just that morning he'd caught Isabel all teary-eyed in the bathroom. When he pressed, all she would say was that they hadn't had a honeymoon.

She hadn't said she wanted one. How was he supposed to know? Read her mind? He'd assumed that they would take a trip for their first anniversary, or something. He had thought that Isabel would not want to take time off with such short notice. He had been wrong. Wrong enough that Isabel had gotten weepy.

He had to do something to rectify the situation, but he couldn't get away from the office right now. Things with St. Clair and Hypertron were too delicate. St. Clair was itching to move, but Alex was advising him to wait. A takeover bid at this point was not guaranteed success. A few days of patience should pay off when Hypertron announced that their newest technology would be late to market.

The computer industry was an unforgiving one.

Alex was still cussing a blue streak in his mind as he opened the back door and stepped into the farmhouse kitchen. The delicious smells of Isabel's cooking did nothing to lighten his foul mood. He'd promised to cook tonight, but he'd gotten delayed at the office, so Isabel had been forced to make dinner. Combined with the honeymoon issue, he wasn't expecting one of their typically relaxed evenings that slipped into increasingly intense sessions of lovemaking.

He had expected the newness of their physical intimacy to wear off and for his constant need for her to abate to less dangerous levels. Neither had happened. In fact, the closer he got to seeing her dad's company destroyed, the more he craved the proof of his and Isabel's closeness and his importance in her life.

She'd never repeated her words of love from their wedding night. He couldn't help wondering if the words hadn't been a reaction to the overwhelming physical pleasure they had experienced together. If so, she should have said them again by now. The pleasure they found together seemed limitless.

He tried to ignore the other possibility: that she had said the words in gratitude for his willingness to try for a baby.

As he walked farther into the warmth of the kitchen, Isabel looked up from some papers she had spread on one end of the big oak kitchen table. Her green eyes were surprisingly warm, and her mouth curved in a smile that faltered when she registered the look on his face. "Rough day?"

He felt like growling, like some kind of wounded bear, but shrugged instead. The day had started off on a sour note—when both his wife and his secretary had decided to get emotional on him—and had only gotten worse. Hypertron had postponed their announcement regarding the release date of their new technology by two weeks.

The stock had dipped slightly from the delay, but nothing like what would happen when they went public with an actual setback in their schedule, which meant a delay in St. Clair's takeover bid. St. Clair had called, irritated and acting as if Alex had something to do with the announcement that had temporarily stymied his plans.

Alex didn't want the delay any more than the corporate raider did. He just wanted it over, so that he could get on with his life with Isabel. The revenge that had once consumed his thoughts now played the role of ugly stepsister. It was necessary but no longer as palatable as it had once been.

"You're here now," she said sweetly, as she brushed the honey-brown silk of her hair over one shoulder.

An overwhelming need for her softness filled him. He craved affirmation that she belonged to him, that she loved him, even when she stubbornly refused to repeat the words. When he was buried deep inside her and she was going crazy under him, he found it all too easy to believe she felt something for her new husband much stronger than desire.

He went to where she sat and pulled her up into his arms. "Yes, I'm here now." And it felt good.

She made no pretense at resistance when his mouth landed on hers, but parted her lips with surprise at his almost angry desire that quickly turned to enthusiasm. She tasted delicious. Sweet and warm, her soft body became pliant against his as he possessed her mouth. Running his hands down her spine, he felt deep satisfaction when she groaned and arched herself against him.

She wanted him. She always wanted him and he could never get enough of her.

Isabel's hands were busy tugging his shirt out of his slacks. Soon, her hot little fingers were roaming over his chest.

He groaned and broke his mouth from hers to trail kisses down the womanly scented column of her neck. "You smell good."

She laughed huskily. "I smell like chicken parmesan."

"No. You smell like my wife and you feel so good against me, it drives me crazy."

"You drive me crazy, too, Alex. I'll never get enough of your touch. I'm hungry for it all of the time."

Her words were like starter fluid on his already raging libido, and the black mood that had been plaguing him began to lift at her sweet honesty. Her emotional generosity had surprised him at first. Given the way she'd been raised, he would have expected that she would be uncomfortable expressing her feelings, but she wasn't. With the one exception that she hadn't again said she loved him, she expressed her desire for him in a thousand different ways. She complimented him. She touched him. She shared her body with him . . . unreservedly.

He picked her up and carried her into the living room because he didn't think he could make it to the bedroom upstairs. Besides, one of his favorite fantasies was making love to Isabel on that pristine white couch.

She gazed up at him, a look of wicked feminine promise in her eyes. "Are we going to eat dinner late again tonight?"

"I need you now, sweetheart." His voice betrayed a depth of emotion that made him feel vulnerable, but he wanted to give her as much honesty as she gave him.

Then you should tell her about your part in the plans to destroy her father's company, a voice taunted him in his head. He blocked it out in favor of kissing his wife breathless again. Laying her across the pale cushions, he immediately began to shed his clothing.

Her emerald eyes widened. "You in a hurry?"

"Yes."

Her mouth parted on a sigh and then she was tearing off her own clothes. He noticed she hadn't been wearing any panties seconds before lowering himself to lie on top of her delectable curves. The feel of her naked breasts against him and the warm cradle of her thighs brought a guttural growl from deep in his body. He wanted to bury himself inside of her. Now.

Using the last vestige of his control, he made himself wait, caressing her breasts with his hand and his hungry mouth until she writhed under him, moaning out a litany of pleasure.

She spread her thighs and grabbed his buttocks, pulling him forward. "Now. Alex. You said you didn't want to wait!"

He hesitated only long enough to slip his fingers inside her to make sure she was ready, and she moaned again.

"Don't tease me. I want all of you. *Please.*"

He would have laughed but he was too close to exploding. Unable to hold his control any longer, he drove into her. Fast and hard, glad that since the first time it had gotten easier for him to enter her. He pounded into her wet, silky flesh over and over again, trying with each thrust to imprint her with his possession.

He wanted to slow down, to let her catch up with him, but he couldn't wait. His control was shot and he thought he was going to come before he could satisfy her, but just as he felt himself go over the edge, she convulsed around him.

"Alex."

He shouted his own release.

Chapter Fourteen

Isabel lay under Alex, his passionate shout still ringing in her ears. They'd made love so many different ways since their wedding night, but never before had he lost control like this. She wondered what had caused it and then decided she didn't care. She liked it, liked knowing that Alex let down his guard completely with her in at least this area.

He was so controlled about everything else, so methodical. He always knew what he wanted and went for it. Look at how quickly he'd talked her into marriage. Well, she was taking a page from his book tonight.

She was going for a honeymoon.

"Am I too heavy for you?" Alex spoke against her neck, where his head rested. Although he asked the words solicitously, she sensed he really did not want to move.

Isabel reveled in the feeling of being needed by her husband. "No, my love."

His head snapped up and his eyes burned into hers. "Say that again."

"No?"

His mouth thinned. "You called me your love."

"Yes." Could he doubt it?

The fierceness in him did not abate. If anything, it seemed to grow. "Am I?"

"Are you what?" she asked, hedging for time, for an answer that wouldn't make her more vulnerable than she already was.

"Your love."

Suddenly, it felt as if her heart were going to pound out of her chest. "You want me to tell you I love you?"

Had Bettina been right? Did she have to show Alex how much he liked hearing the words before he would give them to her?

"Do you?" he asked.

Isabel realized that she couldn't hold the words back any longer. She did love him, and why was she afraid to tell him? He was her husband. He was committed to her. Alex wasn't going to disappear just because she let herself love him. He wasn't a nanny her father could fire.

"Yes, I love you very much."

He closed his eyes and shuddered as if savoring the words. Then he kissed her again, this time with so much tenderness she wanted to cry.

Dinner was stone cold by the time they got to it.

After dinner, Isabel picked up three of the brochures she had been looking at earlier when Alex first came into the kitchen. "I stopped by a travel agent today."

Alex's hand stilled in the act of putting a plate in the dishwasher. "What?"

Ignoring his less-than-enthusiastic response, she repeated herself. "I stopped by a travel agent's office. She's an old friend who used to work with Bettina and me. She had some interesting ideas for a trip."

Alex finished loading the dishwasher, his movements methodical and controlled as usual. He said nothing.

His silence made Isabel nervous, but she wasn't going to back down on this. "She suggested several alternatives, but I like the idea of taking a cruise. There's been a cancellation on a two-week trip to Alaska that sails at the end of the month."

When that idea met with further silence, she decided to give him her other options. "Of course, if you don't want to go on a ship, we could go to one of those all-inclusive places in Mexico. I've got a couple of brochures here you can look at. Then there's always the old standby of Hawaii."

Her own enthusiasm was getting more and more forced in the face of her husband's continued quiet. "Say something."

He shut the dishwasher and turned to face her. "I can't get away right now."

Was that all? "Like I said, the cruise doesn't sail until the end of the month."

"The end of the month might be too soon."

Isabel groped for an answer that wouldn't betray the hurt she felt that he was dismissing their honeymoon so easily. She wanted to be understanding. She really did. "When do you think you could get away?"

"I don't know. I'm sorry, honey. It's just not a good time for me right now." He moved forward as if he planned to take her in his arms.

She stepped back, away from his touch. She needed all of her wits for this discussion, and she didn't have them when Alex touched her. He had rushed her into marriage. He hadn't hesitated to demand her declaration of love. Was it so awful that she wanted this small sign that she was somewhere near the top of his priority list?

She gripped the brochures more tightly. "So, *when?*"

"I don't know," he repeated.

"You must have some idea." He owned his own business, for goodness' sake.

"I don't." He raked his hands through his hair. "Hell, sweetheart, I wish I did. You're going to have to trust me that as soon as I know when I can take the time off, I'll tell you."

His words had a much too familiar ring. How many times had her father put her off with the excuse of pressing business concerns? She wasn't going to tolerate that sort of thing from Alex.

"What about late next month or the month after?" she asked, trying once more to be fair, to trust him as he had told her to do.

The look of anger and exasperation on his face answered her before he could speak. She didn't wait to hear the words of denial that would accompany it. Turning on her heel, she left the kitchen. She heard Alex curse and say her name, but she ignored him.

She supposed that in the scheme of things a honeymoon wasn't all that important. After all, it was the marriage that really mattered, but that realization didn't mitigate the pain in her heart. What was so unreasonable about asking him to name a date for them to go away together? He'd said he had good work habits, that CIS did not come first in his life.

She might react with more understanding later, but right now she didn't feel that way.

She needed time alone. It was late and she felt overwhelmingly tired. She trudged upstairs and got ready for bed. When she had washed her face and pulled on flannel pajamas, she walked right past the bed she shared with Alex. She'd used the bedroom set from her condo to furnish one of the spare bedrooms. She intended to sleep there. Alone.

Slipping between the sheets, she wanted to feel comforted by the familiarity of her old bed. She didn't.

She felt lonely. Her cheeks were wet with tears when she fell asleep.

Alex sat at the large oak table and glared at the brochures Isabel had left lying on it, as if somehow the mess he found himself in was their fault. Isabel acted as if he'd betrayed her when he refused to set a date for the trip. He hoped the deal with Hypertron would be wrapped up by the end of the month, but he couldn't guarantee it. He hated putting her off like this, but he didn't have a choice.

His plans for justice aside, he also had a responsibility to his client. He'd made commitments to St. Clair and he couldn't just dismiss them. But that didn't mean that disappointing his wife didn't bother him.

She'd looked so dejected when she left the kitchen. Like she didn't believe he was going to take her away as soon as he could. Hell, she probably didn't. That look had been so different from her expression when she'd told him she loved him, but if she loved him wouldn't she trust him to keep his word? The thought that her love might not be secure jolted him. He wanted her settled, damn it. He wanted her to believe in him in a way she no longer believed in her dad.

He looked again at the brochures Isabel had dropped on the table and made a decision. He'd have to make arrangements with Marcus, but he was going to prove to Isabel that she had married a man very different from John Harrison. Grabbing the brochures, he left the kitchen and loped up the stairs. He wasn't prepared for the empty bed. The door to the adjoining bathroom was open and there was no sign of his wife.

He found her in the spare bedroom. In her old bed.

The sound of her even breathing indicated that she was already asleep. She thought she could put distance between them by sleeping in another bed, but it wasn't going to happen. Taking care not to wake her, he pulled the bedcovers back. He didn't want another argument right now. He gently lifted her and carried her back to their bedroom. She woke up as he laid her in their bed.

"You came and got me," she mumbled drowsily.

"Of course." Had she doubted for a minute that he would?

She snuggled into the covers. "I'm glad."

He doubted she realized she'd said the revealing words. In her sleepy state, her guard was down. Alex felt his chest expand. She had been angry but had not wanted to spend the night apart. She did love him. She just wasn't sure she could trust him.

He tore off his clothes and then climbed into bed. She rolled into his arms without protest. He kissed the top of her head. "It's going to be all right, sweetheart. I promise."

She mumbled something that he couldn't understand, and then her breathing returned to the deep pattern of sleep.

"Isabel."

Someone was whispering her name, pulling her from her dreams of a long Caribbean cruise with Alex. She tried to ignore the summons. If she couldn't have a real honeymoon, the very least the annoying voice could do was to let her have her dreams.

The voice stopped and she tried to slip back to sleep, but now warm, firm lips were nibbling on her earlobe. "Wake up, sweetheart."

Realizing sleep was impossible, she opened her eyes. The first thing she noticed was that she wasn't in her old bed, for which she felt embarrassed gratitude. It had been childish to abandon their bed in favor of sleeping alone just because she hadn't gotten her way, and she was determined not to do it on such a flimsy excuse again.

The second thing she noticed was the pile of brochures from the travel agency fanned out on the pillow next to her.

She turned her head to ask Alex what was going on and ran right into his lips. He kissed her until she forgot her anger of the night before and her confusion at finding the brochures in bed with her this morning. She was starting to think she should have worn something less constrictive than her flannel pj's to bed last night when he pulled away.

"I like the way you wake up, Isabel."

"I like the way you wake me up," she admitted. "I'm sorry I went to sleep in the spare room. It was stupid."

Warm brown eyes caressed her with their understanding. "I didn't leave you there."

She smiled. "I'm glad."

"You said that last night, too."

She had? Well, she must have been more cognizant than she thought.

He smiled that sexy smile that always sent her heart into overdrive and reached across her to grab the glossy brochures. Then, lifting her into a sitting position, he put them in her lap. "Where do you want to go?"

"When?" she asked, shocked by the unexpected question.

"The first week of next month."

Gratitude and love filled her to overflowing. Not only was Alex not angry for her overreaction the night before, but he wanted to go on a honeymoon with her. She didn't understand why the trip was so important to her, but it was.

"So soon?" She still couldn't quite believe it. "What about your business?"

"Marcus can handle it."

"The first week of next month?" She rattled off the exact dates, wanting confirmation, feeling a little like Cinderella after being invited to the ball. Rattled and very, very pleased.

He smiled again and that killer dimple that turned her insides to mush seemed to be winking at her. "Yes."

"I can wait until things calm down at CIS. Really." She felt obligated to make the offer. After all, it wasn't as if a honeymoon had been on her list.

He shook his head before she finished speaking. "We're going away. Now pick out where you want to go."

She picked an all-inclusive resort hotel in Mexico.

The following Sunday, Alex and Isabel went to Priscilla's house for lunch. Lawrence Redding was also there. When Isabel shared the news with Alex's mother of their upcoming trip, Lawrence had only good things to say about the resort she had picked out, having been there once himself.

Alex enjoyed the look of happiness on his wife's face, and then it hit him: his mother was wearing a very similar expression. Alex knew the reason Isabel looked so happy. She was pleased with him, happy to be married to him, happy about their upcoming honeymoon, and happy with the pleasure they found in each other's bodies.

Why did his mother have that same look of feminine satisfaction deep in her eyes?

After lunch Alex cleared the table, asking his mother to join him in the kitchen while Isabel took Lawrence to the solarium to discuss possible job opportunities.

Alex stacked the plates in the sink while his mother put away the leftovers. "So what's going on with you and Redding?"

Priscilla closed the refrigerator and stood next to the counter. She didn't lean. His mother never leaned. "I've been waiting for this question."

He had a difficult time picturing his mother dating, but particularly to a man as unsettled as Redding. Maybe that's why it had taken him so long to get around to asking. "So, what's the answer?"

Priscilla delicately cleared her throat. "We've been seeing a lot of each other."

"Dad's only been dead two years." The words shocked him. He hadn't planned to say anything of the sort. His mother's private life was her own business and two years was long enough to mourn a husband. But Redding?

Rather than the disapproval he expected in his mother's face, her eyes reflected gentle understanding. "It's time to move on, Alex. It has been a lot longer than two years since I lost your father."

Insides clenching, Alex asked, "What's that supposed to mean?"

"Your father found a mistress I could never compete with and he gave her all that he had to give."

"Dad did not sleep around." Alex ground the words out, praying they were true.

Priscilla met Alex's gaze, her own steady. "No. When would he have had the time? He was much too busy working to sustain a marriage, much less a clandestine relationship."

"So now you want to get involved with a man who can't hold a job?" Alex couldn't believe his mother's attitude. His parents had not been affectionate, but he hadn't thought their marriage was that bad.

Priscilla's eyes narrowed. She drew herself perfectly erect. "Lawrence has no difficulty holding down a job. Each move he makes is voluntary."

Alex ran his fingers through his hair. "Do you blame me for being concerned? Dad might have worked too much overtime, but he was stable. For all we know Redding is looking at you as his retirement plan."

The minute the words left his mouth, Alex knew they were a mistake. His mother's eyes flashed blue fire, and she looked suspiciously like she and Isabel had gone to the same school for irate females.

"I regret the need to say this, but I'm going to. Your father worked far too much. He let his job overrule every other priority in his life including his family. It may come as a horrible shock to you, but I consider Lawrence *my* retirement plan. I want someone to spend my *time* with." His mother's eyes filled with tears, which she quickly brushed away. "I'm tired of loneliness, Alex."

"Damn Hypertron."

"No. Damn your father's workaholic ways," she said fiercely. "He was a heart attack waiting to happen."

The curse coming from his mother's proper mouth shocked Alex, but he wouldn't let her say that Hypertron had no responsibility. "Losing the right to patent his design caused his heart attack. If Hypertron had given Dad his due, he could have relaxed and given you the time you needed."

Priscilla shook her head sadly. "Your father allowed his obsession with the project to take him away from home so much that by the time he finished it, I didn't even know him any longer." She sighed. "Perhaps we could have gotten to know one another again if he put in fewer hours at work, but Ray had no desire to change. He proved that in the hospital."

Alex's muscles bunched as his mother's words penetrated his mind. "What do you mean?"

"His last words were about the project, Alex. He used up his final words to curse Hypertron."

"What do you think they should have been?" Alex demanded, not understanding what she was trying to say.

"Maybe, just maybe, he could have said he loved us."

"He said the insurance was current."

Priscilla laughed, but the sound was hollow. She didn't understand.

"In his own way, Dad was saying that he loved you, that you were taken care of," he tried to explain.

His mother's face softened. "Perhaps you're right, but I needed the words, Alex."

Were the words so important? He'd never said them to Isabel, didn't know if he could. It wasn't something he'd ever said to any woman other than his mother. He could count on one hand the number of times he'd ever used the words at all. After his father's death he'd told his mother he loved her, and once a year later when he found her crying over a photo album.

"So, you're saying because Redding gives you the words, he's a better man than my father?"

He expected her to deny it and was shocked when his mother nodded in agreement. "Better for me at any rate. The words are just that, until they are backed up by actions, and Lawrence has shown me in many ways that I am more important to him than anything else in his life, his work included."

"You don't know that Dad wouldn't have come around if he'd lived," Alex continued to insist stubbornly.

His mom smiled gently at him. "No, I don't know that."

But she didn't believe it. She'd agreed with him to appease him, but her eyes told their own story. His mother didn't hold Hypertron responsible for his dad's death. "So, you're saying it was Dad's fault he had a heart attack and died so young?"

She reached out and touched him. "Does it have to be anyone's fault? Death happens, Alex. It's part of life. Ray's gone but we're still living, and if we do it in the past, we might as well be dead with him."

Isabel put the finishing touches on the picnic basket before sliding the zip-lock baggie with the used home pregnancy test inside. The small white stick had two colored lines, indicating the tiny life growing inside her womb. She sucked in a breath and smelled the fried chicken she had prepared for lunch, glad she wasn't showing any signs of morning sickness.

Isabel hadn't planned to get pregnant so quickly, but considering how often they made love, she shouldn't have been surprised. They hadn't discussed birth control since their wedding night, when Alex had said he didn't want anything between them, so she assumed he knew she wasn't using any.

She blew out a nervous breath.

He'd said that the idea of making love while knowing that a baby could be the result had turned him on. He'd also promised to fulfill her desire for motherhood. *I'll give you babies, Isabel. As many as you want.* It followed that he would not be upset to find out that he had already succeeded in making a child with her. So why did her stomach feel like the US Olympic gymnastics team had taken up residence?

Maybe because of the way Alex had reacted on their wedding night, believing she had married him only to have a baby and was even willing to force herself to make love to him without desiring him in order to get pregnant. She still couldn't believe he had been so blind, but what if he still was?

What if he still saw her getting pregnant right away as an indication that she cared more for the idea of having a baby than for him? Who would have thought a man as self-confident as Alex could have those kinds of insecurities? She had to believe he had gotten over them. The prospect of him reacting badly to discovering her news diminished some of the joy she felt about her condition. She wanted him to be as happy about becoming a parent as she was.

She had to admit that only part of her nervousness came from the prospect of telling Alex about the baby. The rest of her anxiety stemmed from the knowledge that she had married Alex for far more complicated motives than getting pregnant. She'd gone into this marriage with her eyes wide open. She knew she loved Alex and that his feelings for her might be limited to the physical need a man has for a woman.

She had married him because the idea of spending the rest of her life without him hurt too much. She hadn't wanted to lose someone else she loved. She realized that subconsciously she had even agreed to the speedy marriage because deep down she had feared that Alex would change his mind.

Her current emotional turmoil resulted from the fact that regardless of how much Alex had pressed for their union, she felt as if she'd trapped him. Her pregnancy would be one more tie that would bind Alex to her. Amidst her joy at the concept of becoming a mother, there lurked an unholy relief that once Alex knew of his impending fatherhood, he would never change his mind about their marriage.

He was far too committed to family and duty to respond in any other way, even if he wasn't happy about it. And that was what made her feel the icy shards of guilt and trepidation that wouldn't go away.

Alex had never said he loved her. He wanted her. He even liked her. He also needed her.

She had seen it in his eyes. And she knew now that it was not just for sex. He needed *her*, but that wasn't the same thing as love. Or was it? Alex was a man. A man's tender emotions would exhibit themselves differently from a woman's. Wouldn't they?

She took a deep breath and closed the picnic basket, wishing her motives for marrying Alex had been simpler, wishing his motive for marrying her had been love. Because then she would be ecstatically happy right now and she wasn't. Only in discovering her pregnancy had she faced the terrible truth that without love, the family she planned to build could be every bit as empty as the one she had grown up in.

She would have gladly waited to have a baby if only she could be sure of her husband's love. Only that wasn't the way it had worked out. As Nanny Number Five used to say, hindsight is always twenty-twenty. She was pregnant now and she could only hope that Alex loved her, because he certainly hadn't said anything.

She reminded herself that he had been willing to plan a honeymoon although he had something big going on at CIS. Her happiness was important enough for him to sacrifice his own plans—even his work plans. That said something about his feelings for her, surely. It certainly implied more genuine concern than her father had ever shown.

But it didn't tell her diddly about how Alex would respond to the news of her pregnancy. She knew he would accept the responsibility. He would even accept her *right* to get pregnant per their agreement, but would he be happy about the baby? Squaring her shoulders, Isabel decided there was only one way to find out: tell him.

* * *

Walking into the CIS office building a few minutes later she found Miss Richards, that paragon among secretaries, sitting sentinel at her desk.

Her brows rose above the line of her glasses at the sight of the picnic basket, but she merely said, "Good afternoon, Mrs. Trahern."

"Good afternoon, Miss Richards. I'm here to have lunch with Alex."

The secretary looked at her computer screen and clicked her mouse twice. "I don't see an appointment, Mrs. Trahern."

Isabel stifled her irritation and smiled. "Wives do not need appointments, Miss Richards. It's one of their perks."

Isabel did not expect her comment to have the effect it did. Miss Richards's eyes darkened with pain and her face lost what little color it had. She took several shallow breaths but did not speak.

Isabel instinctively reached out to touch the secretary's arm. "Are you all right?"

Taking a deeper breath and expelling it slowly, Miss Richards nodded. "Yes, of course."

Her expression once again settled into a professional mask. "Mr. Trahern does not wish to be disturbed."

"Is he in a meeting?" Perhaps Isabel would have to come back later.

"No." Another strange look passed over Miss Richards's face. "He's going over some new information on an important account right now."

Well, the man had to eat. He could spare a half hour for lunch with his wife. Isabel placed her hand on Alex's office doorknob. "I promise not to keep him long."

* * *

Alex pulled out the spreadsheet of Hypertron's stock prices over the past six months and studied it. The stock had dipped again. Although it wasn't at the low level both Alex and St. Clair had hoped for, it was low enough to begin the takeover bid process. St. Clair would start by buying small chunks of stock, but nothing that should alert Hypertron's watchdogs or put him over SEC guidelines.

It was common enough for investors to speculate and buy stock that was slipping, particularly technology stocks, in hopes that the price would again rise quickly.

Alex planned to meet St. Clair later today to finalize details and strategy. They would discuss other issues as well, particularly the fact that Alex had no intention of letting St. Clair raid CIS for employees. Marcus wasn't going anywhere. He'd see to it.

Damn it. Alex wished he could shake this feeling of impending doom. He knew it had nothing to do with the fear of losing Marcus to St. Clair. Alex was pretty sure that the partnership he planned to offer his second-in-command would guarantee Marcus's loyalty and longevity at CIS.

The nagging feeling of doom shouldn't have anything to do with his revenge plans, either. Everything was in place. Everything except a guarantee of Isabel's reaction to the news that her father's company was going down. She was so damn caring, even toward a man who had treated her like unimportant baggage for most of her life. Isabel should be grateful to Alex if she ever did discover the part he intended to play in the downfall of Hypertron, but his gut told him that she wouldn't be.

" 'Don't frown like that or your face might freeze that way,' Nanny Number Four used to say."

Alex felt as if his dark and chaotic thoughts had conjured her up. Isabel stood in his doorway, a teasing smile lighting her face.

"I told my secretary that I did not want to be disturbed." Hell. *Why had he said that?*

Isabel's smile faltered but did not disappear entirely. "I explained that wives have certain privileges. Disturbing their husbands is one of them."

She waggled her eyebrows, intimating all sorts of disturbances. For once, he did not respond with instant arousal to her obvious suggestion. Their future was too damn precarious now that St. Clair was prepared to make his move.

Lifting a picnic basket covered with a red-and-white checked cloth, Isabel said, "I brought lunch."

As she started to move forward, several things clicked into place in his brain. The first was that if he let her set the basket on the desk, she would see the Hypertron file. He quickly shut the file in front of him and slipped it underneath a newspaper on the side of his desk. Isabel's eyes followed his movements, but he didn't think she had focused on what she saw.

The second was that he couldn't have lunch with her. Not today, because he still had a lot of paperwork to compile before meeting with St. Clair. And because he didn't know if he could give St. Clair unbiased advice toward the destruction of her father's company after spending a romantic picnic lunch with Isabel.

"I can't. I've got an important appointment this afternoon I need to prepare for." His voice came out like a bark, but he couldn't help it. He did not want Isabel asking difficult questions right now. He tried to soften his tone. "I don't have time for lunch today, sweetheart."

She stopped a few feet from his desk, her expression chagrined but not angry. "Surely you can take half an hour out of your schedule to eat."

"I'm sorry, baby, I can't."

She waved the basket in the air and the smell of fried chicken tempted his nostrils. "Not even thirty short minutes?"

"No." The word came out sharp and cutting. He closed his eyes in frustration at his own lack of control.

Hurt registered in her eyes, but her voice came out low and even. "I'll remember to call ahead for an appointment next time."

"Isabel—"

She cut him off. "I'm sorry, Alex. I do understand about work schedules. It's just that I had something I wanted to tell you, and in my excitement I didn't take anything else into consideration. I guess I thought that if I could take the afternoon off, you could, too."

What did she want to tell him? She'd probably booked their trip and wanted to give him the details. He got up from his desk and walked toward her. He didn't want her to leave his office looking wounded.

Cupping her nape, he caressed her neck with his fingers. "We can talk about it tonight at home. All right?"

She nodded, her silky hair moving against his fingers.

He leaned down and kissed her cheek. He didn't dare take her lips. If he did, he knew he would lose the tenuous grip he had on his control. It was always like this with her. "I'll see you later, then."

"Okay." She slipped away from his touch and left the office.

Guilt hit him like a volley of arrows aimed right at his chest. Damn it. He should have taken a half hour for lunch with her. He kept saying that his revenge had nothing to do with her, so why had he allowed it to affect how he treated her? Taking a few seconds to put the file on Hypertron in his office safe, he then left his office intending to beg his wife for a second chance at that picnic basket.

He realized he wouldn't get the opportunity when he walked outside just in time to watch her car pull out of the drive.

Chapter Fifteen

Isabel drove without really thinking where she was going, but wasn't surprised at all to discover herself in her father's neighborhood. She had no intention of stopping by the house. She wanted peace. She needed solitude.

Driving past her childhood home, she turned onto a street that led to a small park. Autumn leaves colored the landscape of the empty play area. Getting out of the car, she walked past the playground equipment and into a stand of trees beyond where the scent of wet bark mixed with damp earth. She had spent more hours than she could count here, by herself. The park had been a refuge from the silent loneliness of her home.

How many times had she come here when her world had fallen apart yet again? The first time she had been barely five and had gotten in awful trouble when the new nanny could not find her. The woman had made Isabel promise not to come to the park alone ever again. Isabel had kept the promise until that nanny left also. Then, she figured all bets were off.

She kicked the wet leaves and tried to make sense of

what had happened in Alex's office. She hadn't been placating him when she told him that she understood schedules, but something told her that that wasn't really the reason Alex hadn't wanted to have lunch with her.

He had acted so distant. So irritated. Isabel stopped and picked up a stick, feeling the wet bark chill her fingers. Why had Alex been so upset? He hadn't even responded to her suggestive comment about interruptions. Alex's physical response to her had been the one thing she could rely on. If he had stopped wanting her, what chance did she have that he would ever fall in love with her?

In a few months, she would be as round as a beach ball. If Alex was tired of her already, how much less attractive would he find her while pregnant? A part of her realized that she was making too much out of his rejection, but that didn't stop her emotions from careening out of control as she walked the paths that had once given her solace.

Her hand dropped to her still-flat stomach as she went over Alex's reaction in her mind once again. He'd moved a file under some papers on his desk. Almost as if he hadn't wanted her to see it. Which made no sense. He would trust her to keep confidential whatever she saw. Wouldn't he?

The thought that Alex might not trust her twisted like a knife in her heart.

Then, like a camera zooming into focus, the image of the file crystallized in Isabel's mind and the knife took another twist. The file had been on Hypertron. Why would Alex have a file on her dad's company? More pieces of their conversation came into sharp relief. Alex had an important meeting he'd been preparing for. What did that meeting have to do with Hypertron?

She remembered her dad and even Priscilla's concern that Alex had been using Isabel to wreak vengeance. Alex had denied the accusation and she believed him. She had assumed that his denial meant he wasn't interested in any kind of retribution, telling herself that a man wouldn't marry the daughter of his sworn enemy.

She had to see that file.

She parked her car next to their house, blowing out a breath of relief when she saw that Alex's Aston Martin was gone. She didn't take time to empty the picnic basket but went straight down to the office. The door was locked. That meant they were all gone: Alex, Marcus, and Miss Richards. Unaccountable irritation rose up at the thought that Alex trusted Veronica Richards with his secrets but not his own wife. She tried reminding herself that Alex wasn't about to tell her about his plans against Hypertron but it didn't help.

She jogged up to the house and snagged the extra key that Alex kept to the office out of the drawer in the kitchen. Hurrying back to the renovated barn, she unlocked the door and slipped inside. She missed on her first try at disarming the elaborate alarm system, but thankfully succeeded before the timed mechanism went off at her unlawful entry. At least Alex had trusted her enough to explain his security system.

Miss Richards's computer had not been turned off. The screen saver flashed bright geometric images. Isabel assumed the secretary expected to return. Pressing the left mouse button, Isabel brought the screen up and smiled. The perfect Miss Richards wasn't so perfect after all. She had forgotten to lock her system, leaving Isabel access to her desktop. Feeling like a cat burglar, she quickly checked the calendar program to see when the others were supposed to return.

Isabel didn't want to believe that Alex was planning

anything underhanded against Hypertron, but her intuition told her to get a grip on reality. Her husband was too hard a man to allow his father's death to go unpunished. She knew Alex didn't see the events the same way that Priscilla did: he blamed her father, or at least his company, completely for Ray Trahern's death.

Alex, Marcus, and Miss Richards were meeting with some person named St. Clair. The name struck a familiar chord in Isabel's memory, but in testimony to how rattled she felt, it took her several moments to realize St. Clair was the man who had hired her to approach Marcus Danvers about employment. No end time to the meeting had been recorded and there were no other appointments that afternoon. They might have planned to be gone most of the afternoon, or they could be back any moment.

Deciding not to waste any time, Isabel went into Alex's office. His desk was clean except for a newspaper folded open to the stock section.

She spied his safe. Of course. Anything as important as revenge would be locked up in there. Alex hadn't told her the combination but she tried anyway. Their wedding date didn't open it. She wasn't surprised. She tried Alex's birthday, but it didn't work, either.

Knowing Alex, he would have chosen numbers that wouldn't be that obvious—but that would be easy for him to remember. She hit her head with the heel of her hand. *Duh.* Pulling the receiver from the cradle on his phone, she dialed Priscilla's number. Her mother-in-law answered on the second ring.

"Priscilla, this is Isabel."

"Hello, dear. How are you?"

Ready to shoot your son. "Fine. I've got a quick question I hope you won't mind answering."

"Certainly. Anything you need."

Isabel's chest grew tight at the warmth in Priscilla's

voice so at odds with Alex's earlier irritation. Darn. She had been told that pregnancy made women more emotional, but she wasn't in the mood to deal with it. Keeping a tight rein on the feelings swirling through her, Isabel tried to think how to word her question without sounding ghoulish and finally decided that bluntness was the only answer.

"What day did Ray die?"

Priscilla rattled off a date. Holding the receiver to her ear, Isabel tried the numbers on the safe's combination. They worked. "Of course. He wouldn't use our wedding date because it's not important enough."

The fact that the safe had been installed long before their marriage didn't diminish her anger toward Alex. His dad had died only two years ago. Alex had started CIS and presumably purchased the safe well before that date.

"What? Are you all right, Isabel?" Priscilla's concerned voice barely penetrated Isabel's anger.

"All right? Yes. Why wouldn't I be?" Just because she was married to a man still living in the past.

"You sound a bit odd. Are you getting enough rest?"

"Yes." Despite the fact that Alex liked to wake her in the middle of the night to make love, she was getting plenty of rest. "Listen Priscilla, I've got to go."

"Very well. I'll see you Sunday, dear."

Maybe. Then again maybe she would be in jail for assault and battery of her stubborn, retaliation-minded husband. Pregnant women have been known to lose control. Isabel hung up the phone absentmindedly as she stared at the contents of the safe. The file wasn't there. Did that mean Alex had taken it with him? Probably. St. Clair must have something to do with Alex's plans for revenge.

Even if he had taken the file, there had to be some kind of backup. After all, Miss Richards was too organized not to have duplicate records. Where would they be? On her computer.

Isabel rushed back into the outer office and did a search for files related to Hypertron. She found an entire subdirectory full of them. Isabel clicked one open and began reading. She was still reading when the outer door to the office opened an hour and a half later.

Alex walked into his office building, and the first thing he saw was his wife sitting in Veronica's chair staring at his secretary's computer monitor. "What the hell?"

Isabel turned her head. Her usual smile of greeting was conspicuous in its absence. "Oh, hello, Alex. How did your meeting with Mr. St. Clair go? I'm assuming your plans to take apart my dad's company are right on target."

A gasp from behind him reminded Alex that Marcus and Veronica had followed him into the building. He had no intention of having this discussion with his wife in front of them. He'd hoped not to have this discussion at all.

"Let's go up to the house and talk about it."

Isabel stood up and stretched. Despite his inner turmoil, Alex's body reacted to the sight. He wanted her. He always wanted her, but first they had to talk.

After stretching, she smiled. It was more a tilting of her lips and her eyes remained cold. "Why?" She swung her hand out to indicate Marcus and Veronica. "They already know the details. Why shouldn't they hear us discussing them?"

A dangerous glitter in Isabel's eyes warned him that although she sounded like she couldn't care less about what she had discovered, she was coldly furious. They needed privacy and they needed it immediately.

He walked forward, took her arm, and then kept right on walking—gently forcing her to follow him into his office. Once inside he released her and she made a beeline for the other side of the room, getting as far away from him as possible.

Taking a tight rein on his temper, he shut the door and turned to face her. "How did you find out?" That isn't what he had meant to say, but it would do for a start.

She glared at him, her green eyes spitting all sorts of accusations at him. "I saw the file on Hypertron this afternoon when I came by for lunch."

"Why did you sneak into my office? Why didn't you just ask me about it?"

The look she gave him questioned his intelligence quotient. "Right. I was supposed to ask you about your plans to ruin my father? Get real."

He walked toward her and she backed away, circling around his desk. That's when he noticed his safe standing open. "You broke into my safe?"

Her eyes shot flames and she seemed to swell with anger. "Yes. And do you know what I discovered?"

"Nothing." He'd taken the file with him. But she had found Veronica's backup documentation on the computer. He wondered how much she had been able to read before his return to the office. Whatever it had been, apparently it was enough.

"Wrong." Isabel's face was pale, with two splotches of red high on her cheekbones. "I found out that our wedding doesn't rate the same level of importance as the date of your dad's death, which you've made the combination to your safe. You're so busy living in the past and plotting for revenge, I don't know why you married me at all."

Why the hell was she so fixated on his safe's combination? Just because he used an important date from the past that was easy for him to remember didn't mean he'd been living in it. "I married you because I wanted to."

"I know you wanted to, but what I can't figure out is why." Then, her gaze filled with horrified disbelief. "Or was I part of it? You told me I didn't have anything to do with what happened to your dad, and I believed you. I was a fool, wasn't I? No man meets a woman and wants to marry her within days! Especially a man as methodical as you." Isabel's voice rose to a hysterical level. "What did you do? Convince St. Clair to call me so you'd have an excuse to come to my office and harangue me? Was marrying me your way of taking away more than Dad's company? You think that you've taken me away from him, too, but you're wrong."

She had completed her circle of the room and stood in front of the closed door. She shut her eyes for a second as if trying to block out the situation, then opened them. Her next words were spoken in a bare whisper. "Dad doesn't care about me any more than you do. You can't take away something someone has already rejected."

He reached toward her, but she jerked away.

"Calm down, Isabel. You're out of control and making wild accusations." He tried to keep his voice level and soothing.

She laughed, the sound hollow and full of pain. He wanted to take her in his arms and make it better, but he could tell that his touch was the last thing she would willingly tolerate right now. How could she believe that he didn't care? She was his wife, not some kind of pawn he would use to hurt Harrison. She had to know that.

He'd never lied to her, damn it.

She took a deep, gasping breath, her hand on the door handle. "I've been out of control and out of my mind since the day I met you. I let you talk me into marrying you. I was naive enough to believe you didn't have any plans for revenge against my father when you assured me I wasn't part of them. But I was, wasn't I?"

This had gone far enough. "No!"

She ignored his denial, her face going a shade paler. "My desire for a baby fell right into it, didn't it? Not only can you destroy my dad's company, his very heart, but you plan to withhold his grandchild from him as well."

Alex felt the breath leave his body in one big whoosh. "Are you saying you're pregnant, sweetheart?"

Was that what she'd wanted to tell him earlier? Elation filled him even as he tried to think how best to handle her increasingly hysterical allegations.

"Don't you dare call me sweetheart, you swine. Yes, I'm pregnant. But if my dad is never going to see this baby, then neither will you!" With that she flung open the door and ran from the office.

Pregnant? The word repeated over and over in Alex's brain, a seductive mantra he didn't want to end. *Isabel was going to have his baby.* Delight coursed through him right along with the wariness and anger brought about by the recent confrontation with his wife.

She wouldn't leave him. She couldn't. She might be pissed as hell and making outrageous accusations, but she wasn't going to walk out on the father of her baby—at least not permanently.

If he had anything to say about it, she wasn't walking out at all. He needed to tell her that he didn't want to withhold either her or their baby from Harrison. He didn't want to use her in any way, and he was going to make sure she understood and believed that. Then, he would explain that he had no intention of letting her go—ever.

* * *

Surprise momentarily halted him in his tracks when he entered the kitchen through the back door. He had expected to find Isabel upstairs in their bedroom throwing clothes into a suitcase. Instead, she stood in front of the sink, tossing food from the picnic basket into the garbage with enough force to earn her a tryout as pitcher for the Portland Beavers.

Annoyingly, his stomach chose that moment to react to the smells of the chicken and potato salad. He hadn't eaten since breakfast, and the sight of the home-cooked meal going into the garbage reminded him forcefully that he hadn't just turned Isabel down but had missed lunch entirely.

A small white stick in a plastic baggie sat on the counter next to the basket. It must be the pregnancy test. He'd seen the pictures on the boxes next to the condoms in drugstores.

Obviously, Isabel *had* meant to tell him about her pregnancy at lunch. He regretted more than ever refusing to take a break with her that afternoon. If only he'd taken the time to listen, they wouldn't be having this argument now. She might still have discovered his role in St. Clair's plans, but she wouldn't have jumped to the totally erroneous conclusion that she was part of it or that he planned to try to keep their baby from its grandfather.

At least she hadn't tossed the evidence of her pregnancy. He took that as a good sign. He didn't want her to regret the baby. Not when he'd only recently realized how much her getting pregnant meant to him.

It was time he told her that much at least. "I'm happy about the baby, Isabel."

She froze in the act of emptying a container of chocolate chip cookies into the rapidly filling garbage container. Damn. Hell hath no fury was right. He could see tossing out the food that was probably spoiled but home-made cookies? She finished her task and turned slowly to face him. Her eyes burned with an anger he'd never seen in her before.

"Because you think I'll let you withhold our child from its grandfather as further punishment? I won't let you do it, Alex. I doubt my father will be any more interested in the baby than he was in me, but I'll do my best to see that they have a relationship."

Guilt rapidly mutated into frustration. Why did she have to assume his every motive was a devious one? "I don't want to do anything to hurt you."

She stared at him, her eyes wide and disbelieving, her hair a tumbled mass around her face. "You don't want to hurt me? Is that why my heart feels like it's been ripped out of my chest? Maybe I should be grateful that this pain isn't intentional."

Couldn't she see that she was overreacting? He had thought that since she wasn't on her way out the door, she had realized her wild allegations in his office had been just that . . . wild. "You don't even like Hypertron." Maybe she thought his sense of justice wouldn't stop with the destruction of the company. "I want to dismantle the company, not destroy your dad."

"It's the same thing and you know it!"

He shook his head in negation. "It is not the same thing. He'll still have his health and his life, which is a hell of a lot more than my dad had when Harrison was done with him."

She didn't back down but stood braced against the counter, her eyes filled with accusation. "Hypertron *is* his life. It's all he has cared about since Mom died. If you let Mr. St. Clair follow through on his plans, Dad won't have anything left worth living for."

She was wrong. Couldn't she see that? "He'll still have you. And in less than a year, he'll have a grandchild. That's more than he deserves, but it's the truth."

Harrison had hurt Isabel by putting that damn company ahead of her needs over and over again. Couldn't she see that the least he deserved was to lose Hypertron?

Isabel shook her head, her normally soft green eyes filled with more pain than Alex could deal with. "He doesn't want me. I'm not enough. I never have been and I can't believe my baby would be, either. In some ways, my dad's already dead inside. Don't kill the only thing still living in him: his love for his company."

Her voice broke on the last word and Alex couldn't take it anymore. He yanked her into his arms. She struggled, but he wasn't about to let go. He pressed her cheek against his heart with one hand while wrapping his other arm securely around her waist and pressing her into his body. "I didn't mean to hurt you. Believe me, baby."

She stopped struggling but still strained against his hold. "But it does hurt, Alex. I feel betrayed and . . . and like our marriage is some kind of mockery, just another nail in the coffin of my father's happiness."

"I married you because I need you, not because I want to hurt you or use you in any way to hurt your father." He whispered the words between dropping soft kisses on the silky tangles of her hair. Would she trust him enough to believe him?

Some of the tension drained from her, but she didn't say anything, just stood acquiescent and yet withdrawn from him within the circle of his arms.

He had to convince her. "Your picture haunted me for two years—"

"My picture?"

Would the knowledge he had opened an investigative file on her only convince her more firmly of his evil intentions? "After my dad died, I wanted to know everything there was to know about John Harrison. That included getting surface information on his daughter."

"Surface information?"

"Where you worked, what you looked like, your relationship with Hypertron. Surface information," he repeated.

He hadn't invaded her privacy, didn't know anything more about her past than what she'd told him. He sure as hell hadn't known she'd started having fantasies of motherhood until he'd found her list.

She shifted restlessly against him. "And you expect me to believe that I had no place in your little frontier justice scenario?"

He rubbed her spine, trying to soothe her, trying to soothe himself. "Yes. I never once considered doing anything to or through you. I wanted to meet the woman in that picture so bad that I'd wake at night from dreaming about you, but I stayed away until you contacted Marcus on behalf of another company."

"You thought I was working for my dad, didn't you?"

At least she no longer believed he'd engineered St. Clair's approach to her on top of everything else. "Yes."

"I still don't understand about the picture—"

"There was something in your eyes—"

"Criminal naïveté?" she slotted in, interrupting again.

"No." His voice came out harsh, but he hated the thought that his actions had made her feel stupid. "Innocence. Softness. I craved what I saw in you and when I met you, got to know you, I was afraid to lose you, so I rushed you into marriage." It was easier to say these things to the top of her head, but part of him wanted to see her eyes and the impact his words were having on her. Was she convinced?

"Did you think you could keep your role in Hypertron's takeover a secret from me?"

"I hoped to," he admitted. "But I figured that if you did find out, you wouldn't just walk away from me if you were my wife."

"Are you sure about that?"

It was his turn to go stiff and his hold on her tightened involuntarily, but he couldn't make himself answer her challenge. The words would have gotten stuck on the lump of fear in his throat.

Alex's stiff posture and silence in the face of her last remark lasted for several seconds before he began rubbing one hand up and down her back again while the other caressed her head. His touch comforted her even though she didn't want it to, even though she knew it didn't mean he was going to give up his awful plans for her father's company.

She had to make him change his mind.

Not just because of her father and what losing Hypertron would do to him, but for his employees as well and ultimately for Alex and their future together.

Isabel didn't really believe Alex intended to use her and their baby against her father. That had been her overactive pregnancy emotions speaking. If she had believed it, she wouldn't have bothered coming back to the house but would be halfway to Bettina's by now. Even in her furious exit from his office, she'd known that her anger and the pain of betrayal had motivated half of what she'd said.

Alex might not live by her code of ethics, but he had his own and he did not compromise them. He said he had no intention of using her, and she believed him, but realized now she'd asked the wrong question that day she'd discovered Ray Trahern's connection to Hypertron.

Rather than asking if she were part of Alex's plans for revenge, she should have asked if he had plans to settle the score for his dad's death.

She grimaced against his chest when she thought about his belief that she would not leave him if they were married. So much for worrying whether he'd be happy about the baby. He was probably relieved by the news, no doubt believing a pregnant wife would be even less likely to walk out the door.

He was right, at least about this pregnant wife. But not because she was pregnant and not even because she'd meant her wedding vows when she spoke them, although she had. No, she wasn't leaving because she believed with all her heart that Alex had meant his vows, and knowing this, her love for him made it impossible for her to give up on him or their marriage.

It wasn't about duty or promises but about love and faith.

She pulled away from him, pressing against his chest until he loosened his hold. He didn't let her go completely, but he did allow enough distance for her to look up into his face. His eyes surveyed her with wary watchfulness while his mouth formed a thin, grim line.

"So marrying me had absolutely nothing to do with your desire to make my father pay for your dad's death?" she asked, the bands of betrayal constricting her chest loosening a little.

Alex's brown eyes turned black with intense emotion. "Nothing."

"You married me because you had some fixation with my picture, and it had nothing to do with the fact I was John Harrison's daughter?" It sounded too implausible to be true.

One corner of his mouth tilted slightly. "I married you because I had and continue to have a fixation with the woman in that picture." And for the first time since taking her in his arms, his eyes flashed a sexual message to her.

She ignored it. "And my dad?"

"Has nothing to do with our marriage."

She wished Alex would let her go. She wanted to think, but as usual, standing so near him was wreaking havoc with her thought processes. She had the feeling that Alex was holding on to her to physically prevent her from leaving if his words did not convince her. Not the behavior of a man who didn't care whether his actions influenced her feelings for him.

She chewed her bottom lip, looking for an angle to take with him that his logical mind would not reject. "What about all the employees? Don't they matter?"

Something like relief flickered in his eyes but blatant irritation swallowed it. "I knew it would be like this if you found out."

"Like what?" she demanded. "Like I would care that you plan to participate in the total annihilation of a sound company for the sake of your personal vendetta against its owner?"

"It's not a sound company. If it were, St. Clair wouldn't have considered it for a hostile takeover."

Of course Alex knew stuff she didn't, which added to her already high level of frustration and hurt. It wasn't as if her dad would tell her if things were shaky at Hypertron. The files she had read on Miss Richards's computer had certainly implied a weakness in Hypertron's market position, but it scared her to have Alex confirm it.

"But I know how this works for you. I researched your company, remember? You aren't a raider. You could have steered Mr. St. Clair toward a different investment or not taken him on as a client at all."

"The point is, I didn't want to."

She flinched at his words, but she couldn't accept that it was too late to prevent the kind of takeover Mr. St. Clair was planning. "But you don't usually work with corporate raiders—"

"I've made the exception before."

"That doesn't mean you have to make it this time."

"Yes, I do."

She closed her eyes against the implacability in his. "Have you stopped to consider how many jobs would be lost?" she demanded, opening her eyes again, but with little hope they would see a change in his expression. They didn't.

"You of all people should realize job security is not guaranteed in this industry."

No way would she let him get away with such a flippant attitude toward Hypertron's numerous employees. "Hostile takeovers, like the one you and Mr. St. Clair are planning, do more than dismantle companies. They tear apart people's lives."

Alex's eyes narrowed. "You don't even like Hypertron. You think the employees there all work under bad conditions."

"Hypertron might not be the ideal employer, but at least it is an employer." She pounded once against his chest. He didn't even flinch. His damn muscles were as unbending as the rest of him. "I never counsel my clients to leave a position without first having secured another one, and I would certainly never countenance a lay-off of this magnitude, regardless of the reasons behind it, but especially not to satisfy one man's need for revenge."

"I'm not just any man, Isabel." Alex's grip on her waist grew painful. "I'm your husband."

"Yes." She couldn't very well deny it.

"I'm also the father of your child." He looked down at her expectantly.

She frowned, not sure where this was leading. "Agreed."

"You said you loved me."

She refused to respond to that.

He didn't give her the option of remaining silent. "Do you love me?" His eyes compelled her to answer and his will pushed against her like a physical force.

She bit her lip to keep from shouting that yes, she did love him, but she thought she might hate him, too.

"Answer me, baby." Then she saw it. The tiniest flicker of insecurity in his eyes. *He wasn't sure.* He confirmed her suspicion when he spoke. "I need to hear the words."

His voice was indeed raw with some kind of primitive, male need. It was similar to how he sounded when he wanted to be inside her but even more intense. Could her love possibly be that important to him? Would it help her to convince him to stop living in the past and start living in the present—with her?

"Yes, I love you. I thought you knew." She had told him. Not often perhaps, but she had said the words.

He shuddered and pulled her close once again. "I didn't know if today changed that."

Alex had some things to learn about love. "I'm not going to stop loving you because you make me angry, but I'm also not going to let my love for you blind me to what you are doing. I can't let you harm all those innocent people."

Releasing her, Alex stepped back. "You mean you don't want me to hurt your father. You say you love me, but you love him more."

Clenching her hands, Isabel glared at her husband. So that was it. He expected to use her love to manipulate her. As she'd thought, Alex had a few things to learn about love, and she was going to be his teacher.

"I'm your wife," she said, tossing his earlier response back at him.

He nodded, looking as wary as she had felt when he'd questioned her earlier.

"I'm the mother of your child."

"I don't know what you're trying to prove here, Isabel."

"Answer me."

"Yes, you're the mother of my baby," he said with exasperation.

"And you're happy about that." This time she knew some of her own uncertainty shone in her expression.

He reached down and gently touched her stomach with one hand. "Very."

"Good," she couldn't help responding.

Then, she said, "I love you."

His wariness returned. "So you've said."

"I love you," she tried again, this time lacing her voice with challenge.

He stood silent, meeting her gaze, testing the strength of her resolve. Finally, he nodded. He also smiled, his gorgeous dimple almost making her forget the point to her words, but she persevered.

"But that doesn't mean I'm going to let you destroy my father's company. My love doesn't make me some kind of doormat for you to walk on."

A bark of laughter surprised them both. "You're too stubborn to be anyone's doormat."

She nodded. Just so that he understood. "You can't go through with your plans with Mr. St. Clair, and I won't let you use me to hurt someone else."

His expression turned pained. "They aren't my plans. They are my client's plans and it isn't my decision whether or not he goes through with them."

She frowned at that, acknowledging she'd have to think more on that angle.

"And, for the last time, *I'm not using you.*"

"But you are using Mr. St. Clair. He's not only your client, he's your instrument of revenge." She'd gotten him with that, she could tell, because Alex's face closed up like a book left on the library shelf.

Then, surprisingly, his dimple showed in his cheek once again. "I'm hungry. Watching you throw away those chocolate chip cookies just about did me in."

"I waited until you got here to do it," she confessed.

"You've got a mean streak, Isabel," he teased. "I hope our child doesn't inherit it."

"Between the two of us, it's almost a given."

His expression turned serious. "I'm not a cruel man."

She sighed. "I think, given the right set of circumstances, you could be."

"You mean like having a client who wants to buy your father's company?"

She couldn't deny it, so she said nothing.

"Do you believe that I have no desire or intention to use you to hurt your father?"

"Yes." But she didn't believe the destruction of Hypertron was a matter of justice and somehow she was going to make him see that.

Chapter Sixteen

Isabel got ready for bed in the master bathroom, her frustration level at a boiling point.

They hadn't discussed Alex's plans for Hyper-tron over dinner or when they returned home. Isabel had tried, but Alex refused all overtures to reopen the conversation. He'd used the excuse that they should be celebrating the news of their impending parenthood. She'd countered that she couldn't celebrate anything, even pregnancy, with the cloud of so many lives being hurt hanging over her head.

They were at a stalemate, neither one having said anything meaningful in the last hour or more.

She came out of the bathroom to find Alex already in bed. He sat against the headboard, his eyes catching hers the moment she opened the door. "I like what you've done to our room."

"Thank you." She headed toward the door.

If he thought he could placate her with compliments after spending all evening ignoring her attempts to talk about such an important issue, he wasn't as bright as she'd always given him credit for being. "I *don't* like what you plan to do to Hypertron." And she didn't like knowing he had married her with ulterior motives. In fact, she hated it. "Goodnight, Alex."

Her hand was on the doorknob ready to pull it open when he spun her around to face him. She gasped. He'd moved so fast she hadn't even realized he'd left the bed.

"You're my wife."

Were they back to that again? She stifled a sigh of irritation bordering on out-and-out anger. "I'm not denying that."

The fingers on her arms tightened their hold. "Let me make this very plain, sweetheart. You are my wife. My wife sleeps in my bed. Is that clear?"

"This isn't the Middle Ages, Alex. I can sleep wherever I want to."

"Fine." He released her.

She opened the door, not quite believing he had given in so easily.

"But wherever that is, I'll be there."

Isabel shivered at the implacability in his voice. He wasn't threatening her. He was stating a fact.

"I don't want to sleep with you," she bit out. "After what I found out today, I need some space."

"And what did you find out today? That your dad's company is not as solvent as he wants everyone to believe. That I have a client interested in capitalizing on that fact. Why do you need space to digest those facts?"

"Maybe not, but knowing you married me so I wouldn't walk away from you when I found out your part in the hostile takeover of Hypertron *is* something I need space to digest." She sounded like a sarcastic shrew and was actually quite proud of the fact.

"That's too bad."

She glared at him. Mr. Sensitive he was not. "What if I decide to sleep on the couch?" she asked a trifle smugly. "There isn't room for both of us on there."

He smiled, the expression sending a shiver through her. "There is if one of us sleeps on top."

She didn't really want to sleep alone. She wanted to cuddle up to her husband, and she wanted him to tell her that he married her because he loved her—not just because he desired her body so badly that he wanted to make sure of getting and keeping access to it through the bonds of matrimony.

It wasn't going to happen and she wasn't going to sleep with him.

"I'm going to the guest room." She didn't raise her voice, but she put every ounce of her determination in it.

Alex's eyes narrowed. "Then I guess I'm sleeping in the guest room tonight, too."

"You aren't invited." Before he got a chance to answer, she added, "I mean it, Alex. I'm sleeping alone."

"So, this is how you're going to try to manipulate me? You're going to refuse to sleep with me until you get your way?"

She wanted to cry. It didn't have anything to do with manipulation. "I just hurt too much right now to be with you," she admitted in a sad whisper.

Alex drew back as if she'd slapped him. She took advantage of the movement and scooted out of the room.

She didn't find the guest room bed any more comforting than she had the first night she'd tried sleeping in it. Alex's accusation that she was leaving their bed in an attempt to manipulate him and the look of pain on his face when she left their room haunted her. Why did he have to be so stubborn?

She punched the pillow and curled up on her side, cuddling the other pillow in an attempt to satisfy the void she was used to Alex filling. It didn't work. She flipped over onto her back.

She didn't belong in this bed, even if she and Alex were fighting. She wasn't accomplishing anything but making herself miserable. Oh, Alex had looked pretty miserable, too, when she'd left their room, but it wasn't worth it.

She wasn't the one into revenge scenarios.

She fidgeted with the covers as she thought about what Alex had said earlier in the kitchen: that her picture had haunted him and he'd found her completely irresistible in person. That kind of admission wasn't to be scoffed at, even if she was mad. His feelings had to run a lot deeper than mere desire and a liking for her company.

She pounded the bed with both fists in disgust. She was never going to get to sleep like this. She wanted to feel Alex's arms around her. She needed assurance that he'd married her for something other than revenge. He might not say the words of love she longed to hear, but when he held her, she always felt at peace and cherished.

Besides, she had just found out she was carrying his child. A woman needed the comfort of her husband's presence after such a discovery.

She tossed back the covers and padded back to their bedroom. She crawled onto her side of the bed without saying a word. From Alex's stiff posture, she could tell he wasn't asleep, but he didn't pull her into his arms.

"Thank you." His voice whispered in the black velvet darkness.

"For what?" But she knew.

"For coming back to our bed." If he'd sounded the least bit arrogantly satisfied by her return, she probably would have left again or made him sleep on the floor, but he didn't.

He sounded humble, which shook her, but still he didn't take her in his arms.

It was a long time before she fell asleep.

Isabel teetered on the brink between dreams and wakefulness. Alex whispered words of need and longing into her ear while touching her in all the places that drove her crazy. His mouth covered hers and the warm, spicy taste of his tongue invaded her mouth. The kiss went on and on and she eventually realized she wasn't dreaming. The arousal of her body was all too real and so was the feel of Alex inside of her mouth.

He slipped his hand between her legs to caress her aching femininity and Isabel came fully awake, but for several seconds of disorientation she continued to respond to his kiss, allowing her body to move against him in utter abandon before reality came crashing back. She was angry with Alex. She couldn't let him make love to her. She stiffened and tried to move away, but he refused to let go.

"Please, baby. Don't fight it. I need you so much. If you want to go back to fighting again tomorrow, we can. But please give me tonight."

The words didn't affect her nearly as much as the desperate pleading in Alex's voice. He did need her and she loved him, but making love right now wasn't the answer. They needed to talk. "I don't want to go back to quarrelling tomorrow—"

His mouth cut off the rest of what she'd intended to say. "I don't want to, either," he whispered against her mouth before the kiss turned incendiary.

That's not what she'd meant. She'd meant they shouldn't make love tonight, but his mouth was robbing her of her ability to think and tell him so. His kisses always had this affect on her—since the first time she'd all but offered herself to him on the doorstep. Part of it was the way her body responded to his, but equally important was the desperation to possess her that she tasted on his lips.

Alex needed her on a fundamental level that she could not deny, but he'd had too many things his way that day. It was time she asserted herself. She pushed against his chest. Hard.

He lifted his head, his face set in stark lines. "Please, sweetheart."

Her heart tripped at Alex's continued pleading. Her stubborn, proud husband was not given to begging, and she reveled at this further evidence of the depth of his feelings toward her. He might not love her yet, but he was close.

"Lie back, Alex. You want to make love, so we'll make love, but we'll do it my way."

He rolled over onto his back. "You can do anything you want with me as long as you don't leave me."

The fervency of his words excited her. Unbearably. And the ache between her legs grew intense. Although they had been married for more than a month and they made love often, she had pretty much allowed him to set the pace and style of their lovemaking. Everything he did felt so wonderful, and it was all so new to her, and she was always too out of control to try anything else. Tonight, that would change.

Tonight, he'd be the one to lose control.

She climbed astride her husband, settling herself against his rigid penis, and stopped. Alex shuddered under her and lifted his hips off the bed, pressing his hardness against her wet swollenness. She gasped as her body gave an involuntary jolt at the contact. Although she loved the way it felt, she needed to set the ground rules. She wasn't naive enough to believe that just because she was on top that Alex would let her control their time together.

"Lie still," she commanded.

"I don't know if I can," he said, but he let his body settle back against the bed.

"I'm in charge and I don't want you to move. At all," she added to clarify.

He groaned. "Honey, is this some kind of punishment?"

She smiled at the strained tones in his voice. "No, I do not consider making love with me punishment."

"We are going to make love?" He wanted her promise.

She nodded and rubbed herself up and down his shaft just once. "Oh, yes. We're going to make love, but we're going to do things my way."

Alex's body went rigid under hers, but he didn't arch off the bed again. She lowered her head to kiss him, slipping her tongue between his teeth mimicking what their bodies would do later. Although he didn't move his head, Alex allowed his tongue to play erotic games with hers and soon they were both breathing heavily.

She broke off the kiss and took her lips on a mapping journey of his body. When she reached his chest she circled his small nipple with her tongue before gently nipping. Alex gave a harsh exclamation and grabbed her bottom with both hands. His fingers bit into her flesh, but she didn't mind. She loved having him so close to the edge of his control.

She moved to his other nipple and gave it the same loving treatment while moving her lower body sinuously against him. Then she gently pried Alex's fingers loose from her hips and slid downward, her mouth blazing a trail of kisses down his stomach. She stopped at his belly button and gave it her entire attention, kissing and stroking the area with her tongue. Alex made mindless noises and forgot to remain still as his lower body moved in a vain effort to find relief against her body.

She delighted in tormenting him by holding herself just far enough from his thrusting manhood that he barely brushed against the skin of her torso.

"You're killing me, Isabel."

From the hoarse tenor of his voice, it almost sounded like it. She moved just a few inches lower. When her mouth closed over the jutting tip of his erection, Alex once again came off the bed. He pushed more of himself into her mouth and she took him, wrapping her hands around the base of his sex and moving them up and down in a steady rhythm. She didn't know if she was doing it all properly, but if the sounds her husband was making were any indication, she'd gotten at least something right.

She loved the taste of him. So male. So uniquely Alex. Touching him like this affected her like his most knowing caresses and her body throbbed with the need to find completion, but she didn't want to stop what she was doing.

Alex took it out of her hands when he put one hand on either side of her head and gently tugged her back. "You're going to have to stop, sweetheart. I can't take anymore."

"But I like doing this." She moved her hands against his shaft again and a small bead of moisture developed on the tip.

His groan sounded suspiciously close to a roar. "Stop, baby. When I come, I want to be inside you."

"But I'm the one in charge," she reminded him while moving her thumb to rub the moisture over his tip.

This time there was no mistaking the sound that came from his mouth as anything but a roar. He put both hands under her armpits and lifted her until she had to let go of his penis, then pulled until she was once again straddling him. "So be in charge, but do it with your body wrapped around mine."

Somehow she felt that his demand diluted the effectiveness of her position, but she was past caring. Her body ached and pulsed in its need to feel him inside of her.

"Okay, Alex." She pushed herself off his chest with her arms and settled her hands over his nipples, rubbing them experimentally with the pads of her thumbs.

He smiled and she knew he planned to return the favor before his hands came up to squeeze her breasts and play with their rigid peaks.

Isabel threw her head back and positioned herself so that his jutting shaft was poised on the brink of her opening. Then ever so gently, teasing both Alex and herself, she lowered her body by centimeters over his hardness. Alex tried to thrust upward, but she lifted her body with his, thwarting his obvious desire to completely seat himself.

"If you don't watch it, baby, I'm going to lose it the second I get completely inside of you." Although the words were meant to be a threat, they came out sounding more like a desperate plea and she laughed.

Her laughter turned to a groan as she took more of Alex's shaft inside her. By the time she had him completely sheathed in her wet heat, they were both panting. She didn't move for almost a full minute, simply allowing herself to revel in the closeness of their joining while she contracted her inner muscles around him.

Isabel could feel Alex's bunched muscles under her thighs and knew he was desperate for completion, but his control hadn't broken yet. She wanted to know that she had the power to push her totally self-disciplined husband past his limits. She needed to know that at least in one area of their marriage, Alex was as vulnerable to her as she was to him.

She kissed him slowly and with lots of heat. "I could do this all night," she lied, as she slid carefully back up the length of his shaft and once again took an excruciating amount of time letting him fill her.

"Well, I can't." Alex erupted up off the bed, tossed her down under him and took over.

She would have laughed in victory, but his mouth covered hers in a hard, carnal kiss while he reentered her ready body. He hammered against her until her entire being was filled with the sensation of their joined flesh. Her pleasure spiraled out of control and she shattered, screaming out her pleasure, but she didn't go alone.

Alex came with a loud shout, his entire body going rigid while she moved under him, glorying in the final spasms of her release. Afterward, Alex collapsed on top of her. She pressed against his chest, needing to take a deep breath and unable to with his weight pinning her to the mattress. He groaned and rolled off of her onto his back, his arms and legs sprawled out.

"You're a tease, you know that?" His voice sounded like he'd used his last reserve of energy to get the words out.

She smiled in the darkness, though there was still a twinge of hurt in her voice when she spoke. "You deserved a little teasing after refusing to cuddle me to sleep."

She'd been wrong. He had a small store of energy left, enough to come up on his elbow and loom over her. "You wanted me to hold you?"

She shrugged, though he probably could not see it. "You insisted I sleep with you. I came back."

"*You wanted me to hold you?*" he repeated, this time his

voice rising. "How was I supposed to know? You were trying your damnedest to sleep without me. You'd even gone to the guest room. I thought if I tried to hold you, you'd have some kind of hissy fit and insist on sleeping somewhere else again."

Were all men this dense? "I do not have hissy fits," she informed him grandly, or as grandly as a totally sweaty, satiated, exhausted woman could.

He snorted.

She was struck by a thought. "So, you waited until I was asleep and set about seducing me?" she asked with mild interest.

He curled his fingers around her waist and pulled her into the curve of his body, this time making it clear that he didn't intend to let go for the rest of the night.

"Not exactly. I waited until I was sure you were asleep and then I pulled you into my arms because I needed to hold you," he admitted. "Once I got your body next to mine, I discovered I needed a lot more than my arms around you."

Well, at least he hadn't found it any easier to sleep without their physical connection than she had. And she'd made him lose his precious self-control. Now all she had to do was make him give up his plans for revenge against Hypertron.

Somehow she knew that wasn't going to be nearly as easy.

"So, what happened last night after you and Isabel went tearing out of here?"

Alex pushed the keyboard drawer in and rolled his shoulders before turning his desk chair to face Marcus. Blue eyes keen with interest belied the blond man's indolent stance. Alex waved his friend to a chair.

"We had a fight."

Marcus's lips twisted cynically. "Yeah. I figured that much. What I want to know is what's happening now."

"What do you mean?"

Blue eyes probed him intently. "I mean are we going ahead with St. Clair's deal?"

"He's our client." That said it all. CIS had never let a client down yet and they weren't going to start now.

"And she's your wife."

Marcus's words reminded Alex of his argument with Isabel. "Your point?"

"I got the impression *your wife* wasn't happy about your part in St. Clair's plans for Hypertron."

"She's not." Unhappy didn't begin to cover it. Try pissed as hell. Furiously angry. Seething. But she'd come back to their bed last night and he knew when to be grateful.

"That's it? She's not, but we're going ahead anyway?"

Marcus's look of disbelief got on Alex's nerves. "Do you have a problem with that?"

"Hell no. She's not my wife."

"Right." She was Alex's and he was determined to keep it that way, but he wasn't going to compromise his integrity to do it. She'd come around. He had to believe that.

"Are you sure you're doing the right thing here?"

Alex's jaw clenched. "I'm sure fulfilling my obligation to my client is the right thing, yes. I repeat, do you have a problem with that?"

Marcus raised both hands in a conciliatory gesture. "Like I said, she's not my wife."

That had been firmly established so Alex just frowned at Marcus, knowing more was coming. Alex had never known his friend to shut up until he got everything off his chest he wanted to, no matter how angry or discouraging Alex became.

"It's just that I'm wondering if you're looking at the big picture here."

"The big picture?" All he could see was Isabel's picture, and not the one in her file. It was a mental picture he carried in his head of her lying on her stomach with the covers bunched up around her hips and her honey-brown hair spread out in wild tangles around her innocent face, relaxed in sleep.

"Right. The big picture. St. Clair's one client. When this deal is done, he goes his way. You go yours. But your wife is still your wife, living in your house, sleeping in your bed, and eating with you at the dinner table."

That's what Alex was hoping. That she would still be there. "You're painting a pretty picture, but I don't get your point."

"The hell you don't, but if you don't want to see it, I'm not saying any more." Marcus's glare was impressive.

Alex glared back. "All right. So I get it. You're saying I should dump my desire for justice, let my client down, and damage my professional reputation because my wife is mad at me."

Marcus's snort said it all. "I'm not saying anything, man. This is your call. You're the boss. She's your wife. St. Clair's your client."

And the whole damn mess was on his head. Yeah, Alex got the picture and this one wasn't quite so pretty. "She's pregnant," he said, piling coals on his own head.

"The hell you say!"

"She wanted a baby. That's why we got married. I wanted Isabel. We're both getting what we wanted." Only now his wife loved him and he wanted that love, as much as or more than he wanted revenge against Hypertron.

"What a mess."

That was Alex's feeling exactly. "I guess you're patting yourself on the back for your no-ties, no-commitments rule right now, aren't you?"

A strange look passed across Marcus's face, but he nodded. "You know it. I wouldn't be in your shoes with a pregnant wife for a million dollars and a fully staffed yacht. Hell, I wouldn't be in your shoes, period."

"Excuse me, Mr. Trahern, but I need your opinion on the new reception area furniture you wanted me to order."

Veronica walked in carrying a thick office supplies store catalog.

Marcus's head had snapped up at her entrance. "Hey, Ronnie. We still on for tonight?"

They were dating? Somehow that didn't surprise Alex. There had been too many hushed conversations and bright blushes from his secretary when Marcus was in the room for Alex not to have suspected something.

Veronica's face looked unusually pale and drawn. The look she gave Marcus made it clear she didn't appreciate his making their relationship public in front of Alex. "I'm going to have to pass on tonight. I've got some things I need to do at home."

Marcus shrugged, his expression relaxed. "So, we can do them together. How about I bring pizza for dinner?"

"No, not tonight."

During this whole time Veronica hadn't met Marcus's eyes, which made Alex wonder if the two had had some kind of lover's spat. Maybe that's why Marcus was being so sensitive about Isabel's reaction to learning about St. Clair.

Marcus's eyes narrowed on Veronica's averted face. "Why not tonight?"

Veronica's knuckles turned white where they clenched the catalog, but she finally turned to face Marcus. "Because tonight I'm not available." She tossed the open catalog onto Alex's desk. "This is the furniture suite I picked out. If you like it, leave the catalog on my desk and I'll order it later today." With that she turned and swept out of the office.

Alex turned to Marcus, who looked pole-axed. "Trouble in paradise?"

"Not that I know of, but it sure looks like it."

"Maybe you should go talk to her," Alex suggested.

"Maybe I better put on armor and a shield first."

Alex laughed. "I survived last night without them, you will too."

"Never let it be said I had less guts than you, but I've still got more brains. I didn't get the woman pregnant and I'm not playing a role in destroying her dad's company. Whatever's bugging her, Ronnie's bound to be easier on me than Isabel was on you." And Marcus's laughter joined with his.

Chapter Seventeen

"The snake!"

Bettina's shriek of outrage acted like a balm to Isabel's wounded feelings. She *knew* her friend would understand. She had just finished relating the previous day's events to Bettina over a double-tall decaf latté. First, she had told Bettina the news about the baby, and both women were still a little teary-eyed from Bettina's over-the-top, happy reaction. Isabel had been loath to share the rest of yesterday's discoveries and ruin the mood, but she needed Bettina's help. In the end, Isabel was glad she had because Bettina's response had been just as emotionally gratifying.

Shifting on the red leather loveseat in her friend's office, Isabel took another sip of her coffee. "Exactly."

Not that she really thought Alex was a snake. She knew Bettina didn't, either. It was just an expression. The right expression. It's what Isabel had called Tyrone when Bettina told her that he'd invited his mother to stay for a month after their first child was born—without asking his wife's feelings on the matter beforehand.

"Alex knew all along he planned this nasty revenge

against your dad's company and married you anyway—
without telling you? Girlfriend, that's low-bellied behavior."

Isabel nodded. "He knew, all right. I'm still a little
unsure what role I'm playing in all this."

Bettina's expressive eyes widened and she tossed her
curling braids back over her shoulders. "You don't think
he's trying to use you for revenge?" she practically
shouted.

Sighing, Isabel shook her head. "No." She wrapped
the fingers of both hands around her drink. "I don't
think he's trying to use me, but I can't figure out why
he married me, either." She voiced the suspicion that
had been gnawing at her. "I'm afraid he did it in a sub-
conscious effort to get one more up on his enemy."

It was Bettina's turn to shake her head. She did it vehemently. "No way. Your man may be a snake, honey,
but he married you because he loves you."

"He's never said the words," Isabel reminded her.

"Did you tell him that you love him?"

"Yes."

Bettina's expression turned thoughtful. "You're married to one stubborn man, girlfriend. It could be a while
before he says the words out loud, but he does love you.
It's in his eyes."

Isabel wished with all her heart she could be as certain of that as Bettina appeared to be. In fact, she'd settle for even half of her friend's assurance. The fact was
that she needed the words, and it wouldn't hurt to know
he put a higher priority on their relationship than he
did on a two-year-old grudge against her father.

Nothing Alex did now could bring Ray Trahern back,
and as long as Alex stayed focused on the past, he wouldn't
be free to love Isabel in the present. Not like she wanted
to be loved, not like she loved him. Completely.

She couldn't afford to dwell on her heart's quandary

right now, however. She had other important issues to re-solve. "I need your help in convincing him to try to change Mr. St. Clair's plans for Hypertron," she said to Bettina.

"I still can't believe that Mr. St. Clair is part of all of this. Why did he want to hire Mr. Danvers?" Bettina sounded every bit as confused by the complicated turn of events as Isabel felt.

"I don't know. At first, I thought Alex had convinced him to do it to give Alex an excuse for coming to see me, but that didn't really make any sense. And something he said last night made me realize that that scenario was really unlikely. I truly don't think I'm part of his re-venge."

He'd just blown her away with that stuff about the photograph.

Bettina took a long sip of her mocha. "Yeah, I can't see Alex using you like that. I can see him wanting some kind of payback for his dad dying and all. Men have such a hard time understanding that they can't control the world and everything in it. Seeing his dad lose the case and then die must have been hard on a man like Alex, but he wouldn't have come after you. He's a fair man. Besides, the guy cares about you too much to hurt you on purpose."

Setting her drink down on a small table, Isabel said, "Why is it that a man can hurt you so much when he's not trying?"

Bettina reached out and gave Isabel's shoulder a strong squeeze. "It's just in the guy chromosome, I guess. I would swear on my mother's family Bible that Tyrone would not knowingly hurt me, but the man has been a sore trial."

At that Isabel laughed. "Try that line on someone who doesn't know just how much you adore your hus-band, Bet."

Smiling, Bettina took another sip of her mocha before setting it next to Isabel's drink on the table. "Okay, so what's the plan?"

"I've been thinking about it all morning, and I know appealing to Alex's compassion regarding my dad would be pointless."

Bettina nodded in agreement. "It's that whole guy-justice thing. 'A man's gotta do what a man's gotta do, even when it hurts.' "

Bettina's excellent impersonation of one of her husband's often-quoted phrases brought a smile to Isabel's lips. "Right. And he already knows I'm mad about it, but he won't budge and I don't want to use our relationship as some form of emotional blackmail."

"So, what are you going to do?"

"I'm going to do what I do best, fight for the employee. I'm going to hit Alex with the reality of what dismantling Hypertron will do to the people working there."

Bettina's eyes lit up with interest. "How are you going to do that?"

"That's where you come in. You are the queen of stats and that's what I need."

"What kind of stats?" Bettina asked, pulling a legal pad and a pen from her desk to take notes.

"I already know the number of employees working there, but I need the probabilities of finding them other employment in the current market, how long that might take, what kind of damage layoffs of this magnitude do to a community. I'm even thinking that getting information on divorce and suicide rates related to layoffs would be good."

Bettina whistled. "Girlfriend, you're getting out the guilt *cannons* on this one."

Isabel nodded firmly. "Yes, I am. This isn't just about my dad and that's what I have to show Alex. It's about a lot of people that are going to get hurt to assuage one man's need for revenge and another man's greed. It isn't right." She set her shoulders. "I might even let it go if it was just my dad. I can't blame Alex for being angry with him, but I can't stand by and watch so many innocent employees be hurt. It would be on Alex's conscience for the rest of his life, and I can't let that happen. I love him too much to let him hurt himself in this way, and I refuse to let his past destroy our future."

In the three days following Isabel's discovery of Alex's plans against Hypertron, his respect for his wife's aptitude for battle strategy increased hourly. He was convinced she'd learned her tactics from guerilla terrorists. Each attack was unexpected and unique to Isabel's style of warfare. She hadn't used the ploy of barring him from her body or her bed, which would have succeeded in at least giving Alex something to fight that he understood and was prepared for.

No, the first day, she went to work as usual, had even called him at lunch just to chat. Prepared for a confrontation on the phone, he'd made an excuse and hung up before realizing that she hadn't once made a reference to her father or his company. Relieved, Alex had convinced himself that even if Isabel didn't understand his need for vengeance, wifely loyalty and her love prevented her from allowing it to drive a wedge between them.

It didn't take more than five minutes after arriving home that evening to realize the phone call had been no more than a diversion, luring him into unsuspecting complacency.

Next to his plate at dinner, he found printouts detailing the number of employees and small businesses that would be affected by the dissolution of Hypertron.

She had included forecasts from statistical averages on how many of those employees represented single-income households and mothers raising their children alone.

Unwilling curiosity forced him to read her "report" and he felt just like she wanted him to—guilty as hell. But he wasn't going to give up his vengeance and disappoint a client because Hypertron employed single mothers. No, damn it. He'd argued that those employees would find jobs elsewhere. Oregon's electronic industry was strong even in the current economic climate.

Isabel hadn't been impressed. Nor had Alex convinced her with the argument that he had a company–client responsibility to St. Clair at this point and that revenge was not his only motive for helping in the takeover. CIS had a reputation to maintain, he'd asserted. Isabel had countered that it was going to be an ugly one when news of his latest client activities hit the media.

Like a fool, he'd accepted an invitation from Isabel to lunch the next afternoon. She had spent the entire time lecturing on the evils of hostile takeovers—until Alex wanted to tape her mouth shut. Not that he said that to her. He wasn't an idiot, no matter what she implied.

And he was too relieved that she hadn't tried to leave him to rock the boat that much. Since the moment he'd realized he wanted her permanently in his life, he'd been afraid she would discover his plans for her dad's company and leave. He'd tried to convince himself otherwise, but deep down he'd thought she couldn't possibly love him enough to stay.

In her eyes, he had used her, betrayed her feelings for him. He still couldn't quite believe her love was strong enough to overcome such imperfection in the man she loved.

So, he listened with as much patience as he could muster to her growing pile of statistics. She showed him charts indicating the average unemployment rate for employees after a layoff of this magnitude.

He had taken refuge in silence, but that hadn't stopped his wife from badgering him with unwanted information. That night over dinner, she quoted divorce rates following a layoff, and this morning she had calmly informed him at breakfast of the increased risk of suicide after job loss.

He refused to vent his growing anger, anger he had to admit was motivated by an increased sense of guilt; she never once asked him to give up his plans for her dad's sake or even her own. She kept her arguments tied strictly to the effects St. Clair's hostile takeover would have on what she termed "the innocent bystanders in this mess—the employees." Men just like his father, she said.

If Isabel had asked him to give up for her sake, he wasn't sure any longer what the answer would be. He thought he could keep her separate from his need for revenge, but she wouldn't let him. Her information bombs were reminding him of why he'd started CIS instead of an investment firm like St. Clair's. He had wanted to build dreams, not tear them down.

He didn't want to admit it to Isabel, but her arguments were making him rethink his position and the advice he'd initially given St. Clair.

In fact, just that morning Alex had found himself researching the possibility of St. Clair's getting a better return on his investment in the role of White Knight than of Corporate Raider. If he could convince St. Clair that investing in Hypertron would be more profitable than taking it apart, Hypertron's "innocent employees" would not be standing in unemployment lines a few months down the road.

Isabel would be happy.

Alex hated that look of censure she wore whenever

they talked about the St. Clair–Hypertron deal. She made him feel like an arsonist who burned down the houses of the elderly for a living. It meant giving up his sense of justice and helping the man he considered his personal enemy to save his business, but even that was a newly hazy area in his mind.

How much of the past was John Harrison or his company's fault? How much had been Alex's dad's? And how much had been no one's, as Alex's mother had claimed, but just life?

Alex was tempted to work late. He legitimately had work that he could do, but even more important, he could avoid a few more hours of his wife's guerilla tactics. Until he knew if he could pull off a White Knight deal with St. Clair, he didn't want to mention to his wife his hope of doing so. Which meant that tonight would be just like every other night since she'd discovered the truth . . . an unpleasantly long one.

Unfortunately for his peace of mind, the thought of giving up time with Isabel—even time spent arguing—was unacceptable. So, like every other day since his marriage, Alex worked with cool precision to ensure he would be finished in time to share an early dinner with his wife.

He didn't want her staying up late. Pregnant women needed their rest. He'd have to talk to her about the possibility of her working part time. Knowing Isabel, she would refuse. That didn't mean he wouldn't suggest it. Arguing about it would be a welcome break from discussing Hyperton's future.

Two hours later, he had the numbers crunched and a call into St. Clair. The White Knight deal looked good on paper. Particularly if rumblings were accurate about Hypertron's newest technology coming to market close to target date. He made a call to his contact at Hypertron and smiled as he hung up the phone. The situation looked good, very good, for a White Knight investor. Now, if Alex could convince the corporate raider, his life with Isabel could go back to normal.

His musings were abruptly cut short when the phone rang and Veronica informed him—in a strained voice that he'd come to associate more and more with her— that St. Clair was on the line, returning his call.

Isabel had taken off early after her afternoon appointment cancelled and was home when Alex came storming up from the office at three o'clock that afternoon. Lost in thought about her marriage, Alex's plans for her dad's company, and the realities of impending motherhood including an inexplicable tiredness in the afternoons, she happened to be looking out the living room window when he slammed out of the renovated barn and started toward the house.

The expression on his face was chilling, and she had a sudden urge to run upstairs and lock herself in their bedroom. Telling herself not to be foolish, she forced her body to remain seated on the sofa. He couldn't be this angry over the article that she'd left on his desk that morning on the psychological effects of unemployment on the displaced employee.

Maybe that particular expression on his face had nothing to do with her at all.

His gaze zeroed in on the house and she felt it lock on her through the window. Sweat broke out on her forehead and her heart began to pound as Alex disappeared around the side of the house. Seconds later, she heard the kitchen door open and shut.

Alex's measured tread announced his movement down the hall toward the room in which she sat. She almost wished he were stomping. Alex in a silent fury was far more intimidating than Alex openly expressing anger.

Soon he stood framed in the entrance to the living room, his eyes dark pools of accusation, his tall body vibrating with suppressed rage. He didn't say anything.

Isabel's insides tightened and she found herself launching into an explanation. "I know you don't approve of my tactics, Alex, but you must realize by now that I'll do anything to protect the employees at Hypertron."

The silent fury in Alex seemed to swell, and maybe it was a trick of the lighting, but did her husband look at least two inches taller?

"Including subverting my company, betraying my trust, and destroying my reputation?" he asked with cold, biting anger.

She sat up straight, pulling her feet from their reclining position on the sofa cushions. He was really overreacting to one small article, even if it had been rather graphic when describing the increase in domestic violence after a large layoff. "Don't be ridiculous, Alex. I'm not trying to hurt you or your company. The opposite is true, in fact. I'm trying to save you from yourself."

Alex's hands fisted at his sides and his knuckles grew white. "You think that telling your dad my plans, undermining my credibility with one of my clients, and betraying my trust in you is somehow saving me from myself?"

She'd been wrong. Alex's loud, soaring rage was definitely worse than his silent fury. In fact, he was downright terrifying. Enough so that it took several seconds for his words to register past her body's urge for flight. *Telling her dad his plans?*

"What are you talking about? I haven't told my dad anything."

Not that she hadn't been tempted, but Alex trusted her. At least she thought he had. She couldn't even convince herself that telling her dad about Mr. St. Clair's plans was a last resort. She simply could not betray Alex.

"If you didn't tell him, then why did I just get through with a damned uncomfortable conversation with St. Clair? I called to try to talk him into a White Knight investment scenario. I thought it would make you happy." Alex gave a derisory snort.

"He called me back to tell me that he'd been approached by Harrison to make a deal." Alex crossed the floor with predatory swiftness until he stood towering over her. "It appears your dad's company is going to bring their technology to market on time after all. The situation looks so good for the stock St. Clair has already purchased that he was in a fine mood. He just wanted to warn me about a leak within my organization. I didn't bother to tell him that my own wife was the culprit."

Shock and pain warred for supremacy in Isabel's emotions as she digested Alex's accusation, and then both were drowned in the most astonishing fury she'd ever experienced. The anger she'd felt at discovering the St. Clair–Hypertron deal had been a tempest in a teapot compared with the boiling cauldron of resentment she felt at the knowledge that Alex believed she'd betrayed him.

How dare he accuse her of being underhanded enough to call her father with confidential information about CIS?

Isabel shot off the couch and shoved Alex's chest until he took two steps backward, enough room for her to stand toe-to-toe with him. He could smolder and tower and intimidate all he wanted, but she wasn't going to let him accuse her of something she hadn't done.

Poking her finger into that rock-solid chest, she shouted, "How dare you accuse me of something so despicable? I'm not the one who entered this marriage with hidden motives, Alex Trahern. I've been up-front with you right from the beginning."

Too up-front. Not only had she fallen in love with a man too stupid to recognize loyalty when he saw it, but she'd been idiot enough to tell him about it. He didn't deserve her love and he sure didn't deserve to know about it.

He didn't look impressed by her anger. "So up-front that when you realized you weren't convincing me with your big guilt-trip about the employees, you told your dad what you knew about St. Clair's plans?" His voice was once again low and filled with chilling rage.

"I didn't need to tell my dad. My 'big guilt-trip,' as you put it, was working. You would have caved any day now."

He'd tried to hide it, but she'd seen how she was getting to him—and arrogant, proud beast or not, he could darn well admit it.

"If you didn't tell him, who did?"

The question acted like a handbrake on all that cleansing rage rushing through her, and her heart did a three-sixty as everything inside her skidded to a halt. If Alex understood the first thing about her love for him—if he loved her at all—he wouldn't, he *couldn't* believe such a thing.

"I don't know, Alex, but it wasn't me." She desperately wanted him to believe her. Needed him to believe her.

Didn't he understand that she could never betray his trust? That the person inside the body he craved would never do something so devious?

Just as she believed, evidence to the contrary, that he had never had any intention of using her to hurt her father. She had ultimately trusted him when he denied having plans to hurt her or her father through her. Her love for Alex made her see the best in him, and it made her capable of believing in his honor even in the face of overwhelming evidence to the contrary.

The key word there was love. She *loved* him and he *desired* her. His feelings for her were based on physical lust—and that did not engender faith in another person. With love came trust, and as Alex didn't love her, he didn't trust her, either.

She let her hands fall to her sides and looked him straight in the eye, though it hurt to do so.

Seeing the accusation and disappointment in his eyes was like being flayed with a cat-o'-nine tails right across her vulnerable heart, but she faced him proudly. "If I decided to call my father with details of that awful hostile takeover, I would tell you first. It isn't something I would try to hide."

He put one finger under her chin, the gentle touch at odds with the leashed anger still evident in his eyes. "Are you telling me that it never crossed your mind to tell your dad about St. Clair's plans?"

She knocked his hand away and glared at him. Did he think she'd lie about it? She didn't have to. The truth was good enough.

"I *did* think about it." She glowered at him, daring him with her eyes to make something of it, but he was intelligent enough to remain silent. "*But* I couldn't convince myself it was a viable option."

"Why?"

Was he beginning to believe her? A spark of hope came to life before she quenched it with a bucketful of reality. Perhaps she could convince her husband that she hadn't betrayed him, but that wouldn't alter the fact that he didn't love her—the fact that he had assumed she was guilty because deep down where it counted, he didn't trust her love for him.

He shouldn't have had to ask that question. The answer was obvious.

"I couldn't betray you because I love you." She felt her voice breaking as weary sadness replaced her anger.

She took a deep breath to control her devastated emotions. He wouldn't understand that reasoning, but it was all she had. She stepped back and to the side, intent on leaving before she lost the precarious control she had over a sudden overwhelming urge to cry.

Alex's hand snaked out to stop her. He took a deep breath. "I know the employees mean a lot to you, Isabel. I can almost understand your feeling justified in telling Harrison."

He hadn't believed her. She wasn't surprised, but it still hurt. She twisted her arm from his grasp. "I'm glad you can, because I couldn't. I suggest you look elsewhere for your leak, Alex, because I'm not it."

Tears burned her eyes. She needed to be alone. She left the room before Alex could stop her again.

Alex watched Isabel rush down the hall toward the stairs and sucked in air, tainted with the guilty knowledge he'd hurt her. *Damn.* If he'd taken a few minutes to stop and think instead of charging over to the house like an enraged rhino, he would have handled that whole scene differently.

So what if she'd told her dad about St. Clair? Contrary to what Alex had claimed in anger, CIS wasn't going to lose over this. St. Clair's career in the arbitrage industry made him naturally cynical. Discovering Alex had a supposed leak at his company hadn't fazed St. Clair in the least. He had been grateful, in fact, that the nameless "spy" had saved him from attempting a takeover bid that would probably have failed, now that

Hypertron's newest technology would be on time to market.

And hadn't Alex already decided to try to convince St. Clair to take a different approach with Hypertron?

Isabel's actions had only preempted his own and he could understand those actions, even admire them. She was motivated by her concern for the employees. It made sense and it was something he respected about her.

Alex raked his fingers through his hair and sighed. The problem, of course, was that he hated the idea that behind his back Isabel had gone to her father. He'd felt betrayed and he'd acted on that feeling of betrayal.

Now his tenderhearted wife was no doubt sobbing her heart out on their bed, if she wasn't packing a bag because she didn't want to continue living with a man who lost his cool and yelled at her. Isabel had looked so hurt when she left.

She loved him and that made her vulnerable to him. He should never have lost his temper.

The guilt he had been feeling toward the nameless employees at Hypertron was nothing compared with what he felt toward his wife right now. And she'd been right—her campaign *had* been working. He'd been feeling very guilty.

Isabel felt Alex's hand on her back, and her body stiffened while she tried to swallow the tears racking her body.

"I'm sorry, baby. I'm so sorry."

She shook her head, rejecting his apology.

He pulled her around to face him. "I am. I can't tell you how much. I don't want to hurt you."

She took a deep, shuddering breath and lifted her

face to meet his eyes. He was sorry? Did that mean that he believed her?

"I should never have lost my temper like that." His face twisted with remorse as he wiped at the wetness on her cheeks with his fingertips. "You've been right all along about the effect on the employees and the community a hostile takeover would have had."

"I'm glad you see that." But did he believe her that she hadn't told her father about Mr. St. Clair's plans?

"In fact, this morning, I was running numbers and trying to come up with a proposal for St. Clair to change his plans from a hostile takeover to investing in Hypertron." He looked at her expectantly.

"That's good." *But did he believe her?*

His face registered disappointment at her response. "I was stupid to get upset about your dad and St. Clair cutting a deal. It saved me time and effort, not to mention the dubious pleasure of helping your dad save his company."

She struggled to sit up, and he helped her to get comfortable against the headboard.

"That's very commendable."

He grimaced. "Not really. I don't like seeing you upset, sweetheart. I would have done just about anything to get you smiling at me again."

That knowledge should have made her feel good, but nothing was penetrating past her need to know if he believed her now.

"So, who do you think spilled the beans to my dad?" she asked by way of finding out if Alex had changed his mind about its being her.

He sighed. "Don't worry about it, honey. It's done now and I can't even say that I'm sorry."

"But I am worried. Either you have a leak in your company, or someone has hacked into your computers. You should be worried, too."

His smile was gentle. "You don't have to pretend anymore, all right? I'm not angry any longer. I realize I shouldn't have gotten mad at you in the first place. I know what a compassionate woman you are, and I should have expected you to take more direct measures when you weren't sure your guilt campaign was working."

So, he didn't believe her.

She crossed her arms over her chest. "But it *was* working. You admitted it."

"But you didn't know that."

"Who says?"

"Look, let's not get into this, okay? I said I don't mind. I know it's not something you'd ever do again."

"Why?" If she'd betrayed him once, why wouldn't she do it again?

"Because the same set of circumstances won't arise."

"You mean you'll make darn sure I don't have access to confidential information anymore?"

His guilty start said it all. Her heart felt numb, so this new evidence of his lack of trust didn't wound her. Perhaps it would later, but right now she was just too tired to care. The emotional upheaval of the last hour, coupled with her afternoon sleepy spells, had resulted in bone-weary exhaustion.

She closed her eyes against the certainty of her guilt in his. "I'm tired."

She heard his sigh as he stood up. "Maybe you should take a nap."

Isabel nodded, opening her eyes, but she avoided looking at him. She settled down farther on the bed and turned on her side to get into a comfortable sleeping position.

She felt the weight of a quilt settle over her and then the firm warmth of Alex's hands as he tucked it around her. "We'll talk more later."

She didn't respond to that assertion. As far as she was

concerned, there was nothing more to say on the subject. He believed she'd betrayed him. She hadn't. End of subject. At least for right now.

"I'd like to go to sleep now."

Leaning down, he kissed her lightly on her temple. "It's going to be okay, sweetheart."

What was going to be okay? A lifetime of living with a man who didn't trust her? She didn't think so, and there was absolutely no way she was going to accept such a situation. She was going to make him see that she wouldn't have told her dad about St. Clair's plans, and then Alex was going to apologize. And this time, he was going to mean it, not simply be sorry he hurt her feelings.

But for now, she needed a nap. Arguing with her husband took more energy than she had to spare at the moment.

Chapter Eighteen

Back in his office, Alex couldn't focus on his work. His confrontation with Isabel kept running through his head. She'd denied telling her father about the St. Clair deal, repeatedly and vehemently.

So, what was stopping him from believing her? It was his certainty that the only other people who knew about the deal, Marcus and Veronica, wouldn't betray him.

They'd had access to information of far more lucrative value over the past few years, and neither one had ever leaked so much as what time he took his coffee breaks. It was this knowledge more than any other that had convinced him so absolutely that Isabel had been the one to tell Harrison about St. Clair's plans. But did that make sense?

She loved him. And he loved her. The knowledge settled in his heart with a pleasant warmth totally at odds with the wariness with which he'd always approached that emotion. He'd been infatuated with her picture and fallen in love with the woman. She was everything he could want out of life: loving, giving, feisty, strong, and so sexy she made him combust with desire every time he held her in his arms.

Alex didn't know why it had taken him so long to come to terms with his feelings, but now that he had, the current situation took on different meaning. Loving Isabel meant trusting her, believing in her.

Would a woman who loved him go behind his back and leak confidential information? No. Particularly if that woman was Isabel. When had she ever shown a hesitation to confront him? And as she'd said—though he'd been too angry to accept it at the time—if she had planned to tell her father about St. Clair, she would have informed Alex of her intentions.

She had too much integrity to skulk around behind his back.

He groaned, snapping in two the pencil he'd been idly playing with. Why hadn't he thought of that earlier, when she was so busy *repeatedly* and *vehemently* protesting her innocence? He'd messed up every way he looked today and it was only getting worse.

Because if his wife hadn't leaked the confidential information, someone else had, and Alex had wasted valuable investigative time acting like a total jerk to Isabel. It was not a comforting thought. St. Clair had said Harrison had gotten the information from CIS, but that didn't mean it was true. Even if it was, the leak could have come from a compromised computer as Isabel had suggested, or one of Alex's field employees could have done some unapproved research while in the office.

Grabbing a yellow tablet, Alex started creating an information matrix with all of the pieces of the puzzle at his disposal. It's what he should have done after the phone call with St. Clair, rather than storming over to the house and behaving like an idiot to his wife.

An hour later, Alex walked into Marcus's office and closed the door. He'd spent the last hour deciding how to proceed and had drawn several conclusions. One of them being he was certain Marcus was not the spy.

The blond man looked up from his computer screen. "Hey Alex, what's up?"

"I've been giving some thought to your idea of expanding CIS into corporate investigations."

Marcus's smile split his face. "Great."

"The problem is, I think I need to take on a partner to head that side of the company. I've got enough work overseeing what we currently do."

Marcus tensed behind his desk. "I guess I thought you'd let me take it on."

"I thought about it, but I can't have my assistant heading another department. It's really the job for a partner." Watching Marcus's expression turn thunderous, Alex thought it really was fitting to use the man's own sense of humor against him. "If *you* were my partner, then everything would pretty much fall into place."

After several seconds of stunned silence, Marcus asked, "Are you serious?"

"Yes. You interested?"

"Yes," Marcus replied.

"Good. Then I've got your first case for you. We've got a spy," he said, repeating the words Marcus had used to gain his attention the day Alex met Isabel.

Isabel finished setting the table just as Alex entered the kitchen. She looked up. "I was beginning to think you were going to work right through dinner."

And part of her had hoped he would, while another part had grown angry at the possibility that he was avoiding her because of her supposed betrayal.

His eyes warily raked over her. "No."

"As I can see."

His lips curved in a grimace. "Isabel . . ."

She adjusted the already perfectly stationed silver-
ware, not wanting to look at him. Her nap had helped
her to gain control over her careening emotions, but
nothing would soothe the wound in her soul from the
reminder that all of her hopes of Alex loving her had
come to nothing.

His hand fell on her shoulder, and she had to fight
the urge to turn into him and beg him to hold her, to
make her forget the pain of their earlier confrontation.

"I'm sorry."

She didn't look up from her unnecessary rearrange-
ment of the cutlery on the table. "For what?"

Was he going to apologize again for losing his temper? She didn't want another one of those apologies.
She wanted him to know he'd been wrong . . . without
her having to argue the point with logic.

She felt his fingers cup her cheek, gently applying
pressure on her to turn and face him. She allowed him
to turn her face until their eyes met. His were full of remorse. She knew hers reflected her caution. She wasn't
going to let her hopes have upward mobility again.

"I accused you of telling your dad about St. Clair's
plans."

"I remember."

"I'm sorry."

"Fine." He probably was sorry he'd accused her.
He'd made it pretty obvious earlier that upsetting her
made him feel bad.

His sigh ruffled the hair at her temples. "No. It's not
fine. I had no business believing you were capable of
doing something so sneaky."

She spun to face him completely, finding herself
trapped between his big body and the solid oak table.
"You don't believe any longer that I was the one that
told my dad?"

"No."

Then the other shoe dropped. No wonder he'd worked so late. He didn't trust her because he'd suddenly discovered an overwhelming love that wouldn't let him believe the worst of her. He'd found the culprit.

"So, who is it?"

He frowned. "I don't know."

"But you found evidence to indicate a leak from within?"

"No." He shrugged. "I'm not convinced the leak didn't originate in St. Clair's office. Marcus is looking into it."

"Let me get this straight." This was important. "You don't have any new evidence?"

"No."

"Yet you no longer believe I'm the culprit?" She had to be absolutely sure of what he was saying.

"Right." His hands settled on her shoulders again. "I'm sorry I ever did. Can you forgive me?"

"Why?"

"Why do I want you to forgive me?"

For such a successful businessman who made his living using his brain, her husband could be thick sometimes.

"Why don't you believe I'm guilty any longer?"

"You're too open to have done it behind my back."

"I tried to tell you that."

"And I didn't believe you. I'm sorry."

She was getting tired of those two words, especially when it was three others she so badly needed to hear. "So why do you believe me now?" Please tell me you love me, her heart begged silently.

"The way you handled your business with Marcus. You could have hidden from me the fact that he'd contacted you, and continued to see me, but you didn't. And the way you've been since finding out about the St. Clair–Hypertron deal. You've been in my face with statistics, arguments, and lectures, but you haven't tried emotional blackmail. You're just too honest to do something like that, and I should have realized earlier that you were too honest to contact your dad behind my back."

So. It made sense to him. No words of love in that little litany of her admirable character traits.

She swallowed her disappointment. She should be grateful for small favors. At least he respected her enough to realize she would not betray him. He'd also apologized, which showed he cared about her feelings even if he did not love her.

She forced a smile of acceptance to her lips. "Thank you. Why don't we eat dinner now?"

He looked disappointed by her response, but for the life of her, she could not drum up one more ounce of enthusiasm for his logical apology.

She shrugged his hands from her shoulders and moved around the table to her seat. "You'd better sit down. Spaghetti isn't all that appetizing cold."

He nodded but watched her for several seconds before complying.

The next morning Alex was sitting at his desk, wondering how to overcome the stalemate in his marriage.

He'd apologized to his wife, told her he believed her and why. He'd told her he trusted her and she had reacted with apathy. He didn't like it.

Not one little bit.

"I've discovered our spy."

Alex looked up and winced at the look on his new partner's face.

Marcus wore the expression of a man ravaged by pain. "It was Ronnie."

"Our secretary?" Alex couldn't take it in.

"Yes."

"How did you find out?"

Marcus crumpled a piece of paper in his hand. "It didn't take a lot of detective work. She left a note on my desk admitting it was her. I found it this morning when I came in."

Considering that when Alex arrived over an hour ago, Marcus had been in his office, he had clearly not dealt well with discovering that his girlfriend had betrayed the company.

"I'm sorry."

"Me, too. I really believed in her integrity."

"I did, too." Alex was sure Veronica had had a reason for doing what she'd done. "Hell, maybe she was trying to save my marriage."

Marcus looked as if he thought Alex had gone one over the legal limit.

"Women understand each other a hell of a lot better than we understand them, Marcus. She probably knew that if I went through with helping St. Clair achieve the takeover, there would be a wedge driven between me and my wife."

Marcus shook his head. "Yeah. So, why disappear without a word to me? If her motives had been so altruistic, she wouldn't be gone."

Alex didn't have a ready response to that.

His new partner turned to go. "I'll contact St. Clair and let him know where the leak was."

"He'll want to know it definitely didn't originate in his office."

"Not likely to have. He doesn't trust his employees. It would be damn hard for one of them to betray him." Marcus sounded like he wished he were as cynical.

And Alex wished he hadn't been . . . with his wife.

Chapter Nineteen

"I know I don't have an appointment, but I have it on good authority that one of a husband's prerogatives is to drop in unannounced on his wife at work."

At the husky timber of Alex's voice, Isabel's hand froze over the file she'd been replacing in the drawer.

She'd used work as an excuse to avoid more heart-to-heart—or rather her heart to his logic—discussions the night before. He'd tried to talk to her a couple of times, but she refused to be drawn. When he took her in his arms after they went to bed, she'd told him she was too tired to make love. It had been true. Pregnancy had taken an unexpected toll on her energy.

Or maybe it was her emotional turmoil.

Alex had held her until she slept.

The last thing she'd expected was for him to show up in her office today. He had a corporate spy to find.

Snapping the file drawer shut, she opened the one below it. "I'll be right with you, Alex," she said, without turning around.

She had been searching for some information she needed before she called Lawrence Redding about a possible job opportunity, and that was as good an excuse as any to avoid Alex for a few minutes while collecting her scattered thoughts and emotions. Part of her was rejoicing that the hostile takeover of Hypertron issue was over. Another part of her was wondering what Alex intended to do instead to satisfy his sense of justice.

She pulled the file on the employer she planned to pitch Lawrence Redding to. It was a consulting firm. They were looking for a consultant with Lawrence's background. She'd felt like a fool when the idea came to her of pitching her old client to the firm. It was the perfect job for a man who didn't like to stay static, and she couldn't believe it had taken her so long to connect Lawrence with it.

A consultant never did the same exact job twice. Something always changed, whether it was the work environment or the work itself. Lawrence would finally be settled with one company, if not with one job. Alex should be happy. Even if he wasn't happy that Lawrence and Priscilla appeared to have found happiness.

Her mother-in-law had called that morning to invite her and Alex to dinner the following evening, saying that she had some good news to share. Isabel felt sure the older couple planned to announce their engagement.

Alex's hand settled on Isabel's shoulder, pulling her around to face him. He leaned past her and closed the drawer she had just opened. "That can wait, can't it?" He smiled, his dimple winking sexily at her. "I hoped you could take some time off this afternoon. I've got a picnic lunch in the car and some things I need to tell you."

He had a lot of nerve expecting her to set time aside for him when he'd rejected a similar offer from her so recently. She had a schedule to keep as well. "I'm a little busy this afternoon, Alex. Maybe another—"

Alex placed a finger gently against her lips.

"Before you turn me down, I should mention that the food isn't homemade. I don't have chocolate chip cookies and I'm not going to tell you I'm pregnant."

She smiled with bitter cynicism. "You make it sound irresistible."

He winced and she noticed for the first time that he didn't look nearly as confident as he sounded. "I know. I didn't tell you what I do have, though. I got the food from Diane's," he said, naming Isabel's all-time favorite restaurant.

"How did you know?" Although they'd been married a little more than a month, they hadn't eaten a meal there.

"I called Bettina. After giving me a dressing down that left me blushing, she became a fount of information."

Isabel grimaced at what her volatile friend had undoubtedly said to Alex. She couldn't imagine her husband doing anything so vulnerable as blush, but if anyone could make him do it, Bettina could. "But no chocolate chip cookies?"

"I've got key lime pie."

Bettina *had* been a fount of information. If Alex had managed to placate her furious friend, perhaps what he had to say would be worth listening to. Besides, she loved him and curiosity about what he planned to say ate at her resolve to remain aloof. He also looked darned irresistible with his dimple and an altogether too endearing insecurity shining out of his eyes.

An insecure Alex Trahern was something she'd never experienced. He always knew just what he wanted and how to go about getting it. What could he want now that he wasn't sure of getting?

"Okay. For key lime pie, you get half an hour."

She expected him to balk at the time limit and wasn't

disappointed. If Bettina had told him about Isabel's favorite restaurant and dessert, she had surely also told him that Isabel didn't have any afternoon appointments, either.

"Sweetheart, I can't even get you to the picnic spot and back in half an hour."

She had no intention of making everything easy for him. Bettina might be placated, but then she believed Alex loved Isabel. Isabel wasn't harboring any such illusions. "Then let's have the picnic in my office."

His face split in a wickedly sensual grin. "Another time, honey, and I'll take you up on that, but today we need to talk and there's not enough privacy to do it here."

She could imagine just what Alex meant by a picnic another time, and against her will, she felt herself flushing. "You'd be lucky."

He nodded, his expression graver than she'd ever seen it. "Yes, Isabel, I would."

She felt herself swallowing a lump in her throat. Darn those pregnancy emotions, anyway. "You have one hour."

He grinned, relief shining brightly in his dark brown eyes, and she had the distinct impression that her small surrender on the time had been much more. Her fears were confirmed later when he drove through downtown Portland and crossed the Ross Island Bridge. She realized she wasn't going to make it back to her office at all that day.

They were on the road that led to Mt. Hood.

"Where are you taking me?" she demanded.

He smoothly shifted gears. "Someplace where we can talk without interruption."

"Does Bettina know about this?" She sensed her friend's fine hand at manipulation along with Alex's indomitable will at play in the current situation.

"She took care of things at your office. They don't expect to see you again until Monday morning."

Considering that it was only Wednesday, that meant Alex planned to do a lot of talking. "What about CIS?"

"Marcus is covering for me."

"I guess you can afford to take some time off now that St. Clair is working with my father instead of you, but what about your spy?"

"Taken care of."

"Already?"

"Yes."

"Who is it?"

"Veronica."

"Your perfect secretary? That paragon of office virtue?" Isabel couldn't quite keep the shock from her voice.

Alex frowned. "Yes."

"Why?"

"I have no idea. I would imagine for the money your dad paid her."

Isabel was sure there were extenuating circumstances. Despite Veronica's overzealous efficiency, Isabel had liked her. She had sensed something had been bothering the secretary the last few times she'd talked to her. Perhaps it had been the thought of selling out her employer.

Isabel felt bad for Alex that he'd been betrayed by an employee he trusted, but she couldn't mourn Veronica's actions. Whatever the woman's reasons, she had done her own part in saving Hypertron's employees from the layoff ranks.

What really interested Isabel was the way Alex behaved about the discovery. He acted as if it didn't matter.

"What are you going to do about it? I assume you have proof."

"She left a confession along with her resignation on

Marcus's desk this morning. I'm not going to do anything about it."

"No revenge? No plans to destroy her life because she wrecked your perfect payback against my dad?" Isabel knew she was goading him but figured he deserved it.

Alex turned his attention briefly from the road and faced her, his mouth set in a grim line. "No."

"Why not?"

Alex shrugged, his head facing forward once again. "I have more important issues to deal with at the present time than punishing Veronica for selling my secrets. She's gone from my company. That's enough."

"Did she leak a lot of information before she left?" Isabel couldn't help asking.

Her curiosity was aroused. The image of the perfect secretary as a corporate spy made an intriguing picture in her mind.

"According to her letter, no. And frankly, we've seen no evidence to the contrary. Marcus is attending to security measures while I'm gone."

"Dealing with your *more important issues*?" she asked.

"Yes."

"Like coming up with a new plan for vengeance against my dad and his company?" She didn't really think he meant to do that, but she wanted confirmation.

"No." His hands tightened on the steering wheel. He slid her a sidelong glance and then returned his focus to the road. "Why don't you take a nap, sweetheart? It's a long drive to our cabin."

In other words, he wasn't ready to talk about those more important issues yet. She wasn't sure she was, either, so she let him get away with the change in topic. "Our cabin—as in a cabin we're renting?"

"As in a cabin we own." Alex adjusted the climate control so that Isabel's vent blew pleasantly warm air on her.

"We have a cabin on the mountain?" He'd never said a word, but then there were a lot of things she hadn't known about her husband when they got married.

"Yeah. Do you ski?"

"No."

"I don't, either."

"Then why did you buy a cabin on Mt. Hood?"

"Property is a good investment."

She should have known.

"Besides, it's quiet."

There wasn't much to say to that. "I'm not tired," she said instead.

Isabel had slept so much yesterday that she couldn't possibly even doze, and she said as much to Alex. He didn't argue with her but popped a CD of Vivaldi in the Aston Martin's stereo.

She was asleep by the second track.

It was still early enough for a late lunch when Alex woke Isabel with the news that they had reached their destination, and her empty stomach let her know that lunch was indeed late. She stepped out of the car, letting her gaze travel around her new surroundings. The small, rustic building they'd parked in front of looked exactly like a mountain cabin should. Its cedar-shake exterior had weathered to a silver gray, and the small front porch boasted a swing big enough for two.

She wasn't surprised that the cabin's shakes had been left in their natural state. The color would suit Alex to a T, she thought. Someday, she was going to buy him a pink shirt or two. The color would go nicely with his multitude of both dark gray and black pants.

A forest of trees surrounded the cabin but did not completely obliterate the view of the small lake. Peering through the trees, she could also make out other buildings surrounding the lake, but their muted presence did not diminish the sense of solitude surrounding the structure standing in front of her.

She was vaguely aware that Alex had carried the picnic basket inside along with two small suitcases. He hadn't come back out after the last trip, and she assumed he was waiting for her. Taking a deep breath, she followed him into the cabin.

From what she could tell, standing in the main living area, there were only four rooms. She could see a small kitchen through an open archway, a bedroom off to her left, and a bathroom off to her right. A large fireplace took up most of one wall in the main living area, and from the sounds coming from behind the cabin, Alex was chopping kindling to start a fire.

A few minutes later, her suspicions were confirmed when Alex came through the kitchen archway carrying a stack of logs and kindling.

She watched as he made a fire with expert efficiency, grateful for that efficiency when the blaze sent a wave of warmth into the room. She'd left her coat in the car and realized she was shivering. "You do that very well."

He looked up at her from his kneeling position by the fire. "I've had a lot of practice. I come up here three or four times a year."

Wrapping her arms around herself to hold in the heat, she nodded. He spread a red-and-white checked tablecloth over a large braided rug near the hearth with the obvious intention of setting the food out immediately.

She was hungry and the nap had helped to relax her, but she still felt as if her nerves had been pulled taut over a stretching frame and left in the sun to dry. She definitely didn't want to wait to have their discussion until after they ate.

"Let's talk first and then have our picnic," she suggested.

Alex's gaze met hers, his brown eyes dark and serious. "You're pregnant. You need to eat."

She frowned. She didn't want him acting solicitous right now. She wanted to stay mad at him. "I'm not hungry. I want to talk." Her stomach growled almost immediately, giving lie to her words. She felt her cheeks heat, but Alex didn't tease her.

"Please, honey, just eat a little something for the baby, and then we'll talk."

She nodded silently, not having much choice. Her body had already shown her up for a liar. She'd look like an idiot if she kept insisting she wanted to talk first.

He smiled with obvious relief, and she got the distinct impression that he was putting off the discussion. Which was really weird. Alex didn't put things off. He was too focused and confident. Yet the jerky way he pulled out containers from the basket and his relief at putting off their discussion implied a nervousness that surprised her. She couldn't see what he had to be anxious about.

She lost her train of thought as the smells of roasted chicken and garlic mashed potatoes reached her nostrils, and she ruefully acknowledged to herself that she was starving.

Alex's eyes were intent and curiously cautious when he asked, "Would you like to serve up while I nuke the hot cider?"

"Sure."

In a few minutes, everything was ready. The room had warmed enough, so she was no longer shivering. She let her gaze settle on Alex's profile. His charcoal gray turtleneck clung to his muscular torso, and she remembered how solid and comforting those muscles felt when she was held against them. It wasn't a sensation she would willingly give up.

She took a bite of her chicken and stared into the flames of the fire. Shifting her gaze back to Alex, she asked, "Are you ready to tell me what those more important issues are now?"

Brown eyes drilled into her with an intensity that was almost scary. "The biggest is figuring out how to earn your forgiveness and get my marriage back on track."

She concentrated on her food while she digested Alex's words. In the end, she chose not to respond to them because she didn't know what to say. She needed his love, not his apologies, but if he hadn't figured that out yet, then she'd wait until he did.

She returned to the discussion they'd been having earlier in the car. "You're a smart man, Alex. I'm sure you'll come up with a new plan for revenge against my dad." Now she knew she was really goading him and this time she felt a little guilty.

"I can't."

She looked up upon hearing the raw passion in his voice.

His gaze burned through her.

She ignored the feelings swirling through her and said, "Of course you can. You're an expert at revenge."

He shook his head and pulled her almost-empty plate out of her hand, moving it and his own to the side. "I've finally accepted something that I refused to believe before."

"What?" The word came out breathless and wispy, but she couldn't help it. She felt breathless and wispy.

Her body was reacting to the heat in Alex's gaze. It was all she could do not to touch him, not to offer him her lips. She figured it would be like this for the next fifty or sixty years and part of her was fiercely glad.

Another part of her, the part that needed Alex's love, felt incredibly vulnerable because of her instant physical response to him.

He leaned forward and cupped the nape of her neck with his hand, gently but inexorably tugging her toward him. "Hurting your dad would mean hurting you, and I can't do that."

His mouth was only inches from her own, their bodies almost as close.

As usual, his proximity had an unsettling affect on her equilibrium, but she managed to get one more word out. "Why?"

There were so many reasons he could give, but only one would heal the wounds in her heart. And she was afraid that reason was the one he would not offer.

He kissed the corner of her mouth, then shifted his head and kissed each of her eyelids. "I can't hurt you because I love you. I love you more than I believed it was possible to love, and I will never again put anything, not even well-deserved vengeance, ahead of you."

She would have frowned at the well-deserved crack, but she was too busy kissing the man she loved. She ate his lips like a starving woman. *He loved her.* Places in her heart that had been lonely and empty for so long filled up at the knowledge.

She couldn't help pulling away just long enough to ask, "Are you sure?"

His eyes held a wealth of love and certainty. "Yes. I'm sorry it's taken me so long to get it, sweetheart. But I do. I love you so much it scares me because I almost lost you."

He'd never been in any risk of doing that, but she thought telling him would only inflate his ego. A woman had to have her secrets.

If her smile was a little wobbly, she could be excused.

"Well, you have me and you're keeping me, Mr. Trahern. Through sickness and health."

"Until death do us part." His voice turned incredibly husky and his eyes filled with moisture when he repeated their wedding vows.

She started pushing him backward, toward the floor. "I love you, Alex. So much."

He let himself be maneuvered into lying beneath her on the red-checked tablecloth. "Even after all the mistakes I've made with you?"

She ran her hands over the hard wall of his chest and felt his immediate reaction. "Yes. I don't love you because you're perfect, Alex."

"Why do you love me?" The question came out stilted because his breathing stuttered as she pressed her lower body against his.

"I love you because you fit the requirements on my list, of course."

She was laughing when he growled and rolled her over until she found herself under him.

Later, she snuggled against him in the big bed he'd carried her to. "It's true, you know."

"What's true?"

"You did fit my requirements."

"Schizophrenic courtesy and all?"

She smiled against his side as she remembered the label she'd applied to him on their first date. "Yes."

"I'm glad no one else fit them first."

"Impossible."

"How so?"

"They were written for you, I just didn't know it at the time." It was true.

She'd never met a man who had all the traits she'd listed and hadn't expected to, either. She'd thought she would end up settling. Instead, she was so happy, she was bursting with it, married to a man who embodied her every ideal.

"No other man could have fit them the way you do."

That kind of thing wasn't coincidence; it was one of life's greatest gifts. The gift of love.

She traced a small circular pattern on his bare chest and remembered something he had said the day before that had gotten lost in the heat of the moment. "Did you say yesterday that you'd already come up with a White Knight scenario for Mr. St. Clair?"

"Yes. That's what makes my reaction even more stupid than it was. I'd already decided to try to save Hypertron from my machinations and St. Clair's plans."

"That must have been a hard decision."

"Not really. Not when I love you so much." He sighed. "Besides, I've been thinking a lot about some things both my mom and your dad said. As hard as it is for me to accept, I have to come to terms with the fact that my dad chose his own path and it wasn't always the best one. He chose to put his work above our family and he hurt us all in the process. Losing his right to patent his designs might have been the catalyst for Dad's heart attack, but like Mom pointed out, his all-consuming passion for his work didn't leave room for eating right and exercise."

She hugged Alex close, wrapping her body around him like a protective blanket. "I'm so sorry."

He turned his head and kissed her. "Me, too. I remember how my dad used to thrive on the stress of his work, and in all fairness that stress probably contributed as much to his death as anything else. I know you don't think Hypertron is a good work environment, but for men like my dad, it's ideal."

"But not for men like you."

He smiled and hugged her close. "No. I've got more important things than work in my life."

She kissed his dimple and asked, "Like what?"

"Like a sexy little wife that I adore who just happens to be pregnant with my baby."

Isabel's happiness threatened to burst out of her. "I love you so much, Alex."

His brown eyes turned almost black with emotion. "And I love you, baby. You are so precious to me."

Her eyes burned with happy tears and she laid her head on his shoulder and snuggled, feeling so content that she never wanted to move from this spot.

"I'm really sorry, honey."

"For what?" she asked, not actually very curious.

She was too fascinated by the play of late afternoon light filtering through the window on Alex's chest to work up much interest in another conversation. She had other things on her mind. There were things she wanted to do to him, things she thought might just drive him crazy. She smiled against his chest in anticipation.

"For ever doubting you. You believed me when I told you that you weren't part of my revenge, but I didn't show the same level of trust in you."

"Actually, you did and that's what gave me hope."

Alex shifted until they lay facing each other. "What do you mean?"

She moved until she could see his face and reached out to brush his cheek. "I'll admit that at first, I thought your accusations meant you couldn't possibly love me."

He looked pained. "That wasn't a very bright assumption."

She almost laughed. "I know, because that's exactly what happened to me. When I read the files on the work you were doing for Mr. St. Clair, I jumped to the conclusion that you must have used me even though I loved you. It was a shock, but when you denied it, I believed you."

"I believed you, too."

She smiled, her happiness a palpable thing. "I know. Ultimately, you trusted me, which gave me a lot of hope that you could eventually come to love me."

"I've loved you for a long time. I think since the first moment I realized your picture hadn't lied. You really were the woman your eyes and smile promised."

He traced a circle on her breast right over her heart. "I trust you with my heart and my future."

She smiled, feeling the dampness in her eyes spill over into a single joyful tear. "Now that you love me, I can trust you with my future, too."

"It feels good, doesn't it?"

She arched into his gently caressing fingers. "Yes. And so does that."

"Good."

Then he went about proving just how good their future was going to be, going every bit as crazy as Isabel had anticipated.

Epilogue

Alex watched his wife as she slept. He would never know—looking at the serene contentment on her face now—that less than four hours ago, she had given birth after a very difficult labor to their daughter: Hope Priscilla Trahern.

His mother had been there for the delivery, but Lawrence had taken her home an hour ago, and the hospital room was silent for the first time. Isabel slept while Alex held his daughter and allowed a few very private, very necessary tears to roll down his cheeks. He had been given so much, and to think he had almost thrown it all away for a chance at revenge.

Isabel was right. Life had its own way of doling out the consequences and blessings. His mother had married Lawrence Redding and was ecstatically happy. It had been hard for Alex to admit, but he doubted she would have found that happiness if his father had lived.

John Harrison was making an effort to spend more time with Isabel. And he had recently revealed to Alex that Ray Trahern really had been his best friend. It wasn't a relationship that Ray had shared with his family, like so much of his life at Hypertron.

The destruction of that friendship and Ray's death had taken their toll on John Harrison, something he had admitted in a quiet moment alone with Alex. Alex had the feeling that the older man had admitted to his own pain in an effort to assuage Alex's disappointment at losing his vengeance. It was a strange idea, but Alex couldn't shake it. It was as if Harrison understood and even agreed that he deserved to lose his company but was grateful that he hadn't.

None of it mattered any longer. Isabel had convinced Alex that the past was just that. He'd even changed the combination to his safe in his office: it was now the date he'd first met Isabel. When he told her, she'd laughed and hugged him, making a much bigger deal out of it than he had thought necessary.

He might never fully understand his wife, but he would always love her. How could he not? She'd brought into his life something far more important than revenge. She'd brought him peace.

Please turn the page for a sizzling
sneak peek at Lucy Monroe's
next Brava romance,
READY,
coming in July 2005 . . .

Lise sat on the porch swing, a throw blanket around her shoulders to ward off the chill. Her white flannel nightgown wasn't warm enough for the winter weather, but she had needed to be outside. She'd spent so much time in her apartment, hiding, the last few months that the outdoors had called to her like the irresistible sirens of old.

The stars that were invisible in Seattle's light-polluted night sky, glittered here overhead and the fragrance of fresh air teased her nostrils. At three o'clock in the morning, the ranch yard was deserted. Even the dogs were sleeping. And she was thoroughly enjoying the solitude.

No stalker could see or hear her. Nemesis did not know where she was and that would change tomorrow. So, for tonight she was determined to enjoy every nuance of the freedom she would not enjoy again until her stalker was caught.

Being drawn to the swing could be attributed to the fact that she'd spent so many evenings of her childhood curled up on it, telling stories in her head and avoiding

the coldness of the ranch house. Only, she wasn't remembering her childhood, or telling herself a story in
her mind, or even plotting her next book.

Instead, she was reliving the volatile feelings she'd
had in Joshua's arms last year on this very swing before
she'd come to her senses and rejected him. Those feelings had been so different from anything she'd experienced with Mike, she'd been terrified. And she'd run.

Just as Joshua had accused her of doing, but tonight
she could not run from the memory. She didn't know
why . . . perhaps because she'd realized today that
Joshua still wanted her and while that desire frightened
her, it also exhilarated her.

His wanting her confirmed her femininity in a way
she was beginning to see she needed very badly, even if
she didn't want to explore the ramifications of it.

But knowing he wanted her impacted her senses almost as much as the kiss had and she was filled with unwanted sexual excitement. If she closed her eyes, she
could almost taste his lips again.

Remembering the moment when his mouth had laid
claim to her own made her nipples pebble with a sting-
ing sensation against her nightgown. Had she ever
wanted Mike this way? She didn't remember it if she
had. Pressing against her swollen breasts with the palms
of her hand, she tried to alleviate the growing ache. It
didn't do any good. Between her legs she throbbed and
she clamped her thighs together, moaning softly.

This was awful.

She was not an overly sexual being. The coupling of
male and female flesh did very little for her. It was a
pleasant way to connect on an emotional level, but that
was all.

This consuming ache was not pleasant, nor did it feel
particularly emotional.

Now she was a physical animal, in touch with primitive needs she'd been certain she didn't have.

In a reflexive move, her hands squeezed her breasts and she cried out softly, unbearably excited by the simple stimulation.

A harsh sound to her left caught her attention.

Her eyes flew open.

"Joshua . . ."

He stood a few feet away, sexual energy that matched her own vibrating from him in physical waves that buffeted her already overstimulated body. He was just as he'd been on the night of the Christening. Only this time he remained where he was, staring at her, instead of joining her on the swing.

His face was cast in grim lines, his naked chest heaving with each breath of air he sucked in. The black curling hair on it tapered to the unbuttoned waistband on his jeans. The shadowy opening hinted at his maleness.

She wanted to lean forward and lower the zipper so she could see it all, which would be incredibly stupid.

Only right that very second, she could not quite remember why, not with her fingertips tingling with the need to act.

She watched in mesmerized fascination as a bulge grew in the front of his jeans. A large bulge.

"Lise . . ."

She looked up.

A gaze so hot it burned her to her soul and inflamed her. They remained like that for several seconds of hushed silence, their eyes speaking intense messages of need while their lips remained silent.

The past ceased to exist.

The present consumed her.

Her reasons for caution melted away as her fear turned to a firestorm of cravings. His presence devoured everything around them, leaving nothing but man and woman communicating on the most basic level.

He took the steps that brought him within an inch of the swing. If she moved it, she would bump his legs.

She shivered at the thought of even that slight touch.

Dropping to his knees with a grace that spoke of leashed power, he knelt in front of her so they were eye level.

Neither of them spoke.

She couldn't.

He reached out and put his hands over hers where they pressed against now-throbbing turgid peaks. The heat of his skin seeped into hers, making her burn with unnamable desires.

When his head lowered to let their lips meet, she met him halfway. She wanted his kiss, desperately.

She concentrated on each individual sensation of his lips slanting over hers, his beard stubble prickly against her chin, his taste . . . like the most irresistible nectar, the heat of his mouth, the warmth of his breath fanning her face. She had never known the intense pleasure she found in his mouth, the conflagration of her senses she experienced when they touched.

Part of her was still cognizant enough to know she should stop him for the sake of her own sanity, but it was a tiny voice in a hurricane of physical sensations.